BOOKS BY JEFFREY POSTON

ACTION/ADVENTURE THRILLERS

American Terrorist: Where is the Girl?
Contagion: American Terrorist 2
Escalate! American Terrorist 3
American Terrorist Trilogy

Joshua Experiment (Call Sign: Raven Book 1)
The End of Everything (Call Sign: Raven Book 2)
The Queen (Call Sign: Raven Book 3)

JASON PEARES HISTORICAL WESTERNS

Courage (Book 1)
Legacy of an Outlaw (Book 2)
Warriors (Book 3)
Manhunter (Book 4)

LEGACY OF AN OUTLAW (THE PEACEKEEPER)

"Poston's [Jason] Peares walks into trouble at every turn. He's tough, quick with a gun, and understanding of the underdog."

—Steven Havill, author of *Privileged to Kill*

"A fast-moving story of guns and gunfighters, with a climactic cattle stampede of Texas-caliber proportions."

—Elmer Kelton, author of *Cloudy in the West*

"An exciting, page-turning traditional western sure to please. Fine work."

—Norman Zollinger, author of *Rage in Chupadera*

"Poston's stylishly written action yarn will generate a strong following among western fans."

—Wes Lukowsky, American Library Association

COURAGE

"Jeffrey Poston understands the craft of constructing his novel and does a wonderful job balancing narrative elements with his dialogue. When his protagonist handles his firearms, you know the author has done his research in describing the action."

—Phillip Hardy, Lulu.com review

A MAN CALLED TROUBLE

"In his first novel, Jeffrey A. Poston has numbered himself among the best writers of westerns working today."

—Biblio.com review Praise for Jeffrey Poston

WARRIORS

"It doesn't get any more real than this."

—D. Brock, Silver City, NM

WARRIORS

A Jason Peares Historical Western

JEFFREY POSTON

LOMAS & TURNER PRESS

Ordering Information:

Quantity sales. Special discounts are available on quantity purchases by corporations, associations, and others. Orders by U.S. trade bookstores and wholesalers. For details, contact the publisher at the address above.

Editing by The Pro Book Editor
Cover design by Deanna Dionne
Interior design by IAPS.rocks

eBook ISBN: 978-0-9916194-1-2
paperback ISBN: 978-0-9863328-2-1

    1. Main category—Fiction/Westerns
    2. Other category—Fiction/Action and Adventure

First Edition

CHAPTER I

"THEY WILL EXTERMINATE US," THE Apache warrior muttered to himself.

Juh (pronounced Hoe) walked slowly down the steep path under the high cliff face. He glanced up at the inaccessible caves of the ancient cliff dwellers. There were no paths from the river up to the cliffs where the caves sat higher than even the tallest trees, so Juh figured the ancient people must have used ladders or ropes.

A part of his mind reflected on the vision he'd experienced earlier in the afternoon. At the same time, he absorbed the beauty of the surrounding land. The sky was a deep, azure blue, and there was not a cloud to be seen anywhere. Even high up in the mountainous pine country, it had been a scorching day.

The leader of warriors stopped his descent for a moment and gazed back up at the cliff face behind him. Only leaders and elders on vision quests were allowed to approach the ancient caves. He looked at the particular rock depression that seemed to call to him hours ago. Below that high cave opening, he'd spent the better part of the day seeking, and ultimately finding, his vision.

He continued his journey down, following the narrow stream of water as it meandered through the wide valley. He crossed, agilely hopping atop exposed rocks, and entered the protective canyon that branched off to the north of the main river valley. Shadows of late afternoon crept over the dozens of tepees lining the banks of the Middle Fork of the Gila River as Juh observed his people attending to their chores. They seemed at peace, and he shared their feeling of security. Only three major paths led into the valley, and warriors constantly guarded these for intruders. Many narrow, hidden trails allowed egress from the valley if needed.

Yet, he knew that safety was a fleeting concept, a temporary dream of false hope where the White man's army was concerned. Just recently, the Black soldiers had journeyed two moons, all the way from the place they called Texas, to join the war against the native populations. Even the oldest and wisest leaders were bewildered by the Black man's involvement.

The warrior leader of the Apache tribe passed children playing in the water. He watched them for a moment and breathed deeply as a feeling of pride and love enveloped his soul. It was followed instantly by a deflating sadness, and he wondered if any of the children playing before him would grow to reach adulthood. As Juh proceeded toward the tepees, he decided finally that the children would not be told of his vision. It would serve no purpose to spoil their young lives by telling them how bleak their future was.

CHAPTER 2

THE GUNSHOT BROUGHT JASON PEARES out of his heat-induced drowsiness. He inhaled a deep breath of hot, dry desert air as the adrenaline rush of impending danger raced through his body. He caught a hint of the pungent odor of sagebrush and the more pleasant, spicy scent of desert evergreens.

When his eyes finally focused in full awareness, he found he already had a gun in his left hand and his Winchester rifle was raised and ready in his right. A dozen years of gun confrontations and a thousand fast draws had ingrained instant reactions in his brain.

He'd been just on the near side of dozing in his saddle, his body rocking comfortably in time with the slow gait of his horse. As he always did in hostile territory, he rode with his Winchester balanced across his lap, his right index finger resting across the trigger guard, and his left hand resting on the butt of a pistol stuck in his belt. Most times on the long trail, he never even bothered to hold onto the reins, usually letting his well-trained horse simply follow the trail.

In addition to his belt gun, Jason wore a double-gun holster. The gun pockets were slung lower than most holsters, placing both gun butts in excellent position for a quick draw with minimal arm movement. Leather straps at the bottom of each gun pocket were loosely tied around his thighs and kept his rig secured. An observer, when he rarely passed one, might have thought him foolish for wearing all that hardware across the scorching desert. Certainly he was uncomfortable, but years of outlaw life had taught him that having weapons ready for a fast reaction to danger was far more important than the inconvenience.

Despite what the army said about keeping the native people under control, Jason knew he rode in hostile Apache land. While he had no qualms with the natives of southern New Mexico, he knew they would treat him as they would any other intruder on their land.

As he scanned the desert around him, pointing his gun and rifle in all directions, the thought finally occurred to him that the sound he'd heard was not the sharp report of a nearby gunshot. Distance had muffled the shot, made it sound more like an echo. Almost as soon as he came to that conclusion, he heard several more distant shots.

He recognized the deep, throaty echoes from the army's standard issue single-shot .58-caliber Springfield carbines. The sharp reports of the Winchester repeaters that raiding Apache warriors preferred answered the army weapons.

Jason tucked his pistol back into his belt and guided his mount toward the top of the low hill where the echoes of battle seemed to be coming from. Atop the swell, he gazed down into the near distance to find a small detachment of soldiers riding rear guard behind a racing stagecoach. Every now and then one of the soldiers turned in his saddle and fired at the half-dozen warriors pursuing a couple hundred yards back. While one soldier reloaded, the other two turned in sequence to take a shot.

Very efficient army tactics, Jason thought.

Whenever possible, Jason liked to avoid well-traveled trails through hostile country, mostly because of the sight below him. The folks in the stagecoach were lucky to have an army escort. Otherwise, the battle would be over already, or maybe there never would have been a battle in the first place.

Jason had chosen his own trail, following a winding path through the low hills north of the main route. That way chances were pretty slim he'd ride into an ambush like the stagecoach had. He narrowed his eyes thoughtfully as he gazed down at the running exchange of gunfire.

Even though the stage driver ran his six-horse team full-out, the warriors should have been able to overtake their prey with ease. The attackers might have lost one or two of their number in the battle, but three soldiers shooting back over their shoulders at six charging warriors with Winchester repeaters wouldn't survive a determined attack. Suspicious, Jason scanned the terrain ahead of the stage from his vantage point.

He knew this part of the southern New Mexico landscape formed a natural depression. The shallow valley stretched many miles wide from the flatlands near Deming, then narrowed as it ran northwest to the foothills of the Mogollon Mountains where Silver City sat. The stage trail below him didn't follow the valley exactly. Rather, it paralleled the Mimbres River north from the valley, allowing stage passengers and the coach horses to have access to water during the long trip.

When the river turned sharply east before continuing north again only a few miles from where Jason now sat, the trail headed west to rejoin the relative safety of the wide valley. The stagecoach company accepted the risk of having extra travel time in proximity to water only because of the army's promise of help in that dangerous stretch of land. Cavalry escorts from Fort Bayard near Silver City or Fort Cummings near Deming assured safe passage of all stagecoaches.

As he searched the terrain ahead of the stagecoach, Jason immediately recognized the warriors' strategy. The trail traced through a series of draws, and no doubt the soldiers hoped to get the stage into the first draw so they could dismount and prepare a defense against their attackers. Already, one of the soldiers raced ahead of the stage to secure the area. Clearly, the army commander knew the warriors were herding the stage into a potential ambush as the pursuing warriors neither gained ground nor fell back. If the attackers had brethren waiting in the next draw, there was no need for the pursuers to accept even minimal losses. All the warriors needed to do was chase the stage into a two-sided ambush and the battle would be over in seconds.

Jason flipped his Winchester barrel down and slid it into the scabbard in front of his right knee. He reached back behind his saddle pack and pulled out his long rifle. The single-shot Spencer was modified with a forty-four-inch octagonal barrel. A powerful scope was mounted to the top of the barrel to allow extreme long-distance shooting. Jason had hit stationary targets just under a mile away with the weapon.

He dismounted and steadied the thirteen-pound weapon across the saddle. He peered through the scope, scanning the trail as it dipped ahead of the stage. As expected, he saw movement in the draw below the line of sight of the approaching stage and soldiers. It would be quite a long shot at the extreme edge of his range. He'd succeed only if his targets stayed put while he tried to hit them from such a great distance, and he'd only get one shot. As soon as the distant warriors knew he had them in his sights, they'd smartly start moving around. Hitting a moving target a mile away could only be the wildest stroke of luck. Regardless, massacre awaited the soldiers and the travelers on the coach as soon as they entered the draw.

Jason turned his attention to the victims, focusing his scope on the racing stage. As near as he could tell, seven or eight civilians filled the big coach to capacity.

Jason had only half a minute to act before the coach and the pursuing warriors were out of his effective range. He wanted to fire a warning shot to discourage the warriors from their raid, but he knew with all the gunfire and the thunder of hooves down on the trail, neither the soldiers nor the warriors would hear his shot. He didn't want to take a life, but he didn't seem to have any other choice. Kill one to save a dozen. It didn't take much brainwork to figure that one out.

The horse whinnied and shook its head, then pawed the ground with its left hind leg.

"Easy, Grady." Jason patted the horse's flank and spoke gently to the animal as if it could understand him. "Things are fixin' to get a bit noisy, but it's nothing you haven't been through before."

Two years back, he'd found Grady waiting patiently by his dying master's side on the plains of western Texas. The grizzled old man sat leaning against a tree in the middle of nowhere, waiting for someone to come along and see to his burial. He'd been gored by a wild steer and trampled by several others, and both his legs were broken in more than one place. The left side of his chest was caved in nearly to his backbone.

"I got careless," the old man croaked when Jason fed him water. "I shoulda quit this work like the missus told me." The old man managed enough strength to grab Jason's arm. "Just take care of Grady for me."

The obedient horse whinnied as if it knew its name, and Jason glanced over. When he looked back, ready to ask after the old man's kinfolk, he was dead.

Over the past couple of years, Jason had come to appreciate Grady. The big roan was tough, yet gentle, and was very obedient. The animal possessed great stamina and had carried Jason through the worst that man and nature could conjure up. He liked its color too. The animal wore a reddish-brown coat that was thickly interspersed with gray.

He related to Grady as if the animal had a personality, and the horse responded to Jason similarly. He'd trained Grady not to react to the sounds of weapons fire and had even shot the Spencer off the saddle a few times. He knew the animal would not spook.

He grabbed a trio of .50-caliber shells from a saddle pocket, locked one into the Spencer's chamber, and took aim. He sighted down into the valley and made his adjustments to account for the half-mile distance and his target's forward movement.

When Jason pulled the trigger, Grady skittered only slightly against the tremendous explosion of sound. The cartridges packed the powerful explosive force of one hundred seventy grains of black powder, propelling a seven-hundred-grain bullet toward its target at more than fifteen hundred feet per second.

The recoil of the weapon slammed against Jason's shoulder, and his right boot slipped a bit. The rifle barrel bounced up, then dropped back down against the saddle, the scope right in front of Jason's waiting eye. In less than a second, Jason ejected the first spent shell and inserted another. He aimed and pulled the trigger a second time in case the first shot missed.

When the scope dropped back down in front of his eye, he reloaded a third time and waited. A .50-caliber bullet with that much force behind it pretty much destroyed whatever it struck.

There were women and children on that stage. Had the battle been only between the warriors and the soldiers, Jason would have left it alone. He had no interest in taking sides in the war between the army and the Apache, but in his mind, war should never involve unarmed civilians.

He mentally counted three seconds and knew his first shot missed. His aim was true on the second shot.

CHAPTER 3

JUH AND HIS BAND HAD been on the move almost constantly for the last six summers. His people spent most of the year in their mountain stronghold of northern Mexico, but they always welcomed the opportunity to journey north and visit with family and friends of Victorio and Nana's bands. Lately, though, the two other leaders rarely had their people together on the Warm Springs reservation north of the Gila at the same time.

When Juh brought his people up into the valley of the Gila River, he learned both Victorio and Nana had taken their people even farther north into the Black Hills and the San Mateo mountains to elude army scout patrols. So, instead of continuing north to Warm Springs, Juh camped his people on the banks of the Middle Fork of the Gila River where it merged with the West Fork. Hundred-foot-high cliffs protected the camp from the occasional high winds that raged through the wide-open Gila Valley. During the extremely hot weather, the cliff walls shaded the camp for most of the day.

Though the US Government had reclaimed the Warm Springs reservation that had been promised to Victorio in exchange for his treaty of peace, the army could never discover with certainty when Victorio or Nana and their people were actually present on the reservation. The army routinely sent out detachments to scout for the Apache, but the mountain landscape made the deployments difficult. Apache lookouts always saw and heard the noisy and carelessly advancing soldiers. By the time the army arrived at a camp, the entire Apache village would have moved. Juh's camp on the Gila River was no less secure. It wasn't as safe as the stronghold in Mexico, but the bluecoats rarely scouted into the high mountain valleys.

Juh's tepee, and those of his wives, sat in the center of the camp. Those of other elders and warriors of status were clustered a comfortable distance from his. He approached the camp from the rear since the doorways of all the homes faced to the east in the Apache tradition. He greeted some of the women and children with a smile as they walked around him, then paused beside the door of the tepee occupying the position of honor to the left of his own as he faced it. The thick hide flap swung to the side as if the occupant had been summoned by some hidden signal.

An elderly woman, stooped with advanced age, walked out to meet him. She stood wordlessly as he greeted her.

"Grandmother," he said. "You look well today."

She nodded and smiled, showing gaps of missing teeth. "I opened my eyes this morning, and I am still breathing. That is no small thing."

Juh smiled in return. Though she was not his blood relative, he called her Grandmother as a name of great respect, as did everyone else. Two generations removed from his own parents, Grandmother was said to be the oldest living Apache of all the tribes. Over a hundred summers old, she was the most respected of all the elders.

Juh always thought her round face held a distinguished beauty, as if she held the wisdom of the ages in her countenance. The outer corners of her eyelids drooped downward and made her look sleepy or unaware. Sometimes he didn't know if her eyes were actually open, but Juh suspected she saw everything and her mind was as sharp as anyone's.

As always, he shared his discovery with her first. "I have had a troubling vision."

She nodded knowingly. "I remember a time when no one had ever seen a White man. In those days, the Apache were hunters instead of warriors. When I was a child, we could travel for two moons in any direction and never depart Apache land. Those days are no more."

Juh nodded and explained what he saw in the cave. "I will speak to the people after the evening meal."

Grandmother nodded, and Juh went into his tepee. The *White-Eyes* had called him a chief. They seemed either unwilling or unable to learn Apache names or customs. To prove how little they cared to learn about his people, White folks sometimes referred to any Apache as Chief, so much so that Juh considered the word an insult. Failure to honor or accept cultural differences was one of the primary reasons why the Apache and the army remained at war. Juh was convinced the *White-Eyes* sought to destroy all they feared and to force change on all they could not understand. There seemed no room in the land for a culture that was different from that of the White man.

He reflected on the new army tactics—sending Black soldiers after his people. Grandmother had told the other elders long ago that the slaves had found a way to find their freedom by accepting the White man's ways and living in his culture, by his rules. She said that, as distasteful and foreign as it seemed, the Apache would also have to find a way to do the same.

The elders of the tribes had scoffed at her notion and had chosen to continue waging war. Now Juh realized Grandmother was right. She had known for years what he had just discovered that very day.

Juh lay on his favorite blanket. As was accorded his status, his tepee was more spacious than all the others, and he could stretch out his six-foot frame twice over without touching the walls, even with his arms reaching over his head.

He sat upright for a while, gripping his hands in frustration. Safe in his solitude, Juh displayed the emotions he felt, a luxury he allowed himself only in private. He banged his fists together a few times.

After a few fitful moments, he simply held his head in his hands and rocked slowly forward and back. Then he banged his fists together again. The Apache and the *White-Eyes* would never live together in peace.

He remembered back so many years ago when his father explained to him the meaning of the term *White-Eyes*.

"The name comes from an old Apache word that really means pale-eyes," his father had said. "Except for some half-breeds, all Apache have dark eyes. Until the White man came into our land, we had never seen a person with eyes of blue or gray or light brown. No one remembers how 'pale-eyes' became 'white-eyes,' but now—just as they call us *Chief*—we call all outsiders *White-Eyes*, whether their eyes are pale or dark."

Finally, Juh lay back and folded his hands across his stomach. He took a deep breath to calm himself, then exhaled in exasperation. Juh was leader of the band of Nednhi Apache. It had taken him a long time to understand why the *White-Eyes* referred to all the southern Apache tribes as Chiricahua. Perhaps it was for convenience, or maybe it was so they wouldn't have to learn all the names that distinguished each tribe.

Geronimo led his group of Chiricahua Apache, Victorio led his Warm Springs Apache, and Nana led the Mimbres Apache. The White man had grouped all the tribes together under one name that they could understand—Chiricahua.

In the beginning, the whites' lack of understanding of such obvious Apache tribal differences angered Juh. In time though, he accepted that it made little difference how they viewed the Apache people. In fact, there were differences in the religions and customs among the White races, but Juh could no sooner explain those differences than whites could describe the different Apache customs.

Juh was a leader, but not so much because of his accomplishments as a warrior, although his deeds in war contributed greatly to his status. As with all Apache leaders, Juh was elected to his position because of his wisdom and his medicine.

He sighed again, acknowledging another major difference between the Apache and the *White-Eyes*. The medicine of the whites was totally different from Apache medicine. Their medicine most often took the form of strange liquids and powders, which they used to heal their sick and wounded. When Juh was younger and first learned of these White men called *doctors*, he found it inconceivable that they would cut into their wounded with metal blades. Indeed, this cutting was a form of healing in the White cultures. In time, the Apache had occasion to approach White doctors when Apache natural methods could not heal a battle wound or a strange new illness. In this regard, the White man's medicine was powerful.

To the Apache, natural herbal remedies of the land were only a small part of spiritual medicine. The Apache made spiritual medicine also for purposes other than healing. A warrior was rarely elected to lead his band if he possessed no such medicine. Those he led must believe in the power of his medicine or they would not follow.

Juh's medicine was his power to foretell the future. Literally, his name meant *He Sees Ahead*. Long ago, his father learned of Juh's ability and named him accordingly. Now, Juh's vision had shown him the future of his people. He'd lead them back to Mexico, and they'd follow him because they believed in his medicine.

After the evening meal, he planned to share his vision as he had done many times before. Over the years he'd proven that his medicine—his ability to see visions of what was to come—was strong. No one ever doubted what he saw in his visions would most certainly become reality.

Juh heard a scratch on the cloth door of his tepee. When he pushed the flap aside, he was surprised to discover the entire area was in the deep shadow of early evening. He'd fallen asleep. His youngest and only surviving son, Daklugie, stood silently for a moment until invited to speak, then he relayed his mother's instructions to summon Juh to the fire. His beautiful wife, Ishton, favorite and best loved of all his wives, had let him rest.

Juh followed his son and took his place in the clearing where his people would eat their evening meal. Ishton's servants had spread skins and blankets in a semicircle in the clearing for Juh and his men. No warriors or leaders from other bands visited, so Poncé, Juh's *segundo*—second-in-command—took the place of honor immediately to Juh's left. Other warriors sat to the left of Poncé according to their rank and fighting reputation, while the elders sat to Juh's right. Women and children sat beyond the warriors and elders.

When all were seated, Juh held up a hand and was greeted by instant silence. He lit a cigarette of tobacco rolled into an oak leaf and smoked it in the ceremonial way, without inhaling. He sucked in just enough smoke to fill his cheeks. He savored the bitter flavor for a moment, then rose and blew smoke to each of the four directions. After extinguishing the tobacco leaf, he sat and raised his hand again, and the women began serving the food as directed by Ishton.

Everyone ate in silence. During the meal, Juh made no conversation, nor asked for any. When he saw that everyone had finished, he looked at the warriors seated to his left. Then he considered Grandmother, the most respected of the elders, seated directly to his right. She nodded to him, a single down-up movement of her head. He nodded in return and briefly considered each of the other elders.

Juh gestured to Ishton seated on the far side of the clearing, and she immediately dismissed all the small children. Only adolescent males in training to become warriors were allowed to remain with the adults.

"We are the *Indeh*," Juh began. "The Dead." He paused to let everyone consider his words. "This I have seen in my vision on this day. The *White-Eyes* will kill us all."

CHAPTER 4

J ASON HAD AIMED TO HIT the warrior's pony rather than the man, but one could never predict exactly how the breeze or heat-induced air currents would affect the path of a bullet during its two-second journey over half a mile.

The first shot missed, but the lead warrior spilled to the ground as Jason's second shot ripped through his horse's flank, just behind the warrior's leg. Another of the riders tried to leap his horse over the first but lost his seat as his mount stumbled. From high up on the hill, the scene seemed almost comical to Jason, as men and animals sprawled to the scrub grass together. The other warriors seemed to sense something unnatural had happened, something more than just felled riders. They pulled into a group and all finally looked in Jason's direction.

As the maimed horse struggled to get up, Jason fired another shot into its head, ending its pain. He also sent a clear message that he could pick off each of the warriors with little difficulty. They understood the message. Calmly, they doubled up and rode away from the stagecoach, presumably back toward the Mimbres River and north to the mountains. One of the men quickly rode his horse to the top of the hill a quarter-mile west of Jason.

With the attack from the rear thwarted, the soldiers halted the stage. They took up a defensive position in front of the stagecoach, carbines at the ready, barrels pointed skyward. The warrior near Jason yelled into the distance. Almost immediately, another raiding party rode slowly into view from the draw.

Jason felt the satisfaction of victory without bloodshed. The ambush was thwarted and both sides would likely realize that battle would now be costly. At the lone warrior's signal, the distant raiding party trotted off to the north. The man turned to face Jason for a moment. His posture and careful movements gave Jason the impression the man was a fierce warrior, a leader of experienced fighting men.

Jason understood the band's strategy. They weren't looking for a victory with minimal losses. They planned on total victory with zero casualties to their own fighters, and they might have succeeded if not for Jason's interference. Even with Jason's help, it was likely the soldiers still couldn't have defeated the band. The numbers were too lopsided. While Jason could have eliminated most of the closest warriors if they'd continued after the stagecoach, the warriors waiting in ambush probably would have eventually won the battle on superior numbers. But no soldier, Apache or army, sent his men into an offensive strike knowing victory could cost the lives of half his men.

The warrior facing Jason from a distance raised his rifle over his head for a brief second, perhaps as a gesture of understanding or an indication of respect. Maybe he was grateful Jason didn't murder his warriors when he clearly had the opportunity and the means to do so. Jason simply acknowledged the gesture with a lazy wave in return and watched the warrior guide his pony to the north.

The band would raid again, but that wasn't Jason's problem. The innocent folks in the stage below him would live. That's all he cared about. He packed away his Spencer rifle and grabbed a handful of grain from a pocket on the left side of his packs. Grady reached his head to the left in anticipation and took the grain from Jason's outstretched palm. Jason spent the next few minutes performing his ritual of gratitude, talking to Grady and thanking him for staying cool under gunfire and not shaking his aim.

He slowly poured a bit of water from his canteen into his hat and let Grady drink his fill. He stuck the wet hat back on his head and took a mouthful of water from the canteen. He held the hot water without swallowing for a few seconds, savoring its wetness as he mounted up.

He finally swallowed and nudged Grady into a walk toward the west. Below him, the soldiers had taken up escort formation again. One soldier rode point a good distance in front of the stage, and two other soldiers took up position on each side. The last soldier rode far enough back not to need a kerchief to protect him from the stagecoach dust. The rear soldier waved up at him, and he returned the gesture.

An hour later, Jason dropped down off the last hill and fell in a half mile behind the stage. He followed the soldiers and the stage back into the flat valley as the trail led straight toward Silver City.

Six hours later, he rode west into the town, straight up Broadway. The stage sat parked at the northwest corner of Broadway and Bullard, and the passengers had already disembarked. A tall, elderly man with curly, gray hair walked diagonally across the street toward the saloon with four brown-skinned soldiers who were leading their horses. Leaning heavily on an ivory-handled cane gripped in his left hand, he beckoned to Jason with his other.

"The rearguard soldier mentioned you're the one who came to our aid out yonder," he said as Jason pulled up. "I'm obliged to you, sir."

"As am I," a soldier said.

Jason dismounted as they spoke. Nearly as tall as Jason and twice as thick in the chest, the soldier peeled his leather riding glove from his right hand. As the soldier offered a handshake, Jason thought the man was nearly wide enough in the shoulders to have to turn sideways to walk through a doorway.

"Happy to help, Sergeant." Jason noticed three gold stripes on the blue sleeve of the man's uniform, near the shoulder. He didn't know what the diamond was for, but he knew three stripes meant the soldier was a sergeant. The man's grip was so strong it almost hurt.

"Lafayette Crawford, Company B, Ninth Cavalry."

Jason nodded at Crawford and started to speak his own name. The elder man interrupted, and Jason saw in the man's eyes a calculated ploy to gain control of the conversation.

"I'm Senator Joseph Bennington," the elder man said. "I'd be pleased if all you fellows would have a drink with me."

"Sounds like a good idea, Sergeant," another soldier added. The two-striper was a short, light-skinned, blue-eyed mulatto.

"As you were, Corporal."

"Aw, c'mon, L.C. Loosen up some, we're off duty now."

The corporal turned and walked into the saloon. The other two one-stripers looked at the sergeant. After a moment, he relented with a nod. The privates hurried after the corporal.

L.C. must mean Lafayette Crawford. Immediately, he realized that Crawford and the defiant corporal had to be close friends. No other way a lesser soldier would speak so familiarly with a sergeant, off duty or not.

"What's your name, sir?" the senator said.

"Jay."

"Jay what?"

"Just Jay."

Jason had taken to introducing himself only as Jay for the past few years. After seven years of outlaw life, he'd won quite a few gun contests, mostly against bounty hunters trying to collect the dead or alive reward for bringing him in. Even after his trial ended with the dismissal of all charges, there had been a lot of revenge-seeking kinfolk that continued to hunt him. His real name drew trouble like flies on fresh cow patties.

"Very well, Jay." Senator Bennington waved an invitation toward the saloon door and Jason followed Crawford inside. The senator brought up the rear. The man had shrewd and intelligent light blue eyes. Jason saw the older man studying him without directly appearing to do so. The senator was sizing him up with discreet glances.

"I've never seen a two-gun rig quite like that before," Bennington said just before they entered. He indicated Jason's gun belt and holsters with a wave of his right hand.

"Had it made special," Jason replied, patting his right holster. The two holsters hung low off his gun belt and the thigh pads were made of extra-stiff leather that allowed for a smooth quick draw. The holsters were positioned so his gun butts hovered even with his palms when he rested his hands at his sides.

Unlike so many other gunfighters, Jason didn't have to reach up or down or across his body to get his guns. With just a quick curl of his fingertips, he had instant contact with his weapons. All he had to do was lift and shoot. That was one reason why he had a faster draw than most. He also was gifted with extremely fast reflexes, and he practiced a lot.

As Jason followed Crawford into the saloon, he noticed the door was a single-wide opening, but it had two spring-loaded bat-wing doors. The big sergeant had an inch to spare on each side of his massive shoulders as he passed through. At the bar to the left of the swinging doors, the corporal was having a heated conversation with the barkeep.

"I told you, ain't no Negroes drinking in my bar. Soldiers or not."

"This ain't your bar," the corporal argued. "Saunders always serves us."

"You see James Saunders around here anywhere?" The barkeep taunted the corporal as he glanced around the room at the few patrons. "I didn't think so. It's just me. Fred." The man smiled, obviously satisfied with his wit. "And Fred don't drink with—"

"I'll have a bottle, Barkeep," Jason interrupted. He stepped to the bar beside the corporal and produced a shiny coin from his pocket. "And a tall glass." Fred snatched up the coin and reached behind him for a bottle and a tall beer glass. When he placed them on the bar, Jason gave him a half-smile that never quite reached his eyes. Fred hesitated, narrowing his eyes, and finally seemed to realize Jason's skin was a very light brown complexion, not white. He reached for the bottle, but Jason moved faster and snatched the bottle and the glass out of Fred's reach.

"I told you, no Negroes drink in here." He sneered at Jason. "And especially no half-breeds."

Jason's eyes flared, and he felt a flash of heat around his neck. He'd learned to hate that word over the years and had gotten into serious trouble about it on more than one occasion. He entertained the thought of pistol-whipping Fred, but he controlled his temper quickly.

"Mister," Jason returned coldly. "I paid for the bottle, and so now it belongs to me. I'll do whatever I please with it." He turned toward the corporal and shoved the glass toward him. Then he uncorked the bottle and started to pour.

The corporal added, "You'd think these folks would be a bit more grateful for what we do for them." One of the privates to the corporal's left nodded in agreement.

Fred announced loudly to the room, "Colored soldiers get paid to keep the Injuns under control around here. Sure, y'all save some White folks from gettin' scalped, but it don't mean I have to drink with y'all."

Jason filled the glass to the rim. He looked into the soldier's blue eyes, recalling that he'd seen a blue-eyed Black man only once before, maybe ten years ago and way over in Kentucky.

"As you were, Levi," Crawford said gently. "We don't want trouble. Let's go over to Big Larry's up on Bullard Street." Sergeant Crawford stepped behind Jason and laid a huge hand on the corporal's shoulder.

Corporal Levi Shelton eyed the tall glass of brown liquid hungrily. "One sip, L.C.? Just to make a point."

"And at what price?" Crawford stepped toward the door. "Let's go." Something about his posture, his demeanor, told Jason the sergeant was a man accustomed to having others following his orders without question. The privates turned with him.

Shelton hesitated. For a moment, Jason thought he was going to take a sip. The man's blue eyes widened in surprise just as Jason started to set the half-empty whiskey bottle down. He heard the familiar sound of metal dragging on a wood shelf followed by the clicks of twin hammers on a double-barrel shotgun being pulled back.

Jason dropped the whiskey bottle and drew his right gun. He had it cocked and pointed at Fred's forehead just as the man aimed the shotgun.

"That would be a mistake, Mister," Jason said.

Beside him, Corporal Shelton set the whiskey bottle upright on the countertop. Jason listened to the liquid pour off the bar and splash onto the floor as he stared at the barkeep.

Sergeant Crawford held up his hands to Jason's left, as if to try to defuse the confrontation. The senator, who now stood slightly behind Jason just to his left, sucked in a breath like he was going to do the same as Crawford. As the man uttered his first syllable, the saloon doors burst open, and Jason heard the sound of boot heels stomp in. The intruder hesitated, and Jason *felt* the newcomer concentrating on him. Heard him suck in his breath like men always did as they feel the excitement of making a play for a holstered gun. Still facing the barkeep, Jason drew his left gun and pointed it at the new threat.

"That's a dangerous thought over there, Mister," Jason said, still staring at Fred. A couple seconds later, he turned his gaze on the newcomer.

CHAPTER 5

Captain Ambrose Taylor topped the last range of low hills west of the mining town of Silver City. He paused and surveyed the town below him.

Four dirt streets housed a gaggle of brick and frame structures. Beyond the limits of the central part of town, he saw a random collection of shacks, warehouses, and corrals scattered across the land, stretching almost a mile to the north and south. He'd seen a dozen mining towns across New Mexico and Arizona, and they all looked pretty much like Silver City.

Nudging his right boot against his horse's flank, Captain Taylor guided the animal down the trail, more or less following the natural contour of the hilly landscape. He merged onto the main east-west road. *Broadway,* he noted as he passed a neatly-painted street sign. Well-dressed ladies and gentlemen paraded up the boardwalks and crossed at the intersections. Workers carrying their bags of tools or supplies crossed the street haphazardly without looking, as if daring horse and buggy traffic to stop them from getting wherever they were going. Office and shop workers left their buildings and merged with the dozens of evening shoppers moving in and out of the stores or restaurants.

Most of the passersby paid him no attention. A few of the well-dressed men cast him a curious glance. When he wore a uniform, he intimidated most men, but he always attracted the powerful leaders. Women found him irresistible too. He knew he wasn't even close to being handsome and had long ago accepted that reality. Women seemed to overlook his unattractive face though, in favor of the ramrod-straight posture and his imposing military bearing.

He wore no uniform today, but still he caught the eyes of two ladies just beyond the boardwalk. Both stood on the second-floor balcony under the awning of a hotel. The raised deck kept the guests free of billowing dust from passing horses. It also allowed the well-to-do guests to look down on people who passed on the boardwalk in front of them. Taylor had the distinct feeling the balcony gave the hotel's guests an air of importance—of being above all the little people who couldn't afford to stay there.

One of the women blushed and looked away, but the other, a full-bodied redhead, matched his gaze. She gave him a suggestive come-hither smile. He entertained the thought of guiding his horse over to engage the woman in conversation, but his orders flashed into his mind.

Avoid all contact with everyone except the senator.

Taylor tore his gaze away. He slouched his posture and tried to pretend he was just another one of the little people, just another ranch hand or miner looking for work. He traveled in a disguise of range clothes, and he'd let his face go unshaven for over a week. He was, after all, on a secret mission to receive special orders directly from the senator, though he had no idea what he was supposed to do with the orders. General Miles had personally given him instructions back at Sixth Cavalry Headquarters in Arizona.

"Meet the senator over in Silver City, do what he tells you to do, and don't return until your mission is complete."

The general released Taylor from all other army duties and responsibilities. He had no deployments to command, no drills, and no training. Now, his one-week journey was about to end. Taylor rode over and dismounted at the stagecoach office on the corner of Broadway and Bullard. He mashed his hat down low over his eyes and scanned the people around him, familiarizing himself with his surroundings.

Taylor wrapped his reins over the hitching rail and retrieved his canteen. He took a long gulp of water. He turned his face up at the hot, foul-tasting liquid, but he swallowed it anyway. Then he hooked his canteen back behind the saddle and walked into the office.

The thermometer hanging on the doorjamb read a hundred and four. *Almost sundown high up in the mountains,* Taylor thought, *and almost hot enough to fry an egg on the boardwalk. Even Arizona hadn't seemed as hot as this godforsaken, high-desert country.*

"Help you, sir?" a voice said in heavily accented English.

The captain glanced to his left and focused his most contempt-filled glare at an elderly Mexican man. *One of the little people,* Taylor thought.

"Senator Joseph Bennington," he commanded. The old man shrugged, so Taylor continued. "He was supposed to come in on the stage." He nodded out the window at the empty stage parked on the Bullard Street side of the building.

The old man nodded with a look of understanding and pointed farther up Broadway, across the street at the saloon. He started to speak, but Taylor turned away without acknowledgment. He left the door open behind him and walked diagonally across the street to the corner saloon.

"Hey there! Watch out!"

Taylor jumped back as a horse-drawn wagon clamored past him loaded with tired-looking warehouse workers. Had he been in uniform, he would have dared the driver not to stop, maybe even at gunpoint. He was no longer an officer who commanded instant obedience with a mere look though. In his range disguise he was one of the little people, and it disgusted him. It made him want to spit.

He crossed behind the wagon and made his way over to the saloon. Then he froze in mid-step. The hind ends of four army mounts stared him in the face. Raised in the East, the horses were larger and stronger than frontier-bred animals. They were purchased specifically to carry soldiers with full rations and equipage on long scout missions. Fort Bayard lay only ten miles east of Silver City. *Army mounts in town could only mean one thing,* he thought.

Colored soldiers from the Ninth Cavalry were in the saloon.

He looked around the town again, his disgust for the desert southwest bubbling up inside him. Even more, he hated all the land's filthy inhabitants he was forced to encounter. Lying Mexican sheepherders who couldn't speak English. Illiterate White miners with no ambition except to get rich on gold and minerals. Texas cowboys with no loyalties to anyone but themselves, not even to their own ranches. Murderous Indian savages who could never be found or killed. And now, Black soldiers.

Taylor hated the West and everyone in it. He turned back to the nearest army mount and removed his hat, then slapped the animal hard across the rump with it. The well-trained animal didn't even flinch. More frustrated now, he swung his arm back to strike the animal harder. Instead, a moment of sudden clarity hit him in mid-swing. The advantage of being out of uniform meant he no longer had to act like an officer. He didn't have to keep his anger under control.

He smashed his hat back on his head and stormed through the saloon's double swinging doors to give the Colored soldiers a verbal lashing. They were to blame for his plight in the new army.

Taylor froze in the doorway so suddenly that the narrow doors swung back and bounced hard against his shoulders. Fear quickly replaced his anger as he focused on the barrel of a Schofield .45-caliber pistol pointed right between his eyes. He had yet to fully realize the fleeting thought that had just tumbled through his brain—a strange desire to shoot one of the Black men in front of him—and was mildly surprised to find his own right hand hovering over his holstered gun. The gunman had yet to look at him, so Taylor entertained a second thought. He wrapped his fingers around his gun butt and started to pull the weapon free.

"That's a dangerous thought, Mister," the gunman said.

The man's thumb cocked the gun. An icy shiver crept up

Taylor's spine as the gunman finally turned his head toward him. He *knew* this man. He remembered the famous outlaw face from Wanted posters he'd seen years back. He gazed into the penetrating brown eyes of Jason Peares.

CHAPTER 6

"THEY WILL KILL US ALL," Juh repeated.

Silence greeted Juh as he returned the stares of his people one by one. The shadows deepened across the mountain valley, but the semidarkness was belied by the bright blue evening sky above.

Juh knew none of his people doubted that he spoke of army soldiers. The elders would understand what he was about to say, but the young warriors might not. War had become a way of life for the Apache—the only life most of the young men had ever known. Each was anxious to prove his courage in battle. These young ones could not truly comprehend fighting an enemy that possessed an unlimited supply of men, weapons, and food.

The Apaches now numbered only a few hundred. Juh knew all his warriors and those of the other leaders, would bravely fight to their deaths against the army's slavery, but when those few hundred were gone, there would be no more Apache. Now Juh knew this would happen in his lifetime.

Juh began to speak confidently. He had a lot to say and hoped he could get through it all without lapsing into an embarrassing fit of stuttering, which sometimes plagued him during his long talks.

"Many seasons past, the great leader Cochise agreed to end his wars against the army. In exchange for this promise of peace, the Great White Father in the east turned the homeland of Cochise into a vast reservation. He made pictures on a paper and called it a map, in case other White men forgot where it was located. 'On this reservation map,' said the Great White Father and his generals, 'all the tribes of the Apache known to the *White-Eyes* as Chiricahua could live in peace forever.'

"Later, he took back the land, forcing the Chiricahua to move to another, much larger reservation called San Carlos. In this new reservation, *Ussen*, the Creator of all things, scorched the ground so harshly nothing could grow. We could not farm the land and there was no game to hunt for food.

"We have always been nomadic hunters, always moving from place to place. This was our way of life. Yet, the army would not allow us off the reservation even to hunt for enough food to feed our starving children. They forced us to stay, to become farmers on a land that could bear no crops.

"At first, the army provided food for us, but it was not our kind of food, and they never gave us enough to keep our bellies full. We became nothing more than animals, pitiful beggars standing in line to take scraps of bacon and flour from the army. Our people starved, and many died in that wasteland where there is little water.

"Worst of all, we could no longer move our homes as had been our custom. After a time, the day came when I had to walk almost half a day just to find a place suitable to move my bowels. But most of our people could not walk far and our camps became filthy with waste and infested with new diseases the Apache had never seen before.

"So we left, as did the people of Geronimo, Victorio, and Nana." He pronounced the last, *Nah-NAY*. "We are always pursued by the army, but at least now we have our freedom."

He paused for a few moments so everyone could grasp the importance of what he was about to say.

"Then the great leader Victorio made peace with the army and was promised the reservation of Warm Springs forever. And the Great White Father took back the land and tried to force Victorio's people, and all the other Apaches, to return to that wretched place, San Carlos."

Juh paused and looked around at his people. They waited and gazed at him, anticipating his vision.

"Today, I saw our future in the ancient caves of the cliff dwellers. I saw smoke form at the entrance of a cave high up on the cliff wall, where none but a bird can reach. And through the smoke, thousands of bluecoat soldiers marched eight abreast into the cave. At first, I saw only the brave, dark-skinned Buffalo Soldiers. Then, I also saw White soldiers. The cave shown to me by *Ussen* must have been very large, for none of the soldiers ever returned. And there was no end to them. From the east they kept coming."

Juh paused again for nearly half a minute.

"We are the *Indeh*. The army will hunt each band of Apache like wild animals. They will keep us moving, chasing us into and out of the mountains until we can no longer gather enough food to survive. Our hidden supplies will vanish as we consume them, and we will be unable to remain anywhere long enough to gather more food to replenish our supplies.

"For every soldier we kill, two more can take his place. For every supply wagon we raid, two more will be sent from the east to the forts. One by one, the Apache bands will be exterminated unless we fight together. All the Apache everywhere must gather and fight under one leader. Only then will we be strong enough to fight against the army.

"I have heard that several of our great leaders are considering joining forces so we can negotiate peace with the army in exchange for a large reservation in the mountains of this place the *White-Eyes* call New Mexico Territory. It will hold Warm Springs and all the mountains around it. There, all the Apache people from all the lands nearby will live in peace.

"The leaders talk of putting aside all our tribal differences and forming an army to defend this reservation, so we won't have to trust the Great White Father to keep his promises." Juh looked around and nodded. "There is even talk of forming new alliances with bands of non-Apache from the north, people we have made war against for many generations." Juh looked up and sat straighter, his resolve clear.

"For many moons I have been against a costly war with the army, and I have been against forming an alliance with other tribes. But now it is clear that we must force peace upon the *White-Eyes* with a strong and unified army of our own. Only then will we be able to prevent their treachery."

Juh paused again, this time looking at each of the elders seated to his right. A couple of the old men nodded at the wisdom of his words.

"Until today, I believed if we kept moving, the army would tire of chasing us down to the border of Mexico where they cannot trespass. Now I know this will never happen. We must join with the other Apache bands.

"In three days, we'll move our people to our stronghold in Mexico and stay there until I can meet with the other leaders. The Apache will form an army like none the *White-Eyes* have ever seen. We must demand peace talks with the army. If they refuse, we will force them into a war that will take the lives of many bluecoats. The mothers in the East will cry every day as we take their sons from them. Their cries will make the Great White Father stop the war against us and we will finally have peace."

Juh inclined his head and signaled the conclusion to his talk with a wave of his hand. Beside him, Poncé, his *segundo*, spoke.

"What of the supply wagons that travel from the southern fort up to the fort by the great river?"

Juh nodded. An Apache warrior serving as a scout at Fort Bayard had been passing information on supply movements to Juh's warriors since they arrived at the Gila River several weeks ago. Usually, the Apache considered scouts that worked at the forts as traitors, but this particular scout had proven his loyalty many times. Juh had successfully raided army supply wagons three times based on the scout's information, and he had lost no warriors in those raids. Even better, the warriors had been able to avoid taking even a single life of a bluecoat, so the army had not pursued the raiding parties.

The new information from the scout indicated that the army planned to escort nine wagons fully laden with weapons, ammunition, vegetables, and seed grain from Fort Cummings to Fort Craig. The soldiers also planned to drive several dozen mules and horses north to replace worn-out animals, but the scout reported that the wagon train would be only lightly escorted since many of the troops from the forts were already scouring the mountains to the east, hunting for Victorio and Nana's bands.

Juh planned an attack that would isolate and capture a single wagon. If successful, his people would have more than enough supplies for the long trip to the stronghold. He figured the army would consider one wagon an acceptable loss and would not pursue the warriors, especially if they took none of the soldiers' lives. If the soldiers did pursue the raiders, they would weaken their defense of the remaining wagons and risk losing more supplies.

"We need the ammunition and food supplies. We will depart tomorrow at sunrise and take the supplies at nightfall the day after tomorrow. Then we will return here to begin the long journey to the south."

CHAPTER 7

"**N**OBODY MOVE. NOBODY BREATHE," JASON Peares said. "Then nobody dies." He was keenly aware that a single movement, even a flick of an eye, might start the bloodbath.

As he gazed into the plotting eyes of the barkeep, Fred, Jason became aware of the other sights and sounds in the room. He heard whispers across the room from other men in the bar who had scurried out of the path of gunfire. He also heard the nervous breathing of Fred, the soldiers, even the yet-unknown man standing in the doorway. The senator, though, was calm.

The room smelled dusty. Jason caught a whiff of mud and cow dung brought in on the boots of hundreds of visitors, no doubt ground into the plank flooring over the years. Jason smelled sweat, from nervous fear and from hard work in the sun, along with the comfortable fragrance of leather—gloves, chaps, belts, hats.

Corporal Shelton and the two privates had already backed out of the line of fire and now stood to Jason's left as he faced the bar. Shelton had turned toward Taylor's sudden entry and had almost pulled his gun free when Jason's command froze everyone.

Jason knew if Fred the barkeep hit him point-blank with a load of buckshot, there wouldn't be enough of his upper body left to recognize. He also knew if Fred decided to try for a shot, he wouldn't be the only man caught in the deadly spray of pellets.

Sergeant Crawford stood close enough to Jason's left to catch some shot too. The newcomer in the doorway had landed himself directly in line with Jason and the barkeep. He'd catch a chest full of whatever was left after Jason was cut in two. Even the senator, now standing slightly behind Jason and to his right, might end up owning a pellet or two.

Facing the bar, Jason focused his gaze on Fred, but kept his ears primed for the slightest sound of movement from the man in the doorway. His right gun was pointed at a spot between Fred's eyes, while his left covered the newcomer. Fred froze still stooped over a bit from reaching under the counter for the shotgun. He had the weapon barely clear of the top of the bar, and it was pointed in the general direction of Jason's belly. His thoughts marched clearly across his face. Just a quick movement and he'd cut Jason down, but he knew he wouldn't live to see Jason's dead body hit the plank floor. Jason could see that clear realization in the man's eyes.

Sergeant Crawford spoke gently. "Think real hard about this, Jay." Jason felt the big man focus his attention on him. "You gonna kill Fred over a drink?"

"It ain't about the drink."

A few silent seconds passed, then Senator Bennington said, "Gentlemen, please." He stepped into the line of fire, as much as the bar would allow. "This isn't going to do anything but get all of us killed." He looked at Fred. "You don't want to die today, do you, Mister?"

Jason watched the barkeep, saw thoughts of a desperate victory fade from his face. Tension left Fred's shoulders and the man relaxed his grip on the shotgun. Jason slowly lowered his gun and thumbed the hammer of his forty-five back to rest against the chamber.

Jason turned his head toward Crawford. "It wasn't about the drink, Sergeant. He pulled first."

"Except he can get away with it and you can't." Crawford paused. "You understand what I'm saying?"

Jason nodded. "Sure. A White man can kill a Black man for just about any reason imaginable."

Crawford nodded. "And not have to worry too much about the consequences. Fact of life in these parts."

Fred added, "Might be a good idea to remember that too. Only way you're gettin' a drink in here is over my dead body."

Senator Bennington slowly reached out a hand and patted Jason's shoulder in a fatherly gesture. "You don't need that kind of trouble, Jay."

Jason shrugged the senator's hand away. "I'm familiar with that kind of trouble, Senator. And it don't bother me none too much." He finally turned his attention to Taylor, his left gun still pointed at the man's chest. Taylor stood frozen with fear, the bat-wing doors still resting against his shoulders. Jason motioned with his gun for Taylor to step out of his way. As the man complied, the doors closed, swinging slightly back and forth on spring-loaded hinges. Jason gave Taylor a long look before putting his left gun away. Taylor glanced away first and seemed to recognize the senator.

Jason left the group and shouldered his way through the doors. Outside, he took a deep breath to calm his nerves and waited while the soldiers stepped out onto the boardwalk beside him.

"I apologize about that, Sergeant." Jason gazed at the last remnant of the sun ducking behind the distant hills. "I just wanted to force the issue a bit. See if he'd back down. I didn't figure he'd get to killin' over a bottle of whiskey."

"Neither did I. But like you said, it wasn't really about a bottle." Crawford adjusted his cap and pointed up the street. "Let's go visit Big Larry up on Main Street. He'll serve us."

"L.C.," Shelton said. "Maybe you can have a word with the major when we get back to the fort. Maybe tell him to put this here saloon off-limits to the troops until the owner makes Fred serve everyone."

"I intend to do just that."

Jason walked in the street on Crawford's left with the corporal, while the two privates walked to Crawford's right and a bit behind him. He raised his eyebrow at the mention of a sergeant, especially a Black sergeant, dictating a course of action to a White officer.

"Will the major do it?" Jason asked.

Crawford nodded. "He will if I tell him to."

Suddenly, Jason had a new level of respect for the sergeant. Shelton explained the army way of conducting business.

"Don't you know, Jay? First Sergeants run the army. The officers are just around to stir up trouble." Shelton and the privates shared a laugh. "Don't make good sense for even a White man to get on the bad side of a first sergeant."

Jason had his explanation for the diamond on Crawford's sleeve. "I don't suppose this Big Larry is *Big Larry Murtock?*"

"That he is," Crawford said. "You know him?"

"I ran into a fellow down in Texas. Said Big Larry Murtock knew the whereabouts of a Colored folks' town up in Colorado somewhere."

"Hmm," Crawford mumbled. "I knew there were some Colored towns over in Kansas and the Indian Territories, what they're calling Oklahoma now, but I didn't know about any such towns out thisaway. Especially not up in Colorado."

Jason started to agree, but Shelton interrupted. "By the way, I'm Levi Shelton." Jason shook hands. "That there's Lee Humphrey." Shelton pointed out a short, powerfully built kid who had yet to need a razor. "And the other's Washington Comer." Looking about the same age as Humphrey and just as dark-skinned, Comer stood nearly six feet tall and was stick-thin.

Shelton continued. "How'd you learn to handle guns so fast?"

"Just woke up one day with a natural talent for shooting, I suppose." Jason thought back over the years. In his first gunfight, he simply closed his eyes and pulled his gun. At least, that's all he remembered. After the fear and gun smoke faded, he realized he'd killed four of the five men who murdered his family. Afterward, the bigoted sheriff of Malden, Missouri gave him little choice. Run or hang.

So he ran. Seven years later they finally caught him and put his neck in a noose on twenty-six counts of murder for all the bounty hunters he'd killed. In a strange turn of events, he was acquitted at his trial in Santa Fe, New Mexico. Despite his freedom, folks never stopped coming for him. There were always bounty hunters who didn't seem to know he was no longer an outlaw. There were kinfolk seeking revenge for hunters he'd killed during his outlaw years. There were reputation seekers who wanted to be the one who beat Jason Peares.

"I practice my skills just like you fellows practice soldiering. But mostly, it comes naturally."

Shelton nodded. "Well, I appreciate what you tried to do back there. Ol' Fred didn't even notice your skin color at first. Bein' a half-breed comes in handy sometimes, right?"

Jason stopped suddenly and grabbed a handful of Shelton's blouse, yanking the man toward him.

"What?" Shelton looked genuinely bewildered. Realizing the corporal didn't even know he'd offended him, Jason released the man's blouse. Then he turned and resumed walking.

"I never liked that word."

"Didn't mean no offense. Hey, I'm a half-breed too."

Jason ignored Shelton's attempt to apologize. "And I certainly don't want to be hearing it from my own kind."

Captain Taylor immediately formed a dislike for the senator. He'd started to introduce himself formally right after Jason Peares and the soldiers left, but the senator silenced him with a dismissive wave of the hand, then grabbed him by the arm and practically dragged him out of the saloon. They stood on the boardwalk for several seconds, watching Jay and the soldiers head around the corner and up Main Street.

Leaning on his cane, the senator hobbled to the corner and resumed watching the men. Taylor followed, silently fuming at his inability to get control of the last few minutes. First, that damned half-breed gunfighter drew down on him without even looking. Then he stared him down and made him look away first. If that wasn't bad enough, the man sneered at him as he walked out. Now this old, crippled politician wanted to drag him around like a puppy dog. He was a military officer, dammit! He was trained to take charge and lead men under any circumstance. Yet in the space of a couple of minutes, those two men robbed him of his ability to command. He had to find some way to get back in control.

"Walk with me to my hotel," Bennington said. The man reversed his direction and hobbled back up the street without waiting for Taylor to acknowledge him. "I'll give you your orders there."

They passed Fred's saloon and stepped into the intersection at Broadway and Bullard. The senator stopped in the middle of the street at the cursing of a wagon driver. It was the same one, Taylor noted, that almost ran him down earlier. Bennington simply stared at the man and stood in the wagon's path. The driver locked his brake against the protest of his horse. He glared at the senator but held his peace. *It's his status,* Taylor thought. He hated even pretending to be one of the little people.

"What's got you so curious about that outlaw?" Taylor asked.

Bennington smiled. "He's the solution I've been looking for."

"Solution to what?"

Ambrose Taylor stood in the middle of the intersection, waiting impatiently for the senator to answer. *The old cripple manipulated me,* he thought, *and made me wait and ask the question.* When he thought he'd burst from the wait, he opened his mouth to speak. The senator interrupted him.

"Powerful people in the government don't want peace with the Apache Indians. Over the past few weeks we've heard disturbing news that leaders of the different tribes are starting to discuss forming an alliance to negotiate peace with the army. We certainly don't want to negotiate with a united Apache nation. If they get organized.... Well, that's completely unacceptable."

Bennington paused and Taylor knew it was a deliberate ploy to make him ask the obvious. He swallowed his resentment and said, "And what does that gunfighter have to do with the Apache situation?"

"Why, he's the key, of course." The senator gestured, and Taylor followed him up the boardwalk toward the fancy hotel he'd seen on his ride into town. "He's going to help us destroy the Apache alliance."

CHAPTER 8

"REALLY?" TAYLOR SCREWED HIS EYEBROWS in confusion. "How can one outlaw affect an entire war?" He followed as the senator hobbled up the steps one at a time from the boardwalk into the expensive hotel. Bennington didn't stop at the reception desk but instead went straight through the lobby to the stairs at the back of the room like he owned the place.

"Why do you keep calling him an outlaw?" the senator said.

"Because he is," Taylor answered. "Or was, rather. I heard he had a trial a few years back and was acquitted." Bennington said nothing, so Taylor continued. "His name is Jason Peares."

Bennington stopped and turned. His eyes widened, then narrowed as if he were considering sinister plans. He chuckled. "This is better than I hoped. I knew he was a killer. I could see that in his eyes. But...*the* Jason Peares." He paused. "You're absolutely sure?"

Taylor nodded. The senator resumed his difficult climb up the stairs.

"Good. A man like that, running from the law all those years, he's a survivor. He has eluded many a posse and bounty hunter. He's killed outlaws and probably Indians too." The senator nodded again, this time to himself. "He'll do nicely."

"For what?"

"Wars are fought on battlefields, Captain," the senator said as they reached his second-floor room. "But they are *won* in political arenas."

Bennington closed the door behind Taylor then pointed with his cane at an ornate couch opposite the door. Taylor sat with his left elbow resting on the open window ledge. A hot breeze blew through his unkempt, blond hair. While Bennington hobbled around the room, first lighting a lamp, then attending to papers on the desk, Taylor studied the expensive suite. The desk sat against the east wall to his left under the only other window in the room. In the middle of the west wall, a lattice double door concealed the sleeping chamber. Bookshelves and other expensive furniture decorated the sitting room, and an exquisite rug covered the center of the polished oak slat floor.

The senator finally lowered himself into the comfortably cushioned chair in front of the desk. He faced Taylor and studied him through dark eyes that reminded Taylor of a predatory bird, like a hawk or raven. About sixty-five, he had well-groomed white hair, mustache, and beard. Tall and slender, his posture was nearly perfect. Taylor wondered what kind of injury caused the senator to need the cane.

"Here are your orders, Captain." Bennington removed a folded letter from his shirt pocket inside his vest and laid it on the desk.

Taylor reached out, but the senator held up a hand in restraint. Curious about the letter, Taylor decided to let the senator have his moment of control and manipulation. Once he had his orders in hand, Taylor would be in command again. That was the nature of the army. Given clear operating orders, an officer could take charge of any situation. But he had to know the stakes and the objectives. Then there'd be no guessing or political maneuvering.

"First," the senator continued, "let me give you some background information." Bennington poured water from a flask on his desk, filling his goblet almost to the rim. Suddenly, Taylor was very thirsty, but the senator did not offer water to him. The old man seemed to be deliberately antagonizing him.

"It is our destiny to conquer our enemies, Captain. First, we pushed the British out, then the French and the Mexicans. We subjugated the Coloreds, and we pretty much wiped out the redskins all over the continent."

Taylor hesitated. "Sir, we *bought* the French out."

Bennington dismissed the trivial detail with a wave of his hand. "The manner of the victory makes no difference. Military or economic, it's all the same. Conquest is conquest. Had the French not sold the Louisiana Purchase to us, we probably would have gone to war over it."

Senator Bennington sipped water delicately. He pulled a white kerchief from his pocket and blotted a drop of water before it soaked into his blue silk vest.

"My point, Captain, is that the US government does not negotiate with its enemies, certainly not when we hold superior fighting forces. Do you concur?"

"Absolutely, sir!" Taylor agreed. No way he'd suggest the army would do anything other than fight to win.

"If we end the Indian Wars without victory—without total conquest—then we will have admitted defeat to an inferior enemy." Bennington toyed with his water goblet but didn't drink. "If we allow the Apache to negotiate, then we're giving them power and control."

Taylor instantly understood. It would be tantamount to admitting the red man was equal to the White man.

"Understand that if we start treating them like humans, they're going to demand human rights and there will be softhearted politicians who will become sympathetic."

"Senator!" Taylor raised his hands in surrender, then slapped his knees. "Don't tell me there are politicians who actually believe these damned savages are people? Why, redskins are no more our equals than the Coloreds or the Mexicans." *Or the Texans for that matter,* he added silently.

The senator shot him a look of pity, one that suggested Taylor couldn't comprehend the larger picture.

"Captain, I appreciate that a good percentage of our population agrees with you, especially easterners. But this isn't about race or color. It's about power and control. The Indians are not civilized men, but they are men nonetheless. Unfortunately for them, civilized men have the power. *We* control this country. And we're not going to share that power or relinquish even a small part of it."

The senator paused again. Taylor had the feeling the man's big picture was about to be made clear to him.

Bennington continued. "These Indian warrior-leaders and the elders aren't fools. In fact, they are very astute. If we give them the right to negotiate, eventually they will learn how to sway public sentiment in their favor. Like the slaves, the red man will gain political support and laws to protect them. If that happens, perhaps they will even gain freedom and American citizenship. You realize what that means, don't you?"

Taylor had no idea, but he nodded anyway.

"It means we won't be able move them when we need their land."

Taylor's expression must have betrayed his confusion.

"Captain, why do you suppose the army took Cochise's reservation back?"

Taylor's job was simply to control the Indians, and he always considered that task synonymous with killing them. Rarely did he need to know the political reasoning behind his orders.

"I really couldn't tell you, Senator."

"Minerals, Captain. Gold, silver, and copper." Bennington paused, apparently to let Taylor absorb the revelation. "Over half our country's known mineral deposits sit within a hundred and seventy-five miles of Tucson. Right under the topsoil of Cochise's reservation land.

"Almost every day, a new mining claim is filed somewhere in the southeastern part of Arizona. What kind of power do you suppose Cochise and his people would have had once they learned how important those minerals are to the economic and industrial infrastructure of these United States? What do you think they'll have once they learn how to use the minerals on their land?"

"Economic power?" Taylor said hesitantly.

Bennington nodded. "Our decision was simple. Give them economic power and control over the minerals or move them and claim the minerals as our own."

"So we moved them to San Carlos."

"Very good, Captain. Now why do you suppose this town is called Silver City?" Thankfully, Bennington didn't force him to answer the rhetorical question.

The senator continued. "By the end of the decade there'll be a dozen mining towns like Silver City, Hillsboro, and Kingston scattered all over these mountains. They'll all be built on land the Apaches claim as their home."

"So they'll have to be moved," Taylor suggested.

Nodding, the senator said, "There are other considerations as well." He paused and delicately sipped more water.

"If we end the wars quickly through negotiation, powerful businessmen in New Mexico and Arizona will lose government contracts worth many millions of dollars. They supply the army with everything from livestock and field mounts to vegetables and supplies. Major weapons manufacturers in the East will collapse virtually overnight without the army to keep them in business.

"Towns near every fort will go bust if soldiers stop spending their pay on drinking and whoring. And political leaders in this particular region," the senator swept his arm around the room as if to encompass the whole of the Southwest, "some of whom are my wealthiest supporters, will be mighty upset when hundreds of unemployed Blacks from the army cavalry and infantry units start settling in their towns. The army is the only home most of the ex-slaves have known since they became free men."

The senator took a deep breath before continuing. "So perhaps you can appreciate how ending the war prematurely might upset the regional and national economies. Now, you can hate the Apache if you desire, or think whatever you wish of them.

But I don't want them subdued or negotiated with. I want them defeated, stuck away on a reservation like San Carlos, not on mineral-rich mountain land where they now live." He paused. "Defeated, you understand? Or killed."

Ambrose Taylor knew then he was nothing more than a pawn in the senator's grand plan. He wondered how much of the big picture benefited the government and how much furthered the senator's own political agenda. He thought he finally understood the larger perspective.

New Mexico and Arizona were far from the political power centers of the eastern cities where he'd grown up, but apparently these frontier territories were not without rich and influential campaign contributors. He realized also how insignificant the power of an army captain really was. How could he even hope to compete for control with a man who wielded the power to influence the country's decision on war or peace with the entire race of Indians? Taylor blinked and realized the senator was speaking.

"If the field soldiers believe they're defending helpless towns and miners from savage Indian attacks, fine. Fact is, Captain, I can respect the Apache for trying to defend their homeland. After all, we *are* invaders. History will no doubt record that the war against the red man began decades ago. The same thing that has happened to Indians all over the continent will happen to the Apache. Unless...."

Taylor waited patiently, but he knew the senator wouldn't continue until he asked the question.

"Unless what, sir?"

The senator sipped again. "Unless they manage to unite all their tribes into one fighting force. The Apache are not like the Plains Indians of the north and east. These Indians are particularly vicious fighters, and they're especially dangerous because they're high mountain warriors. They're trained from birth to be warriors and to fight. These mountains are their home, and they know every canyon and valley to hide in. It will take ten thousand soldiers to drive out even a few hundred Apache. If the various tribes unite to create any sizable fighting force, then the economic cost of such a campaign and the loss of civilized life will be unfathomable."

"We can use the Colored soldiers," Taylor said, shrugging. "Lord knows they're not good for anything else. They don't follow orders, and they can't be trusted."

"Captain." Bennington tapped his cane on the fancy rug. Taylor interpreted the gesture as a warning to curtail his opinion.

"What I meant, Senator, is that the Colored soldiers are just an army experiment."

"That experiment has been going on for fourteen years." Bennington sighed and shook his head. "They're no longer an experiment, Captain. They've proven themselves in battle. And they follow orders extremely well, in fact. I've seen reports from their White commanding officers. Hell, they seem to be better-disciplined, more competent, and braver than White soldiers, because they have something to prove.

"There are some White officers who will *only* go into battle with their Black soldiers. You may not like it, but you'd better get used to it. I have. Colored soldiers are a fact of life and they're here to stay."

"Maybe not. We can station them all here in New Mexico. Then when they fight the Apache, we can blame their high mortality on poor field performance. We could say they can't learn mountain warfare or they're cowards."

"Captain, there are only a few hundred Colored soldiers from the Ninth Cavalry stationed here in New Mexico. Add the entire Tenth Cavalry in Texas and the two Colored infantry units and we've still got only about two thousand fighting men. We'll need five or ten times that number, and maybe even the whole US Army to wage a mountain war against a unified Apache army. If a thousand White soldiers die in an extended Indian war, the resulting public outcry will condemn the president and the army."

"So, what do we do, Senator?" He hated even to ask the question because not having the answer made him feel more like the senator's pawn than an army officer.

"We can't fight them all at once, but we can whittle them down one tribe at a time. We can even campaign against several tribes at the same time, as long as they don't form a single coordinated army. The solution to our problem is to prevent Apache unification, Captain. That is your mission."

Taylor thought the senator was insane, and he knew the senator could hear the ridicule in his voice. "And just how do you expect me to do that?"

"I've received information that Chief Juh has settled in the mountains north of Silver City for the summer. They're holed up along the Gila River. My source tells me this particular chief is very influential among the Apaches, but he is the last chief to hold out against uniting with the other chiefs. You will ensure he stays opposed to the idea."

"I will?"

Senator Bennington nodded. "More precisely, you'll hire this outlaw, Jason Peares, to do it for you."

CHAPTER 9

"**O**NLY A HANDFUL OF VERY powerful people know about this operation outside of this room, Captain." Senator Bennington fixed his hawklike gaze on Taylor. "And I want it to stay that way." The senator tapped the index finger of his right hand on the folded paper holding Taylor's orders.

"After you read your orders, make sure you understand everything with perfect clarity. Is that understood?"

Taylor nodded slowly, feeling a mixture of excitement and caution. He knew he was about to become part of something very important. History would remember the name *Taylor* in connection with the subjugation of the Apache. Or he would carry the total blame to his grave if he was unsuccessful in his mission. Eternal fame or infamy. Promotion or court-martial. The senator surmised he was ambitious, sure, but he wasn't stupid. He'd keep the orders in case things went awry. Let the senator take the blame if he failed.

"What do I have to do?"

"You want to kill Indians, Captain?"

"Hell yes!" He felt the heat of embarrassment as the senator raised an eyebrow at his outburst. He silently cursed himself. The politician was snobby enough without witnessing him lose his military bearing.

The senator passed the folded paper. Taylor read it slowly. At first he narrowed his eyes in disbelief, then widened them in astonishment. He looked over the edge of the paper at Bennington and tried to speak. Finally, he just sat there feeling like his mouth was hanging open. He saw so many parts of the letter to disbelieve, he didn't know where to start.

He finally found his voice. "You have an informant in Juh's camp? An Apache warrior?"

"Not exactly. He's an Apache scout who's been assigned to Fort Bayard for some time now." Taylor started to speak, but the senator continued. "He was captured with his wife and five children, so we offered him the luxury of civilized living and lots of gold for his family if he worked for us."

Taylor had had his share of dealings with Apache scouts in Arizona. Scouting was one thing, but betraying his own people for gold? He had trouble believing even an Indian would do such a thing. They placed so little value on the mineral that civilized men fought and killed for.

The senator shrugged as he explained. "He hasn't seen his family for some time now. He's been feeding carefully parsed information to Chief Juh all summer. I'm sure he'll continue to help us as long as he believes his family is safe."

"Are they?"

"Oh, he'll be joining them soon enough." Bennington peered at Taylor with dark eyes. "Probably as soon as you're finished with him."

Taylor translated the senator's cryptic words into silent instructions. The scout's family was already long dead. As soon as the scout got Taylor's troops to Chief Juh's camp, Taylor could kill him too.

"And General Miles? He supports this?"

"The general does not directly know of the details of the plan, of course, but he owes me a favor," Bennington said.

Taylor took a deep breath. *Must be some kind of favor,* he thought. Taylor felt even smaller and more insignificant than he had a moment before. A part of him admired the power the old man seated across the room from him had to possess to control the activities of a US Army general and troops of multiple forts.

"Why me?" was all Taylor could think to ask.

"I know of your previous accomplishments during the war between the north and the south, Captain. And I've heard about your...shall we say, difficulties adapting to frontier service. I thought you might appreciate an opportunity such as this, one last chance to ascend back up in the ranks where you belong."

Taylor nodded as he reflected on more glorious days. He'd always known he was destined for greatness. He was a New York City gentleman, well connected socially and politically. His father, a respected businessman and aspiring politician, served on several city and state councils with an eye toward becoming a senator someday. His mother was a prominent socialite, always at her husband's side when the proper image was required.

Ambrose Taylor used their powerful connections to obtain a nomination to attend the army's academy for officers at West Point. He'd graduated tenth in his class and became a master tactician during the Civil War. He quickly became one of the youngest officers to ever attain the rank of colonel, due mostly to battlefield promotions for his extraordinary campaigns against the South.

After the war, the army shrank its war-swollen ranks, discharging most of its officers and enlisted men within a few months. Taylor wandered around New York for a few years and even moved into successful business ventures with his brother who had followed in his father's footsteps. While successful, he found life dull and monotonous compared to the adventures of war. Taylor knew he was capable of so much more. He sought to renew his commission in the new army.

The only opportunity available at the rank of colonel was a command position of the Tenth Cavalry, one of the army's newly formed Colored outfits. Taylor vehemently declined the command, even though he knew he was destroying his last chance at a career revival. He called on every contact he had, every politician his father knew, and finally found one last opportunity to rejoin the army as an officer. He took the demotion to captain and filled the billet of quartermaster for a Sixth Cavalry company stationed at Fort Apache in southeastern Arizona.

Five years later, he was still a captain, suffering in anonymity at a thankless job with no unit to command and no hope for promotion. *Ever.* He rarely even got to see action against the savages. Now that he had his chance to fight Indians, he had to command Colored troops...as a captain instead of as a colonel.

Taylor shook his head at his bad fortune. Had he known five years ago this would happen, he would've accepted command of the Tenth. At least he'd have been a general by now, managing regional campaigns. He could have been wiping out Indians wholesale rather than a few at a time in this new, obscure scouting mission.

He sighed and looked up. *Bennington chooses his puppets well,* Taylor thought. The old man knew he would do anything for one final chance at greatness, to find a promotion, or escape the desert wasteland. He had to get away from the detestable people of all the races who called this forlorn place home.

"So I have to command some Colored troops?"

The senator hesitated for a moment. "In a manner of speaking."

Captain Taylor waited, but the senator offered no further explanation.

Finally, Taylor nodded. "I accept the assignment under one condition. Upon completion, I want a promotion to major and a transfer out of this hellhole desert."

"Consider it done."

The senator hadn't even blinked, and for a moment Taylor thought he should have pushed for a jump back up to colonel. That didn't matter though, as long as he'd get out of the Southwest, back to real army work. Or maybe he'd ask for a department assignment back East so he'd at least be around civilized people. Just so long as he never had to see another Colored soldier or an Indian. Or a Mexican. Or a Texan.

"General Miles has graciously arranged for a special unit

from the Sixth Cavalry to be escorted from Fort Bowie to Fort Bayard. They are most likely already here."

Good, he thought. The Sixth didn't have Colored troops. Then he said, "Escorted?"

Bennington said, "This is a unique group of sixteen men, Captain, and they are especially suited for this kind of operation. You'll understand when you meet them. Major Philip Clark, post commander at Fort Bayard, has orders to provide you with mounts, supplies, weapons, and a company of his Colored troops to support this mission."

"And the outlaw's part in this?"

"I would think that much is obvious," Bennington said with another dismissive wave of his hand. "He's a killer, so let him kill. Of course, you may use him however you think is appropriate." The senator pulled a timepiece from a vest pocket and checked it. "I suppose you ought to go recruit him, don't you think?"

Taylor stood, knowing he'd just been dismissed. Bennington reached into a desk drawer and pulled out a red sack and more papers. He tossed the sack in the air. Taylor caught it, instantly recognizing the tinkling sound within. He put the sack in his right front pocket.

"Gold for the outlaw and for yourself," Bennington said. "And for the soldiers in your detail, should you decide they need extra motivation. In these papers, you'll find the names of the troops in your special Sixth Cavalry unit and their...qualifications.

"Also, you'll find a map of Juh's camp and other details that might be helpful." He paused as Taylor picked up the folded papers and stuck them in his back pocket. "Do you have any questions, Captain?"

Taylor had a thousand questions, like how in the world did the senator get a map of an Apache Indian's campsite and an accurate count of the warriors, even with a traitor scout on the army payroll. But he didn't want to give the senator more fuel for his manipulations. He shook his head.

"Very well then." Bennington withdrew a match from the

desk drawer and shoved an ashtray toward Taylor. He struck the match on the desktop and held it up. He smiled at Taylor and gestured knowingly at the paper that held the secret orders.

As Taylor watched the flames consume his orders, the senator added, "You will speak to no one of this operation, Captain. Nor will you make any written account of your activities henceforth. Is that perfectly clear?"

For a moment, Taylor forgot he didn't wear his uniform. He drew his back straight and stood at attention.

"Very clear, Senator."

The senator nodded toward the door and scooted his chair around noisily on the slat floor to fully face the desk. Taylor stepped toward the door and pulled it open. He paused in the doorway and turned back to Bennington.

"You realize what that chief will do if we're successful, don't you, Senator?"

"I'm counting on it."

CHAPTER 10

Jason Peares sipped his beer as he listened to the soldiers chat about various odd topics ranging from the last time each had a woman to the post's latest victory over the Silver City baseball team. He tossed in a forced chuckle every now and again just to be polite.

Jason always felt uncomfortable in social situations. Partly, that was because of his solitary life on the trail. He couldn't even remember when he last kept more than one or two friends at a time. Mostly though, he didn't trust people. He never knew when a new friend might turn out to be someone with an old grudge, hunting him for his outlaw deeds years back. He'd been betrayed more than once. So he kept to himself to avoid that pain. He never gave anyone a chance to get close.

As he watched the four soldiers interact, he admitted to himself he had another reason why he never felt comfortable around people. Being half-Black and half-White, he knew people saw him in different ways. Whites saw him as Black, while Blacks saw him as *not Black*. During his childhood years in school, he always sat alone, ate alone, and walked home alone. The White kids in town called him Black and the Black kids called him White, and they all teased him, sometimes brutally.

He couldn't remember the first time he'd heard the word *half-breed*. He didn't remember when he understood what the term meant and that it was used as a slanderous insult. He didn't remember when he started hating the word.

As an outlaw, he avoided everyone. He rarely had to deal with discrimination or racial teasing. As his reputation as a gunfighter grew, he found no one dared disrespect him to his face. In time, he found himself befriending people in difficult situations.

Maybe it would be a lone Black man on a cattle drive, or a woman brutalized by a power-hungry land broker, or small farmers of all races terrorized by a ruthless cattle baron. He typically got attached to people whose need for Jason's talents were far more important than any concerns they might have about his skin color.

In truth, Jason realized that out on the frontier all men were truly created equal, and they were equally likely to succumb to any number of natural or man-made hazards. On the frontier, a man or woman's value was more likely based on their skills and contributions than on any other factor.

Still, he'd been acquitted for almost five years now, but he hadn't settled down yet. When he stopped to admit his reasons, he knew it had nothing to do with his previous outlaw notoriety. Plain and simple, he was hiding—avoiding the specter of social interaction. He was a loner and was unable to relate to other people. He wasn't sure he knew how. He didn't know if he'd ever get comfortable around other people.

He sat at the table in the midst of four Black soldiers, totally alone, unable to get involved in their conversation or their friendship. He was just about to excuse himself when he heard the familiar sound of Taylor's boots stomping on the boardwalk outside the saloon. Jason was facing the door, so he simply pulled his right holster gun and laid it on the table as Corporal Shelton stopped talking.

All the soldiers turned in their chairs and looked toward the door as Taylor stepped through the open doorway. The man glanced to his left and seemed to study the single door held wide open by a carefully placed chair. Then he scanned the room, his gaze finding Jason's table at the far back right corner of the room. Jason locked gazes with the man, then Taylor turned toward the bar along the right wall.

A moment later he walked over to the table holding two mugs of beer. Hackles rose up and down Jason's spine when the man smiled down at him. He wanted to shoot him on suspicion alone, just to avoid whatever trouble the man was brewing.

"I want to apologize for my earlier error," Taylor said. He handed Jason a glass, then raised his own in toast. Jason did the same and sipped. Taylor looked down at Crawford.

"First Sergeant, I'm Captain Ambrose Taylor, Sixth Cavalry. May I have a word in private with Jason Peares?"

"Jason Peares?" Shelton gasped aloud, and the four Buffalo Soldiers stared at Jason in amazement. Jason shrugged sheepishly and smiled like he was caught telling a small fib.

"I try to keep my name quiet 'cause everywhere I go people seem to know me and most times that isn't a good thing."

Crawford nodded as he pushed his chair back and stood at attention. He seemed to accept Taylor's word that he was an officer and addressed him as such.

"Very well, Captain. We'll be heading back to the fort." He sidestepped from in front of his chair and pivoted with military precision. He motioned to his men and marched toward the door. His men rose with a scuffling of chairs and hurried behind him.

"May I join you, Mister Peares?" Taylor sat down across the table without invitation and shoved the soldiers' glasses aside with a slow and careful brush of his forearm. He eyed Jason's gun and nodded. "Schofield forty-five. A nice choice for a belt or holster gun. Originally developed by Major George W. Schofield about five years ago."

Jason knew the history of the weapon. That's why he chose it as his primary gun. It was the first weapon of its type that incorporated a top-break loader, which meant the revolver could be loaded much faster than other handguns. With the barrel latch released, the barrel could rotate forward and down for easy ejection of the spent cartridges. A shooter could complete that entire process with just one hand. The gun was also extremely reliable and nearly maintenance free.

Taylor said, "I see you use the long-barrel version. I'm told a man can reload a Schofield without looking in about twenty-six seconds."

"On a slow day," Jason said. "I empty and reload in fifteen."

Jason studied the man and made a show of sticking his gun back in his holster. The man *could* be an officer. His posture seemed correct. He wore no uniform and had a significant amount of hair growing on his jaw, but he certainly had the piercing eyes and the presence of someone accustomed to command.

To say Taylor was not handsome was being very polite. His forehead was wide under his unruly, blond hair, and his face narrowed severely with sharp cheek bones over a narrow mouth with thin lips. His sky-blue eyes were too deeply set and too close to his bony ridge of a nose. He appeared cross-eyed as he looked at Jason. His nose began abruptly between his bushy eyebrows, and it ended in a knobby point that seemed to merge into his mustache and his too-thin top lip. His thin nostrils seemed too narrow to pass any significant volume of air, and his lower lip melted into a basically chinless lower jaw.

Taylor looked about forty or so. His mottled skin had seen far too much desert sun, and severe crow's feet indicated the man spent most of his days squinting. Beyond his sorry excuse for a face, Jason found the man to be well-built, though slender, and he stood a tad under the six-foot mark.

"Are you really an army captain?"

"I am. I'm on a secret mission, and I'd like to recruit you. The senator told me how you helped rescue his stage. Knowing your reputation as I do, I would be pleased if you would lend me your skills for a few weeks."

Jason shook his head. "Actually, I'm headed north to Colorado."

Taylor smiled. "You haven't heard my offer yet."

Curiosity made Jason lean forward a bit, but there was something about Taylor that he didn't like. He just couldn't quite put his finger on it. He remembered when he first looked at the man in the other saloon. He saw hatred and repulsion in his eyes then. Now, all of a sudden, the man was smiling at him and trying to recruit him for army business. Jason raised an eyebrow as an invitation for Taylor to provide more details.

"How does twenty dollars a week sound?"

"Sounds like a lot of money." He sipped his beer. "Sounds like gunman's wages."

"You might need guns for this mission, but mostly we'll need you to do some scouting."

"You don't have Indian scouts?"

"Can't use 'em. And I can't tell you all the details until tomorrow after I brief the post commander." Taylor paused. "I can tell you this, though. If you don't accept, we'll *have* to use Indian scouts. Plain and simple, we just can't trust their loyalty on this mission, and a lot of soldiers might die if the scouts turn tail." He paused again. "Including your new friends." Taylor thumbed over his shoulder at the door as if pointing at the departed soldiers.

Jason had trouble believing he was suddenly the single indispensable part of an important army mission. Taylor hadn't even known he existed an hour earlier, and now the mission would fail without his help? It didn't make sense until Jason considered that maybe Taylor came to town recruiting for qualified civilian scouts, and his path simply crossed Jason's at the other saloon. Jason felt comfortable concluding that if he didn't accept the job, Taylor would just continue his search and choose someone else.

"I need to know what I'm getting involved in before I accept."

Taylor hesitated, glancing around the room as if searching for eavesdroppers to his conversation. His expression hinted that he was struggling with a requirement not to reveal anything about the mission. He focused a serious gaze at Jason and spoke so quietly Jason almost didn't hear him.

"We're going to end the Apache wars all over the territory," he said. "Forever."

CHAPTER II

ALL THE WARRIORS AND YOUNG men stood before Juh. As was his custom, Juh studied them for a few moments, giving each a few seconds of his concentration. He believed they benefited from his gaze. Perhaps each felt a measure of confidence or strength from receiving individual attention from their leader.

The warriors dressed well for the supply raid. Most wore only breechclouts and knee-length, hard-soled moccasins, though all but one wore the tops of their moccasins folded down to the ankles. A few wore loose-fitting shirts and pants traded from the peasant farmers in Mexico—perfect clothing for hot weather. The new day had just begun, yet already the air was uncomfortably warm, a prelude to another very hot day.

Juh knew the flatlands by the Rio Grande River would be extremely hot and the warriors would have to travel carefully. Though he and his warriors were well accustomed to surviving in the harsh desert, they respected the power of the sun. Juh would use the sun as an ally against an enemy who did not give it the same respect. The soldiers, fully dressed in their dark wool uniforms would be miserable in the hottest part of the day. Tired and hot, hungry for their evening meal, they might not watch as closely for an attack.

Each warrior wore his bow and quiver draped by a leather strap over one shoulder or the other, depending on which hand each preferred to shoot with. All carried rifles at the ready.

Juh and most of his warriors had long, black hair—an Apache's most prized possession and a symbol of beauty, strength, and courage. The warriors tucked their hair into their rawhide belts, braided to prevent tangling or catching brush when hunting or raiding. Two of the warriors preferred to keep their hair short, just at their shoulders. Strange behavior for warriors proven in battle, but they had earned the right to wear their hair as they pleased without question.

One young warrior possessed long, brown hair. Accused of having White blood in his family line, the youth suffered harshly during his younger years. Juh remembered the young man's parents, though. Like himself, Brown Hair's parents were both full-blooded Nednhi Apache. No one could explain the unfortunate reason the young man was cursed with brown hair, but the name stuck with him. Over the years, he wore his hair and his name with pride.

Brutal harassment by the other Apache children nurtured the youth's toughness, and he grew to become stronger than most of the other young warriors. He was also quicker to anger and more brutal in his response to danger. Brown Hair reserved a special hatred for the White man in his heart, and sometimes his temper was uncontrollable. Other warriors were beginning to talk about his excessively cruel deeds in battle.

When Juh caught the young warrior's gaze, Brown Hair held the stare a bit too long before looking away. The young man was defiant and confident. He was hateful, but dependable. He was a good warrior to have close in a desperate fight, but he was too vicious, too eager to kill. Juh didn't look forward to the inevitable task of dismissing Brown Hair from his band of Apache.

The adolescent warriors in training stood on the fringes of the group. Some tiptoed, moving back and forth, trying to see between the heads of the taller men. He knew them well. They wanted to watch their leader when he spoke, to see his lips move.

"I'll take twenty-five warriors with me to capture the army supplies." Juh spoke carefully, wary of the stutter that tended to creep into his voice at unexpected times. "We'll meet Lives With

The Enemy where the trail passes into the thick stand of trees just before the river turns toward the setting sun. He'll tell us where the army supplies can be found."

Juh nodded at the tall warrior with long, gray hair known as Runs Like The Wind. Nearly sixty summers in age, the warrior still ran long distances faster than all the younger warriors. Whenever Juh's people had time to relax and have competitions, the old man graciously refused to run so someone else could win the prize.

"Runs Like The Wind will stay at the entrance of the valley and watch for soldiers. If necessary, he'll warn the sentries along the ridgeline of any danger. The young warriors in training will remain here at the camp to protect our people." Juh saw a few of the younger men stand a little straighter, chins a little higher. To the Apache, there was no greater honor, no better way to prove one's skills, than defending the elders, women, and children. If any danger threatened the camp though, the best defense everyone practiced was the orderly evacuation of the camp.

Juh saw movement to his left and noticed his son, Daklugie, leading his favorite mount, a powerful black stallion, toward the warriors. A feeling of pride swelled in his chest as he gazed upon the boy. Only eleven summers old, Daklugie was still too young to become a warrior in training. *Another summer,* Juh thought, *and the boy will become an apprentice to a warrior.* He would then cook the warrior's food, run his errands, care for his horse, and observe the rigid rules of the aspiring warrior.

His son's arrival with his mount signaled the end of the meeting. Juh walked over to Daklugie and silently touched him on the shoulder. He swung expertly onto the animal's bare back and grabbed the thick, rawhide thong serving as bridle and reins. By habit, Juh felt for his water jug draped over his right shoulder opposite his quiver. Then he reached for his emergency ration bags with his left hand.

Behind Juh, the warriors mounted their horses as the young warriors in training formed into two lines. Wordlessly, Juh led his men between the lines. Always keeping to Apache custom,

Juh said nothing as he passed Ishton, and he made no gesture of farewell. At the last moment, he glanced down at her. In the briefest eye contact, they shared a private acknowledgment of their love.

As Juh passed the last of his young warriors, he put his horse into a trot. He chose a path that crossed the wide valley of the Gila River and veered gently up to the ridgeline towering high above the south bank. When the ridgeline trail curved south with the river, Juh signaled Brown Hair to join him in front of the long line of warriors.

For a moment, he was unsure how to say what needed to be said, as he didn't want to embarrass the young man. To an Apache, losing face was the ultimate indignity. Though the other warriors followed out of earshot, they were sure to be interested in the body language displayed by the two men. Juh knew he had to choose his words carefully, so he wouldn't invoke an embarrassing reaction from the young man.

"The Apache do not take scalps," Juh said simply. "It's not our way."

The young man tensed but said nothing for a long while. He simply rode his pony alongside Juh. Finally, he spoke.

"The *White-Eyes* take scalps. And some of the other bands of Apache do too."

Juh shook his head. "All Apache leaders have agreed to end this practice."

"Not Geronimo."

"That was many summers past," Juh answered. "He took the scalps of the soldiers who murdered and scalped his beloved wife and child. Now he takes no scalps—like all Apache."

"Then I am not Apache."

Juh knew he'd stretched the truth a bit, since a small number of Apache still practiced the ritual that had been started by the Mexicans long ago. Even now, the *White-Eyes* and the Mexicans still hunted Apache scalps for reward money promised by the Mexican government. In retaliation, a few Apache continued to collect the scalps of their enemies.

Juh took a few moments of silence before he continued. "The hatred in your heart burns as bright as the sun."

"With good reason." Brown Hair's voice crackled with emotion. "One day, when I had never seen a White man before, many soldiers rode into our village and killed everyone they could find. They killed unarmed men and women and children. We did nothing to anger them. We were only farmers and hunters. None had warrior weapons." He fell quiet for a long time.

"I had only lived five summers then. The commander stuck a pole in the ground and his men impaled my father through the chest on it. He lay helpless and dying, watching as the soldiers raped my mother and my three sisters over and over again and then scalped them while they still breathed. My youngest sister was barely older than I. To this day I find it hard to believe that men can be so cruel."

Juh had heard the young man's story before, and he knew many of his people had lived through similar tragedies. He wanted to comfort him with a gentle hand on his shoulder, but he dared not. Such a gesture might be interpreted by the warriors as condescending. Instead, he held his silence and thought about all he'd heard about the young warrior.

When the Apache killed their enemy, many times they dismembered or mutilated the corpses so their enemies' spirits would wander through the next life in shame, forever disfigured as they appeared at death. Brown Hair carried the custom to the extreme, often performing savage cuttings that left little of an enemy's corpse recognizable.

Juh heard more than once that the young warrior exacted his hatred on his enemies while they still lived, then reveled in their agony as they slowly died. Some said the young warrior had performed his deeds not only on soldiers, but also on unarmed ranchers, and once even on a woman and her infant child. Juh said as much, and the young man reacted with a sudden explosion of emotion. He yanked his fighting knife from the sheath at his belt.

"Yes!" he said. "Many *White-Eyes* have fallen before the knife of Brown Hair. My blade has dripped with the blood of their women and children too. Their soldiers kill *our* women and children, so I will kill theirs until there are no more on our land."

"You are Nednhi Apache," Juh argued. "You must follow the ways of our people."

Brown Hair put his knife away and raised his chin in defiance. "I will not change."

Juh nodded but held the young man's gaze. He spoke softly so he wouldn't further inflame Brown Hair's temper. He didn't want the warrior to feel punished.

"The path you choose isn't that of our people."

"Are you telling me to leave the people?"

The young man swayed confidently in time with his pony's gait. On the ground, Brown Hair stood about the same height as Juh. Twenty years younger, Brown Hair was much more muscular, thicker in the chest, and wider in the shoulders. Juh felt no fear or threat from the youth though. He knew his warriors followed him with respect for his judgment and proven warrior skills, and because they believed in his medicine. He led them with equal respect for their skills.

"We don't kill because the *White-Eyes* kill. We kill to defend our people. We take their supplies because they burn ours. The choice is yours. If you follow the ways of the *White-Eyes*, you must leave our people."

Brown Hair finally looked away and sighed. "There are others who feel as I do," he said softly, almost apologetically.

"No Apache has ever been forced to serve in an army or be commanded by another Apache. You know warriors follow a leader only because they choose to, and a leader can only lead with the respect of his warriors. If you choose to follow another leader or follow your own path, you are free to do so. I will not oppose any warrior who chooses to join with you. This is the Apache way."

Juh paused before continuing, his voice soft and gentle. "You are a brave and capable warrior, one of the best I have ever seen. But your heart is twisted with hatred and your actions may bring the wrath of the soldiers upon our women and children. After this raid, you must find your own way."

The young warrior looked at him again, and for a moment Juh thought he would rebel. Brown Hair simply nodded and pulled his horse up to regain his place in the column. Juh continued to follow the trail for half a day until it sloped down to the river where another stream merged from the east. Lives With The Enemy squatted in the short, wild grass by the edge of the water. Greetings were quick and short, for the mood of the raiding party was serious.

Juh tried to overcome his dislike for the traitor and had to force himself to remember the value of the information supplied by the Apache warrior who had chosen to scout for the bluecoats. The man even dressed like the enemy. In spite of the searing heat, the Apache scout wore full-length pants and a long-sleeve deerskin shirt. It was probably the only way he could appease the soldiers, who no doubt felt uncomfortable having an Apache warrior inside their forts.

Juh found himself concentrating on the man, not his words. He even *smelled* like the enemy. His skin reeked of the greasy food they ate, and his clothes carried the odor of the wood they cooked with, of the animals they rode. Juh glanced over at the scout's army horse, a big gray horse with white spots over its flanks. A full saddle and packs were strapped to its back. *What a shameful way to treat an animal,* he thought, *riding it into the mountains burdened with all that weight.*

"Three days past," Lives With The Enemy said, "a caravan of nine wagons with a great number of mules and horses left Fort Cummings, the distant fort inside the adobe walls. They're carrying a lot of food and weapons in those wagons. They'll cross the great river near Fort Craig tomorrow night."

Juh accepted the scout's report and thought for a moment. Quickly, he made his decision.

"We'll ride through the night and arrive at the river crossing before the army. When they have a few of their wagons in the water, we'll attack."

The traitor scout retrieved his army mount and watched Juh lead the raiding party away without farewells. Runs Like The Wind stayed behind. When the warriors vanished into the stand of trees, the runner turned his pony toward the high trail. The scout conveniently moved his horse into the pony's path.

"You'll watch the river? To protect our people from attack?"

The runner nodded. "From that outcrop of rock high up on the ridge." In the Apache tradition he pointed along the trail with his nose.

The scout said, "If the army ever attacks, they'll follow the river as they always do."

"They're foolish," the runner agreed. "It is said the Apache follows the ridges of the mountains, but the soldier follows the streams. If they come this way, they'll take twice as long to reach the camp. By the time they arrive, our people will be gone."

"No, they won't."

The traitor scout nudged his horse closer to the runner. He pulled his rifle from the scabbard, the bayonet already affixed under the barrel. Runs Like The Wind barely had time to register surprise before the scout rammed the sharp, metal blade into his chest.

CHAPTER 12

J ASON RODE INTO FORT BAYARD late the day after Captain
Taylor recruited him. He had slept late in the hotel room
paid for by Taylor's money and then eaten a double breakfast. When he was checking out of the hotel, he discovered
Captain Taylor had departed before sunrise.

Nothing much happened on the ten-mile ride almost straight
east to the fort, but then Jason didn't expect any excitement. He
knew the army's presence in the area discouraged warrior activity, but many years of traveling in unsafe territory—whether
eluding posses, bounty hunters, or hostile native people—gave
Jason a feeling of controlled fear. One could never know when
renegade warriors might feel like they had something to prove by
raiding inside the army's circle of protection.

With that little itch of fear scratching at his spine, Jason rode
with his left hand on the gun stuck in his belt, ready for an
instant reaction to any trouble that might rear its ugly head. He
lightly gripped the reins in his gun hand, while in his right he
held his Winchester loaded at the ready, barrel pointed skyward.

Though he needed only two hours to make the leisurely trip
to Fort Bayard, the searing heat quickly made him drowsy. He
regretted not waking early for the trip. By the time he arrived
in sight of the fort, his throat was parched dry even though he
drank a good measure of water from his canteen. The sweat on
his back seemed to get whisked away into the hot, dry air before

any could soak into his shirt, not that a wet shirt would cool him. The dead-still air hung around him like a blanket.

To Jason's surprise, Fort Bayard had no defensive walls or high-mounted guard posts. The buildings formed a protective perimeter around the central parade ground, and armed soldiers paced at key approach points. As he rode up to the fort, Jason put his rifle away, not wanting to appear threatening to the soldiers.

Though Jason had seen forts before, he'd never visited one. Fort Bayard was much larger than he expected. As he rode through the main entrance, he faced the parade grounds. In the center stood the staff for Old Glory, sided by two large, six-foot cannons. He scanned more than thirty buildings around the grounds, some connected, some standing individually.

Most of the connected buildings formed the long right side of the rectangular parade ground. He saw a few soldiers occasionally walk in and out of those buildings, so he figured those were the barracks. All the fort's buildings were adobe, though the duplexes along the left side of the parade ground seemed newer and in better repair. *Officers' quarters,* he guessed.

The only two-story buildings stood on both sides of the main entrance on the south side of the huge fort. A single Black soldier stood guard at attention by a wooden double door under the porch covering, so Jason assumed the man guarded command headquarters. The other two-story building to his left had to be administrative offices. Jason nudged his horse in front of the covered porch and nodded to the guard.

"Will I find Captain Taylor in there?" He indicated the double door with a brief movement of his left hand.

"Yes, *sir*" the guard returned crisply.

Jason dismounted and stepped onto the covered boardwalk. Noticing no one else around, he felt a sudden sense of kinship with the lone Black soldier.

"Nice day," he said.

"Yes, *sir*"

Jason looked at the man for a moment. "You don't have to call me sir. I'm not in the army."

The man glanced at him briefly, quickly averting his eyes like he'd be shot for just looking. Then he cast Jason another lingering glance and relaxed as Jason removed his hat.

"Sorry, friend," the soldier said. "I thought you were...."

Jason waited, but the man didn't complete his thought, just studied him through wire-rimmed spectacles.

"You thought I was White?" He smiled as the man shrugged his shoulders.

"I didn't mean to offend you, friend."

Jason chuckled. "No offense taken. Believe me, I've been accused of being worse things." He pushed through the right-side door and found himself facing a large desk with another Black soldier seated behind it. The soldier jumped to his feet and stood at rigid attention.

"Help you, sir?"

"Looking for Captain Taylor." Jason heard voices in the adjoining room. Familiar heavy footsteps preceded Taylor's voice. The man stuck his head around the doorjamb and summoned Jason.

"In here, Scout."

When Jason entered the office, he found three men in officer's uniforms standing casually before a desk, behind which a fourth officer sat. First Sergeant Lafayette Crawford stood rigidly at attention behind the three standing officers. Approaching to the captain's side, Jason offered a handshake to Taylor.

"I'm grateful for the room and food, Captain."

Taylor simply gripped his hands behind his back and balanced for a moment on the balls of his feet. "I don't exchange pleasantries with Negroes in front of the men."

"That right?" Jason withdrew his hand. "In that case, I'm not grateful."

The captain turned toward him, head held higher than the day before, chest puffed out a bit more. Today he was clean-shaven and his hair was perfectly combed. Obviously, his status as an officer in uniform gave him some measure of confidence. Jason gave him a smile that he hoped looked more like a sneer as he gazed at the man's pinched, hawklike face with those too-close eyes.

"I'd advise you to separate yourself from that attitude, Scout," the captain said.

"I'm not in your army, and I didn't ask for this job, Captain. If you don't want my services, you can show me the door and I'll go about—"

"If you were in the army, Scout, you'd be heading for the stockade for a comment like that. I hired you to kill Indians, not to be cocky. Is that clear?"

Jason looked him straight in the eyes. "You hired me to *scout* for Indians. I won't kill anyone who isn't trying to kill me. Expecting anything else from me is a mistake." He paused. "Is *that* clear?"

The officer behind the desk stood and cleared his throat. "I'm sure that's what the captain meant. We all get a little excited about the Indian threat in these parts."

The officer stuck out his hand, and Jason accepted it. "I'm Major Philip Clark, post commander. I have no problem with any soldier or scout who pulls his own weight and follows orders."

"Fair enough," Jason replied.

"Let me introduce Lieutenants Nathan Henry, commander of Company B, and Stanley Reeves, my administrative officer." The major nodded behind the men. "I've been told you already know my first sergeant."

As Jason nodded at Crawford, Taylor placed the cap he'd been holding behind his back on his head. "With your permission, Major, I'll see to my other troops."

The major nodded, and Taylor turned to leave. He cast a sinister glance that brought chills to Jason's spine, as if the civilized talk of the previous day had never occurred and they were suddenly sworn enemies. In that instant of eye contact, Jason knew he could never turn his back on Taylor.

"Well, then," the major said, seating his heavy frame in his straight-backed chair. He leaned forward, resting his elbows on top of the old desk. "Gentlemen, this is a secret mission. Everyone is confined to the post until your departure at first light tomorrow morning." He looked at Jason. "Do you have a problem with that, Scout?"

Jason shook his head. The prospect of having a role in a secret operation filled him with excitement, but the thought of serving under Captain Taylor's command worried him a bit.

"What exactly is our mission?" Jason said.

"Captain Taylor will fully brief you on your assignments in the field tomorrow," the major replied. "In fact, I don't know all the details myself. I've received written orders from General Miles of the Department of the Arizona Territory to support Captain Taylor's expedition. Colonel Hatch, commander of the Ninth Cavalry, has also ordered me to cooperate fully. I intend to do just that."

Major Clark studied his officers and Jason for a moment. "I do know this much. A particularly murderous Apache renegade chief called *Hoe* has settled in our area. He and his warriors have butchered women and children here and in Mexico and sometimes in Arizona, and he has refused to surrender to the San Carlos reservation. He and most of his warriors have been lured out of their camp on the Gila River. Unfortunately, the majority of my troops are still in the field pursuing Victorio and Nana. Tomorrow, Captain Taylor will lead a force consisting of the remainder Company B and his own troops from the Sixth Cavalry." He paused.

"Your mission is to capture Juh's entire camp. We will hold them under guard here at the fort until Juh surrenders and returns back to the reservation. Any questions?"

Major Clark glanced at his officers first, then at Jason. Jason had several questions, but since the other officers held their peace, he decided to do the same. The major turned his attention to Sergeant Crawford.

"No questions, *sir*," the sergeant said stiffly.

"Very well, then. You're dismissed, Scout. First Sergeant, will you find him a bed in the barracks?"

"Yes, *sir.*"

Crawford pivoted smartly, and Jason turned to follow. The major called out.

"Scout, I assume you have references who can confirm your scouting and tracking skills."

"None that you can verify before tomorrow morning." Jason felt pleased with his witty response, but he sensed the major needed more explanation.

"The ones that caught up with me usually ended up dead, but I eluded some of the best posses and bounty hunters in the business for ten years." He shrugged. "I also lived with Arapaho warriors for a few months one summer as they migrated through northeastern Arizona." During that time, he'd learned much of their ways of hunting and tracking. "I think my skills are adequate for the task of scouting."

Jason gave the major what he hoped was a disarming and reassuring smile, but he could tell the major was still unconvinced, so he decided to throw out a famous name.

"I'm sure Marshal Gallagher can vouch for me." Everyone all over the west knew of Marshal Gallagher's reputation.

Major Clark narrowed his eyes. "I know the marshal." He paused. "You rode with his posse?"

"I rode *from* his posse. He trailed me for two years and all he got for his troubles was two dead men."

The major nodded. "They say the marshal always gets his man."

"All but once."

CHAPTER 13

CAPTAIN AMBROSE TAYLOR STEPPED OUT onto the porch, still fuming at the scout's insolence. The door guard made a convenient target for his frustration.

"Come with me, Soldier."

The guard hesitated, started to object, but Taylor cut him off before he uttered a word. "Well?"

"I'm on guard duty, sir. I can't leave my post."

"What's your name, Soldier?" Taylor said, sneering. He bared his teeth and stepped closer until his nose almost touched the guard's.

"Private Hartley Tucker, *sir!*"

"Well, Private Hartley Tucker, you Black—" Taylor quickly caught himself and left the rest of his planned insult unspoken. "How would you like to spend some time in the guardhouse for disobeying an order?"

"No, *sir!*"

Taylor just looked at the man and felt his hatred boiling up again. This man, Tucker, embodied everything he hated about the Southwest. The man had yellow teeth, bad breath, and dark skin. He was tall and scrawny with round, wire-rimmed spectacles that made him look puny. Taylor reveled in the man's dilemma. He had to abandon his post or refuse to follow orders.

"I suggest you come with me, then. Is that clear?"

"Very clear, *sir!*"

He wanted to call the man a couple of choice descriptive

names but decided to keep his thoughts to himself. The army had changed over the last ten years and had grown soft. Words Taylor once so commonly used to address the inferior races now repeatedly got him censured by his own softhearted commanding officers.

The army had accepted the Colored troops into the ranks, but Taylor had not. Additionally, the army demanded tact and courtesy from officers when addressing civilians of any race. Army doctrine now referred to them as hosts and neighbors since army posts were basically a part of their towns. Taylor knew his contrary attitude had gotten him passed over for promotion several times.

He glared at the soldier and glanced around to see if anyone might be eavesdropping. It was Private Tucker's fault he was still a captain in the post-Civil War army. It was Tucker's doing and that of all the other Colored soldiers like him.

When Taylor refocused on the private, he realized the man was trembling. He stepped back from the soldier and took a deep breath to control his anger. The knowledge that the success of his mission would catapult him back to the top comforted him. When he completed the senator's plan, he'd get an instant promotion and have his pick of any command he wanted.

"You know where my special troops are?" He didn't give Tucker a chance to answer. "Take me to them."

Captain Taylor followed the soldier across the parade field and around a squad of marching troops. They entered the log gate of the twelve-foot-high walls of the guardhouse courtyard. The private marched stiff as a board, eyes darting to the side. The stock of Tucker's Springfield carbine sat cupped in his right hand, the barrel resting against his right shoulder, moving in time with his precision march.

Taylor compounded Tucker's discomfort by interrogating him about his past as they crossed the empty courtyard.

"You're just like all the rest of your kind, aren't you, Private?"

"Yes, *sir!*"

"Where are you from anyway, and how'd you get into my army?"

"Texas, sir. I was a teacher, but I couldn't find work at any schools for Negro children, so I enlisted in the army."

"Ever been in battle? Ever shot anyone?"

"No, *sir!*"

"You afraid, Private?" Tucker didn't answer. "Ever seen the black of an Indian savage's eyes up close when he's gettin' ready to shove his blade in your gut or cut your scalp off?"

Tucker said nothing as he walked. Captain Taylor hadn't seen any real combat on the frontier either, mostly because he spent the majority of his time stuck in an office doing quartermaster work. He certainly hadn't seen any Indians up close, but the words made for good drama against a scared man.

They entered the stone building and passed through the guardroom. The lone attendant, a young, dark-skinned private, jumped to attention, but the captain ignored him and pointed for Tucker to lead the way straight back to the central prisoner room. A dark hallway led to cells full of White soldiers previously attached to the Sixth Cavalry.

"Listen up, men!" Taylor announced. The soldiers lined up at the bars of their cells. Taylor noticed that none stood at attention, and most had an expression that bespoke only mild interest. He didn't expect more.

Major Clark told him the men had all been transferred to Fort Bayard from prisons at forts in Arizona, serving time for every manner of misdeed from desertion to murder. They arrived yesterday by wagon with their hands and feet shackled. Taylor supposed he should have at least taken time to learn the names of the men who would serve under him. In truth, though, he didn't care about the men or their names or their crimes. He only cared that they performed their jobs and followed orders.

"No one here has less than two years to serve for his crime," Taylor said flatly. "You can either spend that time in prison or accept a special assignment." Taylor scanned the haggard faces. "Do you want the assignment?"

"What do we gotta do?"

Taylor regarded the man who had spoken. Quietly, he said, "It's a yes or no question, Soldier." A moment's silence preceded a wild outburst of answers in the affirmative.

"Good. We'll ride at first light. Try to desert and I'll shoot you in the back. Complete the mission, and I'll pay each one of you two hundred dollars in gold nuggets and commute your prison sentence."

"Captain, sir," drawled the same soldier. "What does *commute* mean?"

"It means you go free with an honorable discharge."

Taylor was greeted with a thunderous applause. When the men quieted down, one asked, "So where's the money, Captain?" The man wore a hint of a sneer on his face.

"The gold is in the bank of Silver City," he lied. He had no intention of telling the men that he carried the gold on his person. "Your mission will be to follow orders and make sure I stay alive, or you won't see any of the gold."

Captain Taylor turned away abruptly and noticed that Private Tucker was staring at him, mouth agape. "You like gold, Private?" Tucker nodded. "What would you do for two hundred dollars and an immediate honorable discharge? No, make it *five* hundred. This is your chance to get away from all this bad living and the fear of fighting."

Taylor saw the greedy thoughts race across the soldier's dark face as he considered more money than he'd earn in almost five years. Tucker was a thinker, not a fighter. Taylor could tell that just by looking at him. Sure, he'd learned the discipline of military training, but he'd fold on his first scouting mission. He didn't belong in the army.

"I reckon I'd do pretty much anything, sir."

"Glad to hear that." Taylor turned to leave. "I've got a special job for you."

CHAPTER 14

"**P**LACE LOOKS DESERTED," JASON SAID as First Sergeant Crawford led him toward the center building of the row of barracks. Only one squad of about twenty troops performed marching maneuvers on the parade field.

"We normally keep four companies here, two infantry and two cavalry. Most everyone is out in the field, chasing renegade Apache all over the Black Range and the San Mateo Mountains northeast of here."

Jason started to ask why the men marching weren't out scouting but thought better of it. Obviously, someone had to protect the fort or escort stagecoach travelers and the mail down south and back. "So who's going to defend the fort when we all ride out tomorrow morning?"

Crawford glanced sideways, a bit of a smile creasing the corners of his mouth. "I suppose the major and Lieutenant Reeves will." Crawford paused in front of the open doors of the barracks and motioned behind the east wall. "Sink is out thataway."

"Sink?"

"The latrine ditch." The sergeant shrugged like it should have been obvious.

Jason nodded and looked behind him. The land to the west behind the officer's quarters sloped gently upward toward a rounded hilltop. Then he noticed something he hadn't seen before, a gaggle of shanties at the end of the row of well-tended duplexes.

"What's that?" Jason nodded toward the shacks.

"Houses for maids, laundresses, and the few married enlisted men." Crawford pointed into the distance to the northwest and Jason saw a fairly large boxlike structure. "We get fresh water from there."

Jason raised an eyebrow.

Crawford explained. "Our spring-fed water hole used to flow right through the swamp where livestock and pigs water. Had a lot of sick men back in those days." The big man shook his head. "You wouldn't have wanted to be here back then. We enlarged the spring and built some wooden pipes and brought the water down to that filter box you see there." Jason couldn't really see any details of the wood structure, but he accepted Crawford's description.

"The water passes through charcoal and sand then is stored in a tank. When we need water, it's delivered down here by water wagon." Jason heard the pride in Crawford's voice.

"Sounds like you had a hand in building that contraption?"

Crawford nodded. "I supervised the whole affair."

The barracks building consisted of two large squad rooms, one on either side of a wide hallway. The first sergeant showed Jason to a bunk in one of the squad rooms.

"Supper is in four hours in the dining room." He pointed at the back wall of the building. Jason figured the dining room lay beyond the wall, accessed through the main hallway. "I'll be in my office," the man said. He turned and walked down the hallway.

The interior of the huge room seemed dark after being outside in the bright light, and the air was thick and heavy even though several small windows were open. Jason removed his gun belt, lay down on his cot, and covered his face with his hat. He fell asleep immediately, awaking what seemed like only minutes later to the sound of voices and boots shuffling on the hardpacked earthen floor.

The supper bell sounded, and Jason filed into the dining room behind the rest of the troops. Long rough-plank tables with smoothly sanded benches formed the only furniture. Jason figured the room packed full could seat maybe a hundred men. The twenty men of Company B sat comfortably at tables in the center of the room.

Jason passed through the food line as the cook piled some slop-looking food on his metal plate. He selected the table with Shelton and Crawford. Toying with his bread for a moment, Jason studied his plate. He thought he recognized chunks of beef and potatoes in the mix, along with some vegetables. The whole affair was drowned in white gravy. He turned the stuff over a bit with his well-used spoon and heard a snicker. When he looked up, he realized everyone in the room was staring at him.

He grimaced and said, "I'm assuming this stuff is edible." The troops around him erupted in laughter and Shelton, seated next to him, slapped him on the back with his free hand.

"You gotta love army food," Shelton shouted over the din. "Ain't much to look at, but it's the best free food in the territory."

Jason shoveled a healthy portion into his mouth. "Tastes a lot better than it looks." He cleaned his plate fairly quickly and joined the line for seconds.

When Jason finished his second serving, he heard men at the tables around him sharing stories of the day. He sensed the camaraderie in the room but still felt like an outsider. He thought hard, trying to manufacture comments that he might use to join in a conversation. A couple of times Shelton asked him questions, but he muttered only brief answers in response. Soon, even Shelton abandoned him. He wanted friends, but he realized he didn't know how to *not* keep them at arm's length. He busied himself with picking at the leavings on his metal plate.

Jason cast brief glances at the soldiers. Except for Shelton, all were dark-skinned. The soldiers all seemed to accept Shelton as part of the family. Jason figured they'd probably accept him too, if he let them.

"Hey, L.C.," Shelton said. "What's Cap'n Taylor up to?"

Crawford shrugged. "He hasn't seen fit to confide in me. I just follow orders."

Jason heard a mutter from the table behind him and somehow knew the comment was aimed directly at him.

"When you're done scouting, he wants me to shoot you in the back."

Everyone else in the room must have heard the remark also because silence suddenly filled the room. Jason swiveled on his bench to face Private Tucker, the guard he'd first spoken to when he rode into the fort.

"And?"

Tucker couldn't look him in the eye. "If I don't do it, he'll find someone else."

CHAPTER 15

JUH AND HIS WARRIORS RODE along the ridgelines whenever possible, to avoid the kinds of ambushes they often arranged for the bluecoats. They traveled through the night, stopping only briefly to rest the horses and to relieve themselves. Whenever they came upon water, they let their horses drink their fill, but most of the streams were dry, parched creek beds. Lack of water and the intense heat had forced the warriors to travel more slowly than Juh wanted. He couldn't remember a summer as dry or as hot.

The hours passed slowly, and the sun scorched the earth under his horse's unshod hooves. The air seemed to get hotter by the minute as he and his men descended the last foothills before reaching the river the *White-Eyes* called the Rio Grande. From the distance, he could see even the great river suffered the wrath of the sun. Its brown, slow-moving waters flowed shallower than he'd ever seen.

Juh raised his hand to signal a halt. The ridge where he sat sloped steeply down into the flatland. The almost featureless ground stretched farther into the flats. It was barren of everything but rocks, wild grass, and an occasional sagebrush, and it swept in a gentle slope toward the river five miles distant. Down by the river, he noticed a small gathering of army wagons.

He and his warriors were late. He had intended for them to be in position to observe the arrival of the wagon train so they could pick the proper time and place for their ambush. Even as he adjusted his plans in his mind, he struggled to determine what it was about the sight below that troubled him.

"Where are the rest of the wagons?" he said almost rhetorically. The warriors gathered around him, and Poncé nudged his horse beside Juh's.

"There should be a lot more," Poncé agreed. "Maybe the rest fell behind and are coming soon."

Juh shook his head. "Lives With The Enemy said they were moving horses and mules too."

The warriors debated the issue for a moment, then Juh made his decision. He pointed to a water-worn crevasse that stretched down the slope toward the river. Such steep-sided crevasses were common, formed by storm water that rushed down out of the mountains. Most times the crevasses were only a few feet wide, completely invisible except from only a few paces away.

"We'll hide our horses in the gully below the ridge then approach the army camp on foot."

One warrior stayed with the ground-tied horses as Juh and his warriors jogged downhill toward the army camp. The last mile was especially tiring as the gully shallowed out so much they had to jog crouched over to avoid the possibility of being seen. Then the ground became loosely packed dirt and sand that consumed their energy, requiring two paces forward just to take one normal step. Finally, when the ground flattened out, they had to crawl and slither over the last hundred paces before reaching the trees and brush lining the river.

Carefully, the warriors made their way into the trees and crept south about a mile until they could see the enemy. Fear and alarm flooded Juh as he gazed upon the camp from behind bushes. He saw only six soldiers patrolling the clearing where the path led into the water. That was far too few to defend against an attack. Where were the rest of the soldiers and the animals they were supposed to be transporting?

Juh signaled two of his warriors who were best skilled in silent movement to hunt around the camp for signs of other soldiers. An hour later, both returned and reported there was no evidence of any additional soldiers anywhere around. Juh could see three of the wagons lined up at the water's edge, ready to cross. The last wagon sat a few hundred paces behind the other three, attended by only a single soldier.

Through narrowed eyes, Juh observed the suspiciously inviting target. It had to be a trap. With hand signals he instructed Brown Hair to approach the last wagon and check its contents. He didn't have to tell the young man to avoid contact with the soldier. All his warriors knew a completely silent approach was their strongest ally if they were to capture an enemy supply wagon and escape.

Juh watched as Brown Hair crept through the tall grass around the clearing. The young man left his rifle and bow with the warriors so he could travel quickly and quietly. He stopped just before crossing the trail to approach the lone wagon, studied the ground for a moment, then backtracked. When he could safely squat without being seen, he turned toward the warriors and made hand signals.

The wagons are all empty. The tracks are too shallow for heavy supplies.

The Apache army scout Lives With The Enemy had betrayed them. For what reason, Juh could not understand, but the man deliberately led them to ambush an empty wagon train. He was just about to communicate his thought to his *segundo*, Poncé, when panic gripped his gut.

The traitor scout had drawn them away from their people. The camp on the Gila River was almost completely defenseless, except for the young warriors in training. If the traitor led them to the false supply wagons, he might also have told the soldiers the location of the Apache camp. If the army captured the entire tribe, Juh and his warriors would have no choice but to surrender.

For a moment, Juh entertained the thought of killing the few soldiers before him in retaliation. He contained that thought quickly though. This was no time for vengeance. They had to get back to the camp immediately.

Juh quickly motioned for Poncé to lead the warriors back to the horses and hurry back to camp. Poncé sent a warrior running ahead to scout point, then he and the main body of warriors followed.

Juh motioned for Brown Hair to return. As the young warrior slowly navigated the brush, Juh reflected on another difference between the Apache and the soldiers. Army officers always led from the front of their soldiers in attack or retreat. An Apache leader's position during an attack was in front of his warriors. During escape or retreat, the leader took his position at the rear of his men, as this was the most dangerous place to be. It was the best place for the leader to defend his men if the enemy pursued and attacked from the rear.

Juh watched Brown Hair pause to check his surroundings before slithering across a barren stretch of ground. He'd just started moving when gunshots echoed from the distance in the direction where they'd left their ponies.

Brown Hair froze in clear view of the soldier that raced around the solitary wagon. Juh brought up his rifle and squeezed off a shot as the soldier aimed at Brown Hair. He missed, but his shot distracted the soldier's aim. A bullet kicked up dirt in the young warrior's face. Brown Hair was on his feet in an instant, charging the soldier as Juh shifted his aim to cover the other soldiers.

Even as Juh fired at soldiers behind wagons, he kept glancing at Brown Hair. Armed with only a knife, the young warrior grappled with the soldier, finally slamming his blade into the man's chest and wrestling him to the ground. Juh fired a few more shots and glanced over again to see the young warrior raking his knife around the sides of the Black soldier's head.

"No," Juh shouted. "Don't take his scalp!"

Brown Hair ignored him, just stood and stuck his foot against the soldier's face and yanked on his hair. Even from the distance, Juh could hear the wet sucking sound as Brown Hair tore the man's scalp from his head. The soldier screamed in agony and the young warrior stood over him, yelling his war cry at the other soldiers. He threw the scalp at them, but it landed far short.

The other soldiers seemed stunned by what they'd seen. By the time they reacted, Brown Hair had descended upon his prey again. Juh fired more shots, not wanting to watch as Brown Hair quickly and expertly worked his blade on the screaming man.

When the young warrior completed his task, Juh snapped off a few more shots as they retreated into the brush and moved north to the crevasse. They stumbled in the dry dirt-sand, trying to keep low and out of sight. An hour later, Juh realized the full impact of the trap the traitor had lured Juh and his men into.

CHAPTER 16

HEAVING DEEP STEADY BREATHS, JUH and Brown Hair paused at the place where they'd left the horses and studied the signs. Poncé and the others had paused there also, studied the scene, and moved on.

The warrior left behind to care for the horses lost a struggle, a vicious hand-to-hand combat that cost him his life. The tracks indicated his killer wore large army boots. A big soldier ambushed him and knifed him, judging from all the blood. Then he slit the throats of three of their horses, then shot the rest, probably when they went wild at the scent of blood. No doubt, Poncé and his men took the warrior's body with them to be buried in an unmarked grave in the vast hills where the enemy would never find him. From the soldier's elongated steps, Juh could see the attacker had scrambled up the steep bank of the soft-sided crevasse. He escaped across the desert land, probably to return soon with many more soldiers.

For a moment, the horrifying death scene before him stunned Juh. Once before in the years past, he hid in the brush while soldiers slit his pony's throat. The animal trumpeted its death throes, still standing as it gasped for air. Juh, much younger then, could only watch in sadness as the animal suffocated on the blood it sucked in through its shattered throat. Finally, his pony had collapsed, still struggling against death for long minutes.

He shook off the distant memory and tugged on Brown Hair's

arm. As Juh followed the tracks of his warriors, he noticed the lone soldier's tracks led to the massacre by the same path they now used to escape. Somehow, the soldier found their tracks earlier and followed them. Juh didn't believe it was coincidence. Lives With The Enemy must have told his masters the most likely routes Juh and his warriors would take, and the army had men searching those routes.

A chilling thought entered Juh's mind. The army knew Juh and his warriors were in the area. The soldiers knew exactly when they would arrive. The traitor had helped them set the decoy supply wagons to lure the warriors here. Many other soldiers had to be scouting the hills for their tracks. Now came the challenging task of escape.

Killing lone army scouts would be an easy task if they encountered any. Leaving a trail of dead bodies or missing soldiers though, would only serve as a beacon for the rest of the searching troops.

Such overly optimistic thoughts were short-lived as Juh and Brown Hair caught up to Poncé and the other warriors half an hour later at the head of the water-carved crevasse just under the ridgeline. Silent hand signals confirmed that dozens of infantry soldiers lined the nearest ridges and the flatland, approaching from the west and the south.

Even though the sun was setting, they could not possibly elude all the patrols. He and his warriors had only one escape route. They were being herded to the north, forced away from their camp.

CHAPTER 17

J ASON SHARED AN EARLY BREAKFAST of more of the same gravy-potato-beef mixture smothered over eggs, bacon, and some thick, square, rock-hard biscuits that could only be chewed after soaking up some gravy. Shelton called the biscuits *hardtack* and said it was part of a soldier's standard field ration because hardtack could last for days, or even weeks, without rotting if it was kept dry.

After breakfast, the twenty-six remaining men of Company B and the sixteen Sixth Cavalry soldiers from the stockade departed Fort Bayard under the command of two officers. Captain Taylor led the column accompanied by Lieutenant Nathan Henry.

First Sergeant Lafayette Crawford had informed Jason that since he was the company scout, he would either ride up front with the officers or follow between the officers and the soldiers. However, Captain Taylor told Jason to ride back with the Black soldiers. The White soldiers of the Sixth Cavalry followed the officers, while Jason, Crawford, and the rest of Company B of the Ninth Cavalry brought up the rear.

Jason had never ridden in an army formation before, and he found the experience unnerving. The army mounts were all bigger than Grady, and Jason felt somehow inadequate among all the big men with their big animals and overstuffed packs.

The noise was almost overwhelming too. Jason listened to the unending sound of gear and weapons clattering. In addition, the smell of horse dung was ever-present from the start, as the army mounts dropped almost constantly.

The column struck out north from the fort on the wood haul and sawmill road. They rode the entire day, stopping only for an hour to rest and water the horses. Because of the hard mountain trails, no mess wagon or cook accompanied the soldiers, so they ate a noon meal of hardtack and beef jerky.

The column followed hills and valleys northward, skirting the Piños Altos mining town. The heavily burdened horses labored into the higher altitude over gradually steeper hills as the brush merged into trees and pines of medium height. Eventually, the short-cropped, brown grasses along the well-traveled trail gave way to lush, green mountain wild grass, heavily carpeted with needles from towering pine trees of the higher altitude.

Jason could have enjoyed the ride through the high country, except that he rode with a group of men preparing to make war. He'd spent most of his outlaw years outrunning posses and bounty hunters in mountain ranges all over the frontier, and the high country was his favorite place to be since most times it was peaceful and serene. He felt no sense of calm riding with the army.

As the column topped a series of ridges, the air grew thin, and the pines yielded to a wide variety of trees with leaves of different shades of green and yellow. Rocks and boulders dotted the hilltops and steep, brush-covered valleys bordered both sides of the ridge.

Late in the evening, the column dipped down to the Gila River as it wound through a series of canyons. Finally, they arrived at the junction where the East Fork joined the main branch of the river.

By the time Jason and Crawford pulled up, Taylor was already involved in an animated conversation with an Apache scout. Jason noticed the scout looking away a bit, accepting Taylor's abusive language. The stone-faced look on his countenance could have been submission or contempt. The captain angrily dismissed the scout and shouted orders for his men to dismount and prepare for the evening meal.

Lieutenant Henry rode over to Crawford and repeated the same orders, though in a more civilized tone. Several men picketed the Company B horses downstream and stood guard. Jason tended to Grady himself and had just started to lead the horse to the bank of the stream when he heard a gunshot. Instantly, he spun toward the source of the sound and grabbed for his holstered Schofield guns. Across the clearing, a soldier from the Sixth stood over the body of the Indian scout. Taylor stomped up to the man.

"What do you think you're doing, Corporal?"

"You said we could kill Indians, sir," the soldier pleaded. "I thought he was going for a gun." Jason could tell by the smirk on the corporal's face that the man was lying.

Taylor just shook his head. "Stow that weapon, Mister." Then he turned away.

Jason suddenly felt a knot in his gut. Captain Taylor had just condoned the killing of another scout with barely a half-dozen words of mild admonishment. Jason turned back to Grady and removed the saddle. As he pulled the blanket off the horse, he mumbled a few gentle words, more to relax himself than for the animal's comfort. The horse nudged his side and whinnied softly, and Jason imagined Grady understood him. He let the horse feed on the lush green grass at the water's edge.

As Grady ate, Jason checked his guns, more from habit than for any practical reason. With both Schofield holster guns and his Colt belt pistol fully loaded, he turned toward the gathered men of Company B. He saw Shelton, Crawford, and another soldier seated together and he headed over to them. He felt a tickle on the back of his neck, a familiar warning sign that pulled his attention across the clearing. Both officers sat watching him, maybe talking about him, but Captain Taylor's dark-eyed gaze seemed filled with hatred. Jason looked away, and his gaze touched on the body of the Indian scout that lay almost within reach of the Sixth Cavalry camp. Shelton must have seen the concern in his eyes.

"You better watch your back, Jason," Shelton said as Jason sat down beside Crawford. "I've seen the captain's type before. Probably won't give as much thought to the death of a Black soldier or scout as he did for that Injun."

Jason nodded. "He seems to have taken a special dislike for me."

The third soldier, a private named Silas Nance, chuckled. "Seein' as he hates all of us, you should consider that an honor." Jason and the three men shared a quiet chuckle.

Shelton changed the subject. "How'd you tear your sleeve, Silas? Seems like when we left you at the fort three days ago, you were a corporal."

Jason glanced at the man's right arm. In the waning light, he saw a sliver of cloth torn at Nance's shoulder. He imagined someone ripping the stripes away, tearing the fabric in the process.

"Had me a disagreement with the lieutenant." Nance shrugged. "Got to carry the pole around for six hours too."

Shelton explained for Jason's benefit. "We got us a hundred-pound log we get to carry around on our shoulders behind the neck when we mess up." He imitated like he was holding a log in place behind his neck with his arms. "I've seen grown men break down in tears carryin' the pole around in the heat of the day."

"They can't break me," Nance said. The private was a big man, Jason saw, though not as huge as Crawford. With dark skin almost blue-black, he possessed sharp, narrow facial features. High cheekbones and a wide flaring nose made him look intense and dangerous. Jason could imagine a White officer looking at a dark and serious face like Nance's and seeing a threat, whether Nance intended to be so or not.

Nance continued. "I tossed that pole at the lieutenant's feet when I was done too." He paused. "Well, that's when he put me in the stockade for two days."

Shelton said, "Was that before or after he took your stripes?" The men laughed again.

"They can't break me," the private repeated.

"They aren't trying to break you, Silas," Crawford countered. "They just want some respect."

"Here we go again." Shelton rolled his eyes. "They have this conversation at least once a week." Jason sat with Crawford to his left and Nance to his right. Shelton sat opposite Jason. Nance continued as if Shelton hadn't spoken.

"I ain't gonna be nobody's proper *boy*."

"That's not what I'm sayin', Silas. But you've got to accept things the way they are."

Nance chuckled again. "Things like what? Like they're better than we are?" Crawford started to object, but Nance continued. "That's what *they* think. The lieutenant and the major, heck even Colonel Hatch, they all say we're good soldiers. And they recommend us for medals when we fight just as well or better than the White soldiers. But we never get any, do we?"

"Come on, Silas," Shelton broke in. "We got some medals."

"A few. But not as many as *them*."

Jason listened to the exchange with interest. He sensed the men had rehearsed their viewpoints frequently and thoroughly. Nance seemed to want to recruit Jason to his way of thinking, but Crawford seemed obliged to provide the counterpoints.

"Look," Nance said. "The bottom line is, they'll be nice to us and help us get along in *their* army, as long as we accept White superiority."

Crawford nodded. "You'll get no argument from me on that. But if you accept things the way they are and quit rebelling so much, maybe you can keep a stripe or two on your arm." Nance waved away the argument.

Shelton chuckled. "He's a little short in the brains," he said, nodding at Nance. "Can't quite figure out the kinda stuff that'll make life easy on hisself."

"Yeah, well, maybe I can't read or write—"

"But he's got frontier smarts," Crawford said quickly. "Can't think of anyone I'd rather have fightin' with me in a tight spot."

"Sure," Shelton agreed. "Ten years of fightin' Injuns and he's never been shot or wounded. Just gets promoted and busted a couple of times a month."

Jason sensed the pride within the group and directed a question to Private Nance. "What do you do when you have to fight together?" He nodded to the White soldiers across the clearing.

"We fight together just fine. I've holed up in trenches and fought off ambushes right alongside White soldiers many a time. Usually, the only color that matters then is the enemy's."

Shelton nodded. "Until we get back to the fort."

The soldiers laughed again.

"These fellas are different though," Crawford said, looking across the clearing. "They're convicts. Most of 'em never got along in the army. I'm guessin' over in Arizona, they never seen a Black soldier before. They ain't gonna be easy to get along with."

Nance sneered. "Might be us fightin' against two separate enemies tomorrow."

"So what do you do in a case like that?" Jason said.

Crawford shrugged. "We follow orders. That's the army way."

"And what do you make of Captain Taylor?" Jason said.

"You spoke against him yesterday," Crawford said. "In front of the officers. I suppose he didn't take kindly to that."

Jason nodded. "I'm beholden to no man."

"I agree that's a good personal policy to have," Crawford added. "But that surely is *not* the army way."

Nance chuckled and said, "White folks are born thinkin' they're better'n us. Or they learn it in school or some place. Like the first sergeant said, you challenged his authority."

Jason started to respond but noticed Nance looking over his shoulder. He heard footsteps approaching, and when he twisted to see who Nance was looking at, Jason saw Private Tucker. The man stopped and seemed to wilt under the gaze of the four men. Jason scooted over closer to Nance and patted the ground between himself and Crawford, inviting Tucker to join them.

"Hey, Killer," Nance said with a chuckle. "I heard about you. Come to do Jason Peares right now?" Tucker sat cross-legged like the other men and ignored the barb, so Nance continued. "Read any news lately?"

Tucker nodded and adjusted his spectacles. "I read an article in the *Army and Navy Journal* about Lieutenant Henry Flipper, the army's first and only Black commissioned officer. Seems he's having a hard go of it. Always under investigation or being accused of one thing or another."

"A Black officer?" Nance said shaking his head. "Now there's somethin' I wouldn't wish on a broke-leg dog."

Shelton agreed. "Who's he gonna command?"

"He's assigned to the Tenth Cavalry," Tucker said. "The other cavalry unit for Black soldiers. But they won't give him a command. Assigned him to the quartermaster post or stuck him in the administrative office or something."

"Well," Nance said with a sigh. "That's why they call us *Buffalo Soldiers*. 'Cause we stand up strong under all kinds of circumstances."

Jason glanced over at Nance. "Buffalo Soldiers?" He hadn't heard that term before.

"That's what the Injuns call us, anyways. They respect the buffalo as a strong adversary. Somethin' spiritual about bravery an' such. We kicked their butts a few times, so now they respect us."

"Actually," Shelton interrupted. "I thought it was because our hair reminded 'em of the buffalo's fur."

Nance scoffed at the idea. "That's the White man's idea. Always trying to degrade us. Any fool that thinks our hair looks like a buffalo hide ain't never seen that animal!"

Shelton defended. "I don't mean up close. From a distance, maybe."

Private Tucker cleared his throat. "Actually, those are only two of the speculations on how Colored soldiers became known as the Buffalo Soldiers. There's another possibility how the name came to be, and it's more accurate in my opinion." He fell silent, but Jason and the other three stared at him expectantly. Tucker finally continued.

"I read in a Colorado newspaper a couple of years ago that the Texas Plains Indians—Comanche, I think— first saw Black soldiers from the Tenth Cavalry during a winter scout. It was darned cold, so the soldiers were all wearing buffalo hides because they hadn't been issued any army overcoats. So the Indians called 'em Buffalo Soldiers. I suppose that's how we got that image drawn on our unit flag."

Jason recalled seeing the image on a flag at the fort. It was a soldier on horseback, hunched over against the wind, wearing a buffalo coat. The group fell silent for a few minutes. Without discussion, Shelton prepared five plates of cold beans and biscuits.

"Let's pray," Shelton said. He recited some words that Jason thought appropriate for the situation. Something about keeping the soldiers safe from attack in the next few days, from sickness, and from Captain Taylor and his Sixth Cavalry troops. A chorus of *Amens* followed Shelton's words. When the soldiers opened their eyes, they seemed to sense that Jason hadn't participated in the prayer.

"You ain't gonna pray with us?" Shelton said.

"I don't pray."

"What?" Nance shot Jason a quizzical look. "Ain't you a Christian?"

Jason hesitated for a moment. "I don't profess to be of any religion." He caught Crawford's gaze.

"That's all right, Jason. God loves you anyway. He'll save you."

Jason snorted his contempt and immediately wished he could take the noise back. "You boys go on praying to your God. Here's my savior." He pulled a Schofield pistol from one of his holsters. "When I'm in a pinch, I pray my pistols have full chambers." He stuck his gun away.

Tucker asked quietly. "You don't believe in God, do you?"

"Which God? Your God? Or maybe the Apache God, whatever they call it. Or maybe Captain Taylor's God."

Nance narrowed his eyes. "There's only one God."

Jason chuckled. "You pray for safety while the Apaches pray for deliverance from the soldiers. Maybe Captain Taylor's prayin' for a perfect world where God wipes all the Black men and red men off the land." He paused as the men stared at him. "Where is this God of yours that would let His children hunt and kill each other like this?"

No one answered the question, and the men ate in silence. Afterward, Crawford addressed all the men of Company B.

"We'd better turn in and get a few hours of sleep." He assigned the first shift of guards. Jason noticed Tucker's hand was trembling.

"Scared?"

Tucker said nothing. He clamped his hands together and started to get up.

"Give me your hand." Jason held out his own and waited.

"I ain't gonna hold your hand!"

Jason gestured again. "Your hand, Private!" he said in a commanding voice. Tucker reached out hesitantly, and Jason gripped his hand hard. "When you get afraid out there tomorrow, remember this."

He thrust their hands out into the center of the group. Shelton nodded and put his hand on theirs. Nance did the same and Crawford placed his massive hand on top of the pile. Jason looked Tucker in the eye, then made brief eye contact with each of the other men.

"It's all right to be afraid, Private. When you are, trust us. We're your flesh and blood." Jason shook the pile of hands. "You look out for us, and we'll look out for you."

"Besides," Jason continued with a wry grin. "You don't get courage first so you can go fight bravely. You fight bravely first, then you find courage from that experience."

He released Tucker's hand and the other men withdrew their hands. For a moment, Jason gazed at Crawford, thought he saw the deep understanding of a kindred fighting man. Instantly, he knew they both had experienced the same kinds of life-and-death situations over the years. They both nodded at the same time.

"Scout!" Captain Taylor's voice broke the feeling of camaraderie. Jason looked up at the captain as he walked up behind Shelton. "What're you doing sittin' on your rump? Get out there and do some scoutin'!"

Jason stood and faced the obnoxious officer. In his side vision, he saw the men of Company B staring. Lieutenant Henry stood a pace behind Taylor and watched the confrontation with concern. The soldier-prisoners of the Sixth slowly got to their feet. Some reached for weapons.

CHAPTER 18

J ASON NODDED AND SAID, "WHAT are your orders, Captain?"
Taylor narrowed his eyes and Jason got the feeling the
captain wanted him to respond differently. "Come with me."
He looked at Nathan Henry. "You too, Lieutenant."

A sergeant from the Sixth Cavalry joined the meeting with
Captain Taylor, Lieutenant Henry, and Jason.

Lieutenant Henry spoke. "Captain, my first sergeant should
be included in this briefing. He's the highest-ranking enlisted
man present." Only then did Jason notice that the White sergeant wore no diamond on his sleeve.

"It's bad enough havin' one of 'em near me." Taylor talked
about Jason as if he were invisible. "I'll not have two."

"Sir, it's highly inappropriate—"

Taylor pointed a finger at Henry. "Lieutenant, I'll tell you
what's inappropriate." He pointed at the men of Company B
milling around across the clearing. "No Negro soldier is going to
be giving orders to any White soldiers in my command. I don't
care if he *is* a first sergeant. Is that clear?"

Taylor spoke loud enough so that all the soldiers heard—
White and Black. A few of the White soldiers snickered, behavior
that Jason found curious and unsoldierlike. Then he remembered, these men spent most of their service time in the stockade.

"Very clear, Captain," Henry returned coldly. "But I object.
These Negro soldiers are among the bravest fighting men I've

ever served with. They've proven themselves in battle and some have been decorated."

Jason watched the exchange with curiosity. He admired the lieutenant for not backing down, but Taylor puzzled him. When the man walked into the Silver City saloon in civilian clothes, he seemed like he wanted to kill Jason for no good reason. An hour later, he was profuse in his apologies and wanted to recruit Jason. Next day, he was hateful again.

"Lieutenant, do I need to relieve you of command?"

Lieutenant Henry hesitated, and Jason sensed his struggle between the need to defend his men and obey his commanding officer. One of the bad points about the military, Jason figured, was that authority rested on the man with the most rank, good judgment notwithstanding. Besides, Lieutenant Henry had to know he couldn't buffer any abuse the captain threw at his men if he was back at the fort.

"That won't be necessary, Captain."

Taylor stared at him a moment more, then unfolded a map he'd retrieved from a saddle pocket. He squatted and spread the map on the ground. Jason saw the three forks of the Gila River winding through valleys. Heavily drawn hatched lines showed the contours of steep canyons.

"According to our dead scout," Taylor nodded at the body that lay in the grass by the water, "Juh's camp is here." He pointed on the map where the Middle Fork joined the West Fork. "They ought to be just inside this canyon here, right on the Middle Fork, back about a hundred feet from the junction."

From the map, Jason surmised the canyon walls rose above the Middle Fork a hundred feet, maybe higher. That would provide a measure of protection from the elements, making that area great for a campsite. The main branch of the Gila River, however, wound through a valley that was maybe a quarter-mile wide with no protection from wind or intense sun.

"We'll capture them here." Taylor pointed to the junction. "You, Scout, will see that our departed Indian scout rounded up of all the lookouts near the camp. If he missed any, you will hogtie them and bring them back here. Kill them only if you have no other choice. Chief Juh and his warriors won't surrender if we kill a bunch of their people. Clear?" He paused, and Jason nodded. "And be quiet about it," he added, focusing an intense gaze at Jason.

Then the captain nodded to Lieutenant Henry. "Lieutenant, we'll ride in at first light and corral the entire camp. You will lead your men around this bluff here." He indicated a canyon a mile east of the Apache camp veering off to the north. It joined the Middle Fork half a mile north of the camp.

"You will have the responsibility to make sure no one escapes to the north. Scout, you will have the same responsibility to the west. When you've seen to the lookouts, you'll report back here, then take three men and watch the West Fork up where the valley narrows. Follow the same path as the lieutenant, then diverge west at this point."

Taylor indicated the connecting canyon again. His finger traced north along the Middle Fork past where the lieutenant would station his men. A few miles up, another canyon connected over to the West Fork valley. Taylor's finger moved back south a couple miles and tapped a place on the map where the valley narrowed just south of the canyon, where the West Fork turned sharply to the west.

Taylor glanced around as if making a decision. "Take the Negro school teacher and those two over there." He pointed out two burly, White soldiers. "Questions?" He paused half a heartbeat, then stood and folded his map. "Good." He looked at Jason.

"Get moving, Scout. And, Lieutenant, watch your back. Before he died, that Indian scout said only half the warriors left with Juh. I expect those that stayed behind will put up a fight."

Jason went back to his horse and prepared for his part of the mission. Private Tucker stepped over to him as Crawford conferred with his lieutenant.

"After I get back, the captain wants you and me and those two over there to close off the West Fork and collect any Indians trying to escape."

Tucker followed Jason's gaze. "Those are the ones he said would help me when...."

"When it's time to kill me," Jason said. Tucker looked away and fidgeted with his wire rims. Jason said, "If I judge the captain right, he'll have those two shoot the both of us. In the back, most likely."

"What're we gonna do?" Tucker whispered.

Jason studied the man. "When we go off with those two, I'll try to get 'em in front and keep 'em there. You stick right behind me and watch my back. I'll take care of them when the time is right. But if you see them making their play, give me a signal. Then just keep your head down. Let me handle the gun work. It's what I'm good at."

Jason mounted up and looked at the deepening shadows. The enormity of his task suddenly struck him. He had to find an undetermined number of Apache lookouts in the dead of night. Get close to them without being heard. Capture or otherwise incapacitate them.

All without firing a shot that would alert the Apache camp.

CHAPTER 19

FOUR TIMES, JUH AND HIS warriors backtracked, trying to find a southern route through the line of soldiers. Each time, they were forced to turn around as they came close to encountering patrolling soldiers. One or two of the warriors might have had a chance to sneak through in the darkness, but Juh knew his people at the camp needed more than one or two fighting men. They needed the entire war party to defend them. Yet, he could find no way to get all his men through the line of soldiers. A single mistake would betray the warriors and the soldiers would know instantly where to concentrate their search.

Reluctantly, Juh led his men to the north, away from the decoy army camp. A gnawing panic nagged at the edge of his mind as he feared how his people might suffer. The camp's survival plan relied on the safety of the land, the numerous escape routes, and sentries to aid the few older warriors and younger warriors in training. No doubt, the traitor would find a way to eliminate those advantages.

As he walked, Juh silently prayed to *Ussen* to care for all his warriors' wives and children. He remembered his vision of three days ago.

We are the Indeh.

About midnight, Juh gathered his warriors together.

"I fear for our tribe," he said solemnly. "We've got to find a way through the line of soldiers. They found our horses, so they know fairly closely where we are. Instead of trying to surround us and kill us, they're just trying to herd us to the north."

"But why?" Poncé said. "This just doesn't make sense. The army always wants to kill us, never let us live."

Wishing for another vision to explain his enemy's strategy, Juh just shook his head. "I don't know. But I know our people are in trouble. We may already be too late."

All present understood the danger their people faced. Yet, all knew of the impossibility of the entire war party sneaking past the soldiers undetected in the night. The moon shone bright, and the soldiers were keeping all-night patrols.

Poncé spoke. "If the soldiers wish to find us, let them." Juh raised an eyebrow and nodded for his *segundo* to continue. "Let me take two of our fastest runners. We will distract the soldiers and make a lot of noise. We'll make the soldiers think they've found our entire war party and we'll let them chase us to the north where they want us to go."

He pointed at Juh with his nose. "The rest of you go west through the canyons of Cuchillo Negro. I remember places in the canyon where the walls are so close together only two horses can walk side by side."

Nodding, Juh added. "We'll use the steep path up the south wall. It's difficult, but we can get through there if we're careful."

"That's right," Poncé agreed. "While the soldiers chase us, you can get the warriors back to the camp."

Juh located a small depression in the flat land, a dry stream-bed. They discussed details for a few minutes, then rested under the watchful eyes of two lookouts. Ishton's beautiful face filled his mind as he gazed up at the stars.

Juh's raiding party had followed the East Fork of the Gila River away from camp and crossed the Black Range. They'd headed almost straight toward the rising sun to find the army camp on the Rio Grande. Now, to elude the patrolling soldiers, they had moved maybe ten miles north. If Poncé was successful in drawing the soldiers farther away to the north, Juh and his warriors could head back west, skirting the northern peaks of the Black Range. Then they'd run straight southwest until they came to the Middle Fork, following that branch of the Gila River south until they came to the camp.

Running such a great distance would challenge even the best of the warriors, yet Juh recalled the distance training he received as a young warrior. His father required him to collect a mouthful of water at the camp river, then run into the mountains where there was no water. He and the other young warriors were not allowed to drink the water they carried in their mouths.

When he reached the camp at the end of his run several hours later, he had to return the same amount of water to a cup or repeat the run. It had been excellent training to build stamina, Juh remembered fondly, and he gladly prepared his young warriors to perform the same feat throughout the years.

The upcoming task would be different. Without horses, he and his men had to run through the hottest time of the day. They had to find a way to cover an impossible hundred fifty miles over mountainous land. This was not a training exercise where they could simply be told to do it again. If they failed, their people would die.

CHAPTER 20

I N THE DARKNESS, JASON RODE quickly up the valley until he judged himself to be within two miles of the Indian camp. He left Grady tied in a stand of trees and packed his guns in his saddle pack, except one he kept tucked in the front of his belt. He knew if he used it even in an emergency, he'd betray the entire mission. He changed into his hard-soled moccasins—a gift from the Arapaho warrior he'd spent time with years before. Jason rarely wore them because they had special meaning for him, but tonight he needed them for silent movement.

Armed with a six-inch carving knife on his belt, a ten-inch buffalo bone knife tied to his right calf, and a gun he dared not use, Jason picked his way along a path until he topped the cliff that paralleled the north bank of the Gila River. He found the guards quickly and easily despite the darkness. Their dead bodies lay at key vantage points right where Jason expected to find sentries. All young men, some barely out of their teens, each killed by a single stab wound in the chest or back.

The Apache scout, though employed by the army, was apparently friendly with the camp. Jason saw no signs of struggle, as if the Indian just rode up for coffee, or whatever activity warriors engaged in to pass the time and rammed his bayonet into his unsuspecting victim's chest or back.

Jason wondered if the lookouts were to report back to camp periodically. Maybe they had assigned shifts. If so, they might be missed long before morning and their manner of death and the soldiers' presence would be discovered. He dragged each of the bodies away from the cliff and covered them with rocks, certain they wouldn't be found in the dark. Then he made his way back down to the river where he'd picketed his horse. He exchanged his moccasins for his boots, then rode back to report to Taylor what he'd found.

Midnight had long since come and gone, and when Jason arrived at the camp, he found the captain smoking a pipe, leaning against a tree. He wasn't sure how he expected the captain to react to the news that his Apache scout had killed the lookouts instead of capturing them, but the man simply muttered just loud enough to be heard.

"Fewer Injuns to kill later."

Stunned, Jason made his way over to the sleeping men of Company B. Crawford's huge bulk was easy to spot even in the darkness. He tapped his boot gently against the first sergeant's leg to wake him. The sergeant pulled back his blanket and stood quickly, and Jason got the feeling the soldier was already awake.

"As hot as it is, how can you men sleep under blankets?" Jason whispered.

"Habit," Crawford said. "Keeps the bugs off." He shrugged. "Well, unless they manage to get under the blanket."

Jason nodded. "Let's talk." He led the way down to the stream and away from the army encampment. He saw another shadowy form detach itself from the ground and follow them. Corporal Shelton joined them out of earshot from any listeners, and the three of them squatted by the water's edge.

"First Sergeant, is there something going on here I need to know about?"

Crawford gazed at Jason, then looked around. "You know everything I know. Why?"

Jason repeated what Captain Taylor told him. "But the major said we're going to take these people as prisoners."

"That's my understanding."

Shelton interrupted. "Out here, most folks believe the only good Indian is a dead one. I have to say I agree with 'em too.

They're not at all like us, Jason. If an Indian kid's old enough to use a gun, he's old enough to make war on us. If he's holdin' a gun, we have to kill him. Otherwise, he'll kill some of us."

Crawford nodded. "There's some folks in these parts that believe Indian babies ought to be killed too, so they don't grow up and become warriors."

"Same with their womenfolk," Shelton added, "so they won't have babies."

Jason had lived with Arapaho warriors and their families, but he'd never been involved in a war. He sat back on his haunches. "You fellas believe all that fool talk too?"

Crawford knelt beside Jason and put a gentle hand on his shoulder. "The army don't make war on women and children. Like most people around these parts, the captain was probably just referring to warriors he'd have to face in the future."

Jason took reassurance by Crawford's opinion. Since he'd first helped the sergeant three days ago, he'd felt a bond growing between them, a feeling of implied trust. This business of scouting wasn't simply a job anymore. He was already hip-deep in a savage war where the enemy used kids as warriors and the army killed warriors who were kids.

He started to thank the men, but Captain Taylor's voice boomed into the night, ordering his sergeant to roust all the men. All the soldiers ate and packed within half an hour, and the column prepared to ride. An hour and a half later as the eastern sky began to brighten, Jason followed Company B away from the Sixth and headed north through a steep-walled canyon. Two privates from the Sixth fell in behind the column.

Private Tucker eased his horse beside Jason's. "They got behind us."

"Don't worry," Jason said. "They won't try anything with all these other troops around."

Tucker nodded and looked away. "Their names are Hicks and Burdine. I think they're gonna try it as soon as we get far enough away from the rest of the company."

"Relax, will you?" Jason looked at the man. "You're too scared and nervous."

The canyon opened up into the West Fork valley and the lieutenant led the column back to the south along the river toward the Apache camp. Jason threw a parting wave at Shelton and faced the two prisoner-soldiers.

"I'll lead," he said simply.

"Like hell you will!" The man named Hicks kicked his horse into motion and glared first at Jason, then Tucker. "We'll lead. You fall your Black ass in behind us."

Burdine added, "Where you belong."

Jason smiled as the men rode ahead of him. That was easy enough.

CHAPTER 21

CAPTAIN AMBROSE TAYLOR FELT ALIVE again. After so many years, he finally had a command in a campaign that would make a difference in the war. He told Major Clark and all his men they were about to end the Apache wars. Senator Bennington's plan had far different objectives though. Taylor was about to strike a decisive blow to the heart of the last renegade Apache chief to hold out against either surrender or unification of the tribes.

Victorio, the famous leader of the Warm Springs Apache tribe, had surrendered twice, Taylor recalled. Even the wily old Nana had come into that wasteland, the San Carlos reservation, at least once. Geronimo also spent time there with his band of followers.

Captain Taylor once visited the outpost serving that wretched reservation. Sometimes the summer days were so hot, he'd seen the savages cooking food on flat stones because the army couldn't provide enough firewood. Most times, the corrupt supply contractors got paid by the government then stole their own firewood and sold it elsewhere. Same with beef and other food suppliers. The harsh desert land didn't provide enough resources to sustain the Indians. Taylor smiled at the memory. San Carlos was indeed the perfect place for the heathens.

Regardless of the inhumane conditions, the army forbade the Indians from leaving the reservation. When some of them did leave, they took a few bold followers with them and hid out in the mountains. If they didn't return on their own, the army hunted them down and forced them to return.

Juh, on the other hand, was the only Apache chief never to surrender, and he refused to meet with army officers to discuss terms. Instead, he led his band of warriors around the Southwest with impunity, stealing food and livestock from ranchers and killing anyone who saw him. Taylor was going to put an end to Juh's savage Indian attacks and get himself written down in history as the man who turned the tide against the Apache.

When Juh returned to his camp, he'd have no choice but to go on the warpath. When he did, the army would respond and hunt down and kill all Apache everywhere. The Apache war would continue for a long time, Taylor thought as he pulled his saber, eventually ending not with the Indians' surrender, but with their annihilation.

He glanced at the brightening sky. Just before sunrise, the sentry replacements that the dead Indian scout warned of would just be preparing to go relieve the dead lookouts, and the rest of the Apache camp would be getting about their morning business. Company B had plenty of time to get in position where they couldn't interfere, and Jason Peares was out of the way, probably laid up in the stream with a bullet hole in the back of his head by now.

The captain snickered aloud at the thought. The outlaw could've been a part of history but instead chose to stand against Taylor. How could he *not* want to kill Indians just for the pure joy of the hunt? The outlaw completed his part of the mission. He took care of the lookouts. That's all Taylor cared about.

The burly Sergeant Troy Stevenson rode up beside him at the head of the formation and nodded. The sergeant issued commands and the sixteen prisoner-soldiers prepared their Springfield rifles. Taylor grabbed the reins of his horse in his right hand, the same hand that held his saber, and unfolded the flap of his holster with his left. He pulled his Remington revolver and addressed the sergeant.

"Round up everyone in the camp first. We'll see to any stragglers afterward." The sergeant nodded. "Get two men up high, north of the camp, to make sure Lieutenant Henry and his Black soldiers don't interfere."

"Yes, sir," Sergeant Stevenson said in acknowledgment. A glimmer of a smile shone in his eyes. "I may have to open fire on them to keep them out of the camp."

"Sergeant, you have a problem with killing Indians and Negroes in the same day?"

"Absolutely not, sir!"

"Good, because it won't weigh heavily on my conscience either. Let's go."

Taylor raised the saber over his head and spurred his mount into a fast gallop. He and his men covered the last mile to the Apache camp quickly. When he guided his horse to the right, around the outcropping that shielded the Apache camp from view, he saw just what he expected.

Frightened, half-naked Indians panicked and ran out of their tepees, scurrying everywhere. Those who reacted first ran to the north, only to turn back as they discovered the waiting men of Company B.

Less than five minutes later, all of the tepees lay in shambles, pulled over by the rampaging soldiers. Taylor's men had all the people crowded together near the edge of the water, the soldiers' weapons aimed and ready. An elder man with long, gray hair stood and gestured solemnly at Taylor.

"Shut up!" Taylor commanded. He watched the man for a moment, listened to the unintelligible gibberish. Then he leaned over in his saddle and swung his saber with all his strength. He felt a brief rush of exhilaration as his blade completely severed the man's head.

The Indians, seventy or so, Taylor guessed, erupted in screams again. But when the captain moved his horse into the group, raised his saber, and leaned over as if to strike, they quieted quickly.

"Good," he said. "If you don't shush that nonsense, I'll cut all your heads off." He pointed to the dead elder with his blade. "Now which one of you is Juh's wife?"

The Indians cuddled together, sobbing and trembling in fear. Women clutched their children protectively and young men sheltered the women with their bodies. Old men sat silently, stone-faced, as if familiar with the situation. Taylor screamed at them again, asking for Juh's wife, but the entire group stared back at him uncomprehending.

He backed his horse away from the group. "Corporal," he shouted at the nearest soldier. "Shoot that one there. In the tan shawl."

The soldier didn't move, just glanced left and right at the other soldiers. "But sir, she's just a girl."

"She ain't no girl! She's an Indian." Taylor nudged his horse close to the corporal's. "And when she grows up, she'll have a dozen babies. You want that?" He didn't wait for a response. "Now shoot her!"

The corporal, a blond kid about twenty years old, shook his head violently. "I can't!" he said teary eyed. He yanked his reins to the left to turn his horse, then cried out in pain as Taylor thrust his saber into his back.

In one fluid movement, Taylor withdrew his blade, turned, and shot the girl with his revolver. He shouted again for Chief Juh's wife, but no one answered. Just as he opened his mouth to shout again, one of his soldiers rode in from the back of the camp.

"Sir, looks like a couple dozen got away. Hid in the reeds over yonder and got up into the rocks."

Taylor nodded and looked to his right at Sergeant Stevenson. "Kill them all."

CHAPTER 22

IRST SERGEANT LAFAYETTE CRAWFORD SAT on his mount to the left of his lieutenant. The Buffalo Soldiers of Company B, Ninth Cavalry, spread out across the stream of the Middle Fork, carbines pointed to the sky. Each mounted man had a ten-foot interval between himself and the next. The line of Company B stretched from the sheer cliff wall on the west side of the canyon to the trees on the east side. Crawford's mount stood in the center of the stream as they waited.

A small group of Apache, five women and children and one young man, ran around the bend in the river. When they saw the waiting soldiers they stopped, then turned and ran back toward the camp. Distant shouts told Crawford those few collected others who also sought to escape that way.

Crawford waited silently, anger simmering inside. He thought about how hot the day would be. He wanted to wipe sweat from his brow and pull his sweat-soaked blouse away from his chest, but years of military training and discipline wouldn't allow it. He certainly wouldn't discard his military bearing in front of his officer or his men, despite his discomfort.

His mind drifted and he found himself wishing the army would provide a more reasonable cotton uniform instead of the heavy, blue wool they wore all year. He felt the suffocating heat already, and the sun hadn't broken over the cliffs yet. He listened to the birds flittering in the trees and the water trickling over the rocks in the stream. When he looked down, he let his eyes defocus so he could enjoy the peaceful hypnotic undulations as the slow-moving water reflected the cloudless sky.

All he had to do to help capture an entire Apache village was sit on his horse and look intimidating. That wasn't so bad, but still he felt cheated for not having a more important and active role in the operation. For nearly fifteen years, he'd watched and participated in campaigns where Black men distinguished themselves as superior fighting soldiers. In those same years, he'd seen a hundred officers like Captain Taylor discredit the Black soldiers, relegating them to minor duties in major battles.

Crawford had been decorated for bravery three times and nominated twice for the Medal of Honor. Yet, this wasn't the first time he'd been stuck out of the way while other soldiers, White soldiers, got all the credit for doing the real fighting.

On the other hand, if Chief Juh was as crucial to the campaign against the Apaches as the major thought, and if Crawford could help capture him and end the war just by sitting on his horse, then so be it. He'd lost too many men under his command to hope for a quick end to the fighting.

Then, a chilling thought struck him. What would he do when the frontier wars against the Apache and other tribes ended? Where would he go when the army no longer needed him? All he had known for the last fifteen years was army life on the Texas and New Mexico frontiers and just about everywhere he'd been stationed, the local townsfolk were none too friendly, even when he saved their lives.

Crawford jerked back to reality when he heard the first gunshot. Then the rapid sounds of coordinated gunfire echoed off the canyon walls. Lieutenant Henry quickly ordered the men into motion in a loose battle formation with skirmishers on the wings. Led by the lieutenant, Crawford, and the private carrying the United States flag, Company B rode smartly around the bend that opened to the valley where the Apache camp sat.

At first, Crawford couldn't believe what he saw. The villagers ran every which way, screaming and dying as Taylor and his men laid down withering fire that cut through women, children, and elders. Beside Crawford, Lieutenant Henry raised his right arm, preparing to give the familiar command to charge into battle. Crawford suspected his orders would be to prevent the slaughter, but he never got the chance to hear those orders.

Just as the lieutenant uttered his first sound, Crawford heard the familiar sound of a bullet slicing through the air. The long-distance shot ripped Lieutenant Henry from his horse. Less than a second later, Crawford heard the gunshot. Even as he spun to see the lieutenant was dead, another bullet tugged at his own collar.

He yanked his reins hard to the left and bellowed, "Fall back!"

Crawford knew without looking that soldiers from the Sixth fired at them from the eastern bluff high over the canyon. If Taylor could order the heartless massacre of Indian women and children, he would have no problem ordering his men to ambush the Buffalo Soldiers he seemed to hate even more.

The tidy column collapsed immediately as the men of Company B broke formation and raced back around the bend in the river. Bullets continued to slam into the backs of the retreating soldiers. Four men were hit and two fell from their mounts. Three horses fell. As soon as they reached safety, Crawford barked out commands.

"Corporal Shelton! Set up a defensive perimeter. Make sure they don't sneak in on us."

"Already on it, L.C."

Crawford dismounted and grabbed a wounded man from his horse. As he laid the unconscious man gently on the bank of the stream, he hollered for his sharpshooter.

"Sharps!"

"Here, Sarge," came the reply from behind Crawford.

"Take a spotter and find yourself a good position to take those shooters off that bluff."

"Can't do it, Sarge."

Crawford looked behind him and saw why. The man, Corporal Benjamin Chapman, had a gaping bloody hole where his right shoulder should have been. Only the tattered remnants of the sleeve of his blouse held his severed arm in place. The man swayed, finally falling to his left knee. Crawford stepped over quickly to catch him as he fell sideways. The man gasped in pain and his eyes froze wide open, glazed over in shock.

Corporal Shelton came running. "I have a defensive line set up, L.C. They can't attack us here."

"Who's got ambulance duty?"

Shelton looked away. "He's face down out yonder in the stream. His horse got hit too, so we got no bandages or medicine."

"Give me your blouse." As he spoke, Crawford pulled off his own, ripping the buttons with the swipe of his hand. "Assign two men to see to the wounded."

Shelton threw his blouse down beside the first sergeant and raced away. Almost immediately, Crawford noticed the gunfire from the adjoining canyon had ceased. He called for Silas Nance while he wrapped Chapman's exposed shoulder. Another private arrived to tend to the other unconscious soldier.

"Private Nance, scout the next canyon. And keep your head down."

Private Nance left immediately, only to return half an hour later. "They's gone, Sarge. Left nothin' but dead Injuns behind."

Crawford considered the report. "Corporal Shelton, take two men and secure that bluff. I don't want to see another ambush unless we're doing it."

Shelton picked two men and left immediately. Crawford split half his men into a detail to retrieve their fallen members and escort the dead and wounded back to the fort. Not knowing the full situation at the Indian camp and the whereabouts of Captain Taylor and his men, Crawford sent the injury detail back through the canyon they used to approach the Apache camp. The route was longer, but safer.

An hour later, Crawford and six of his troopers rode into the Apache camp. The first sergeant counted sixty-six bodies. No warriors, he observed wryly. Only women, children, old men, and a few boys who had no time to grab a weapon and put up a fight. He stood still for quite a while, trying to find a reason for the massacre. Around him, his men shifted uneasily, waiting, he knew, for him to make a decision. The shade line crept over him as the sun cast its first rays of light into the canyon. Crawford's massive upper body glistened with moisture.

Corporal Shelton's voice interrupted his thoughts. The man had made his way down from the hundred-foot-high bluff and entered the camp from the West Fork valley.

"Some of the Indians escaped to the west, First Sergeant. Captain Taylor's tracks go that way too. I figure he and his men went after the survivors." When Crawford nodded, Shelton asked, "We goin' after them?"

"How far ahead of the captain would you say the Indians are?"

"Judging by the tracks, I'd say they got a good half-hour advantage. Maybe more."

Crawford nodded. "The Apache have been outrunning the army for twenty years, and they've been surviving here longer than some of our troops have been breathing. There's nothing we can do for them they can't do for themselves." He turned to face the rest of the men.

"Grab your shovels, men. Let's get this dead soldier buried." Crawford looked over at the blond young man's body and noted the stab wound in his lower back. "Probably refused to fire on the unarmed Indians and got killed for it." He looked around at all the dead bodies as the men pulled tools from their saddle packs. "These poor souls deserve a decent burial too. Then we'll report back to the fort."

To Shelton he said quietly, "Murdering women and children takes about the lowest form of trash that ever lived. Major Clark will likely recall one of his officers from the field to hunt the captain down and arrest him."

"I'd handle it another way, L.C." Crawford could tell by Shelton's voice he was suggesting the unthinkable.

Crawford shook his head. "No way a Black enlisted man is

going to be ordered to arrest a White officer, no matter what crime he's committed."

Shelton snorted his contempt. "I'm not thinking about arresting him."

"That's not the army way."

"And what about Jason?" Shelton said as Crawford turned to start digging. "We just gonna leave him?"

Crawford kept digging while he spoke. "I'm guessing Jason Peares can take care of himself."

CHAPTER 23

THROUGHOUT THE MORNING, JASON MANAGED to keep Hicks and Burdine either in front of him or beside him. Private Tucker stuck to his backside like a shadow. Now they hid by the trail as voices and scuffling sounds drew near.

The canyon from the Middle Fork had led them into a wide prairie two miles north of the narrow part of the canyon, where the West Fork turned sharply to the west. Through the canyon, the river was little more than a creek. Tall grasses and reeds grew out of the water. Plenty of bushes and trees filled the narrow pass, almost overgrowing the footpath siding the stream of water.

Jason had picked the ideal location to round up the escaping Apaches. The Indians had to cross an open area devoid of shrubs before continuing on the path through more trees. Jason stood in the shade under the east cliff wall just at the edge of those trees. Taylor's two privates crouched in the sun behind some shrubs, sweating, Jason observed with satisfaction. They covered the open area from across the creek. When the Indians came through, they'd be caught in a vicious cross fire if the warriors decided to put up a fight.

Standing beside a huge vertical boulder, Jason motioned for Taylor's men to keep silent and still. A quick glance to his right showed him that Tucker hid out of harm's way behind a thick tree, a couple paces behind him. When Jason could hear the murmured whispers of Indian language, he judged them to be in the open area. He stepped from beside his boulder and leveled his Winchester at the chest of the first warrior that approached him.

Then he froze.

The woman who led the group seemed so startled by Jason's sudden appearance, she stumbled forward, stopped only by the pressure of his rifle barrel on her breastbone. She gasped, uttered something in her unfamiliar language, and thrust her chin forward in defiance, as if daring Jason to kill her. A young woman, about fifteen, and several other children and elders stumbled over each other behind the woman Jason now faced. He glanced at the younger woman, her belly swollen with child, and then he scanned the group. Jason gazed at nearly thirty people, and all looked as surprised as he felt. He took a step back in confusion.

"Where are the warriors?" he mumbled to himself.

An older woman stepped up beside the defiant woman Jason mentally named *Leader* and grabbed her arm, trying to pull her back. Jason just started to lower his rifle when an explosion of sound startled him. He blinked, then saw the old woman jerk sideways and knock over *Leader* and the young pregnant woman. He saw the look of shock on their faces as the old woman's blood sprinkled them. The crowd panicked as everyone turned to run in any direction for safety. Jason jerked his head toward Private Hicks.

"What are you doing?" Jason shouted. "They're just women and children!"

Hicks laughed as he slammed another shell home. "Cap'n said kill Injuns." He brought his rifle up as Private Burdine swung his weapon to cover Jason.

"And you," Burdine added. "That's what we aim to do."

Instinctively, Jason knew he'd never get his Winchester around toward Burdine in time. He knew he'd never work the lever fast enough to hit both men. Instead, he dropped the rifle and grabbed for his right holster gun. In a flash of controlled panic born of thousands of practice quick draws, Jason pulled his gun and fired a single shot at Burdine. The private's own shot went awry as his head jerked back under the bullet's impact.

Hicks hesitated as he aimed into the scattering crowd of Indians. He seemed to sense his life was over if he pulled the trigger. Jason didn't wait, just fired twice more. As Hicks fell, Jason turned back toward the leader of the group as she and the pregnant girl got to their feet. Most of the other Indians had scattered, but some stood grouped behind *Leader*. He just started to tuck his gun away when one of the Apache boys moved suddenly.

Jason dropped to a crouch, drawing his left gun at the same time. He fired just after the boy released a kid-sized version of a battle axe. At first Jason was surprised the tomahawk flashed by, missing him by two arm lengths. Then, over the echo of his gunshot, Jason heard a grunt behind him. Slowly, he turned his head and saw Tucker pointing his Remington pistol at him. The private's aim faltered, and he dropped the gun, reaching instead for the axe stuck in his shoulder.

Jason looked back at the fallen Apache boy, maybe twelve or thirteen years old. A woman had taken the boy into her lap and pressed a piece of cloth torn from her skirt against the tiny hole in his shirtless chest. But he lay staring at Jason, one hand reaching for the bloody cloth. He winced but bore his pain silently. For a brief moment, emotion squeezed Jason's heart and he felt tears water his eyes.

"Aw, hell," he muttered.

He closed his eyes for a moment. Then he looked from the boy to *Leader*, then back to the boy again. He shook his head and stepped backward toward Private Tucker, though still wary of another attack. Jason tucked his left gun away. He grabbed the handle of the axe but kept his gaze on the Apache. Bracing a boot against Tucker's chest, he pulled the axe from the private's shoulder. The man cried out in pain, but he stayed on his feet.

"You put on a real good performance," Jason said, finally looking at the traitor. "Suckered me good."

"I'm sorry," Tucker said through clenched teeth. "Had to get you to trust me." The private wobbled unsteadily. "Cap'n offered me five hundred dollars. I'm sorry," he repeated.

"Sorry?" Jason glanced over his shoulder at the boy who still lay staring back at him. "That kid saved my life and I shot him for it. For five hundred dollars!"

The rest of the scattered Apache survivors began to gather in the clearing behind *Leader*. Jason turned to face them. He saw the woman glance down at his Winchester near her feet. Jason caught her gaze and tucked away his right gun, hoping she'd take it as a gesture of truce.

"Don't let them kill me," Tucker pleaded.

"Don't worry, Private," Jason said over his shoulder to Tucker. "They won't kill you."

Jason looked at the dying boy and tried to communicate his sorrow in the gaze, but his eyes were clouded by tears. Then he spun, put all his strength in his arm swing, and yelled with the effort as he buried the blade of the axe deep in the middle of Tucker's forehead. The man's eyes crossed, and Jason kicked him in the chest. Tucker flopped to the ground and twitched for a few seconds, then he lay still.

Jason took a deep breath as a sob of sorrow shuddered through him. He wiped at the tears with his sleeve and turned toward the desperate group of Indians as he reloaded his guns from cartridges in his holster belt.

The army wanted the Apache tribe captured, and he'd done just that. As he thought more about his options, he realized he didn't want to wait around for the rest of the troops to arrive. When Captain Taylor discovered Jason shot three of his soldiers, he might overlook the fact that he'd rounded up the escapees. He was fairly certain the captain wouldn't give him a chance to explain events, though he figured Taylor wouldn't care much about Tucker's death.

On the other hand, if Jason rode away, Taylor could easily set the entire US Army on his trail, not only for killing the soldiers, but for disobeying orders and letting the Apache escape. He pondered his situation for a long time as the woman in front of the group continued to stare at him. A young boy about ten came to her side and picked up the Winchester. The woman spoke some words the boy seemed to ignore. She reached out to him, gently grabbing him by the shoulders.

Mother and son, Jason guessed, watching the woman's protective body language. The boy held the weapon by the barrel with both hands, but when Jason stepped forward to take it, the gutsy kid didn't let go. Instead, he placed the barrel against his own chest and spat defiant words at Jason.

Before Jason could respond, the crowd parted, and a very old Apache woman hobbled toward him. She stopped and exchanged a few words with *Leader*, then she began speaking to Jason with words and slow careful gestures in a way that demanded his attention. The old woman spoke a strange formation of words, not familiar, but not unintelligible. She communicated through pronunciations of sounds he'd never heard before.

Jason spoke French and Spanish passably, but the old woman's language was completely foreign to him. Her words seemed based more on tonal rhythms, a combination of nasal and vocal productions, some of which seemed to originate deep in her throat.

Though Jason had no idea what she'd said, he nodded anyway. He took the Winchester that the boy released. In that instant, Jason knew he wanted no further involvement in the Indian Wars. Hired to scout against warriors, he instead found himself confronted by elders and children. He'd seen misguided soldiers blinded by hatred try to murder these people. Yet, the old woman had sensed his lack of conviction. Somehow, she knew Jason wouldn't hold them. She gazed at him through narrow slits of wrinkled eyelids and nodded.

Jason stepped off the path and waved with his hand for the Apaches to leave. Several of the Indians lifted the dead woman's body and carried her away. He caught the dying boy's gaze again as others carried him away, and he watched him until the people disappeared into the trees to the west. Then he headed north across the expanse of prairie where he'd left Grady with the army horses. He wanted to reach Lafayette Crawford before Captain Taylor reported back to Major Clark. Once he explained events, he'd see just how much power a first sergeant really possessed. As he mounted up, he heard distant gunfire in the direction where he'd let the Indians go.

His better judgment told him to simply ride away. He knew he should just ride through the canyon and get back to the fort. He should leave the Apaches to their own business.

Intense discomfort tugged at his conscience, as he remembered how calmly Taylor's man killed the Apache scout and how the captain offered a Black soldier money to shoot Jason in the back. When he considered what Hicks and Burdine tried to do, Jason began to wonder if all the prisoner-soldiers had orders from Captain Taylor to kill Indians under any circumstances.

Maybe Taylor's mission wasn't to capture the tribe at all. Maybe his orders were to murder them. Conveniently, Lieutenant Henry and his Company B were tucked away on the Middle Fork where they couldn't interfere.

Jason spurred Grady into a trot back toward the West Fork. He approached through the trees until he was half a mile from the sound of the gunshots. The trail stretched across the open valley and wound up along the side of a set of hills. Most of the survivors were far in the distance, but half a dozen had only journeyed a mile. At first, Jason didn't understand why the main group would leave the slow ones behind, but then he quickly remembered that the escaping Apache had neither weapons nor warriors to protect them. Escape was the only way to survive.

In the near group, Jason could make out the pregnant girl and the old woman he instinctively thought of as *Ancient One*. Three women and an elder man tried to carry a stretcher of tree branches holding the boy Jason shot. Several other elders trudged along as fast as they could. The gutsy boy who had stuck his chest in front of Jason's Winchester earlier, and another slightly older youth, stayed behind the slow group as their only protection.

Four of the soldiers surrounded the two boys, circling them, shooting into the ground around them. The taller boy tried to hold off the soldiers with a short lance, merely a long tree branch with a sharpened point. The gutsy boy ran at one of the horses brandishing a knife in his hand, but the soldier pulled his rifle, flipped it deftly in the air, and caught it by the barrel. He swung the weapon like a club as he raced by, catching the boy on the side of the head with the stock. The boy went down, and the soldier brought his mount around as he stuck his rifle back in the scabbard. He charged as the boy tried to get to his knees.

Jason shook his head and realized everything he feared about Taylor's soldiers was true. He pulled his single-shot Spencer. As he dismounted, he talked gently to Grady as he always did when preparing to shoot the long rifle. He chambered a .50-caliber shell and took aim, realizing he was committing himself to life as an outlaw again. He'd already killed three army soldiers. In a moment, he'd be guilty of killing more.

Maybe Sergeant Crawford and Corporal Shelton didn't make war on women and children, but the rest of the army did. After today, he knew he'd never be able to explain his actions to anyone who would listen. Army soldiers, Black and White, would pursue him. He'd become an outlaw again. He'd have to run.

Where would he go this time? Where *could* he go? The frontier wasn't nearly as vast as it seemed ten years earlier. There were too many towns and telegraph wires now. There was too much civilization on the frontier.

Maybe he could hide in Canada or Mexico. Maybe he could find his way down to South America. He'd heard a man could lose himself down there for years and never be found. Surely, they'd never heard of Jason Peares beyond Mexico.

As he peered through the scope, a distant part of his mind wondered what his new bounty would be. Considering his previous reputation and with the full might of the government behind the warrant, the price on his head would start high—probably a few thousand in gold. Might even start where it left off before, at ten thousand.

A small price to pay, Jason thought as he watched the boy

look up at the charging animal and duck his head in a futile protective gesture. Jason hesitated, then took a deep breath and let half out.

He pulled the trigger.

CHAPTER 24

A FEW YEARS BACK, JASON HAD seen a hunter take down two buffalo with a single shot from a .58-caliber buffalo gun. Though his Spencer rifle possessed a slightly smaller bore, the cartridges packed almost the same power. A seven-hundred-grain bullet propelled toward its target by the powerful explosive force of one hundred seventy grains of black powder would cover the half-mile distance in less time than it took the charging horse to cover one ten-foot gallop.

When Jason pulled the trigger, the Spencer kicked up, then fell back down in front of his waiting eye. He had a head-on angle of about thirty degrees on the charging animal. Just as the horse's front hooves descended over the Apache child, Jason's bullet struck the massive front of the animal, expending its tremendous kinetic energy inside the animal's chest cavity. The horse stopped instantly, knocked back on its hindquarter by the impact, and the soldier catapulted through the air over the boy. He rolled, dazed, and reached to unclasp his holster gun.

Jason calmly reloaded and fired a second shot. The soldier's body possessed a small fraction of the mass of the horse and the Spencer's bullet struck the man's back and exploded out of his chest with a messy expulsion of blood, bone, and flesh.

Jason had no need to watch his handiwork. He merely sighted on the three remaining soldiers. One was slow to react, as if he didn't understand what was happening. Maybe he'd never seen a sharpshooter at work, firing a rifle from so far away the bullet arrived more than a full second before the sound of the gunshot. He simply turned in his saddle and stared into the distance. Jason rewarded him with a bullet in the chest.

The two other soldiers fled back to the east, smartly riding fast and erratic. Jason chased them with several shots but missed. He'd given them something new to think about though. On the other hand, there was no way an army unit would ride without its own sharpshooter. Jason had to be careful Taylor didn't get his own man close enough to take him out.

A few minutes later, Jason reined Grady up beside the uninjured, well-trained army mount. Its rider lay on his back in the saddle, empty eyes staring at the sky. The other soldier lay on his side, his chest a bloody mess from the bullet's exit wound. Jason rummaged through the saddle packs on the dead horse and collected a canteen, a Springfield single-shot carbine, a pouch of twenty rounds, and a partially full sack of hardtack, dried beef sticks, and coffee. He frowned. The soldiers only carried enough rations for a four-day scout.

From the dead men, he gathered two half-empty Remington pistols and a handful of .45-caliber shells. He found another canteen and rifle with ammunition on the waiting army horse and removed all the other packs. Then he walked Grady over to the group of elders who stood watching him nervously, as if waiting to see what he would do. He led the army horse by the reins, then stopped in front of them and addressed *Ancient One*.

"Here," he said, patting the saddle. "Why don't you take a ride?"

The old woman said nothing, but the boy Jason saved moved over to her and spoke. He took her by the arm and helped her up in the saddle with Jason's assistance. Next, they helped the pregnant girl up behind *Ancient One* and one more elder woman climbed up on the horse's rump. While they mounted, another elder Apache rummaged through the army saddle packs. He left the camp supplies and coffee in a pile alongside the trail. He kept the bedroll and blanket tied behind the saddle with the horse's feed bags.

While the other boy and the remaining elders kept a safe distance from Jason, the younger boy seemed eager to help. Without instruction, he began tying the wounded boy's travois behind the army horse. Jason knelt beside the stretcher and found the boy's wound had already been covered with a natural poultice. The remedy would do the boy little good, and Jason was surprised he still lived. He cursed his accuracy. By instinct, Jason had shot the kid in the high center of his chest. He looked sadly into the boy's eyes.

"I'm so sorry." He touched the side of the kid's face with his palm.

Before he was ready to let the boy go, the pregnant girl nudged the horse up the trail. Jason watched the kid for a long while, then turned to a young girl and two elder women. He indicated for them to mount Grady.

Jason retrieved his Spencer and Winchester and ammunition for them, and he tucked his spare guns in the front of his belt. Then he hung his ration kit and canteen over opposite shoulders. He watched Grady move away up the trail and bent over to pick up the spare army weapons. He knew instantly he wouldn't last an hour in the intense heat carrying fifty pounds of guns.

"Hey!" He called out to the survivors after they had walked a few steps ahead of him. They all turned. "I guess this isn't any time for mistrust. If you're gonna shoot me, it might as well be now." They simply stared at him, uncomprehending.

Jason gave the Springfield rifles and ammunition sack to the elder man and the youngest of the elder women, then gave the other woman the two army pistols. He pulled his own two spare guns from his belt and gave one Colt to each of the two boys. He let the gutsy kid carry his Spencer and kept the Winchester to himself. Then the group started out again.

Jason had a nagging feeling he and the Apache refugees didn't have even a minute to waste. They were a woeful excuse for a rear guard, but they were all that stood between the fleeing elders and children and another massacre at the hands of the army.

CHAPTER 25

A FTER ONLY AN HOUR UNDER the hot sun, Jason felt like his feet were baking inside his boots. At that moment, he would have given anything for his moccasins, but since he and the rear guard had fallen back to delay the soldiers, he knew would be pursuing them, his supplies, and Grady, were far in the distance. He would never have admitted he was uncomfortable, especially when the elders and the two boys bore their discomfort without complaint. The boys seemed like they were simply on another afternoon stroll in the mountains. This was their normal way of life, but Jason suspected the temperature was hotter than even they were used to.

Ahead of Jason, the old man ripped a vine from a bush, tied it around the stock and barrel of his rifle and draped the weapon over his shoulder. The woman at his side did the same. Jason suddenly realized how heavy his eight-pound Winchester felt and decided to follow the old man's example. When he draped the weapon over his right shoulder, he felt immediate relief in his arm.

He paused and took a sip of warm water from his canteen, then gazed back along the trail. It ran fairly straight to the east for about half a mile, but he could see no one. *They'll be along soon,* he thought, as he turned to follow the Apache.

For the next two hours, the trail wound leisurely upward along the sides of the north hills that paralleled the West Fork. Jason looked over his shoulder frequently because he couldn't see more than a hundred feet back along the trail. If Taylor and his men got within rifle distance, Jason and the Apaches had no chance to survive.

Before he fully realized the change in the terrain, Jason entered a fairly narrow section of the trail that wove along the steep side of a cliff. Huge rocky outcrops jutted away from the wall, and the trail wove in and around the rocks. Though the trail was plenty wide enough for a man to navigate, it was narrow enough to give a horse a rough going. For a long while, the land on the uphill side of the trail was steep enough to reach out and touch while standing up, and the downhill side dropped off steeply three hundred feet down to the river.

Jason was toying with the idea of setting an ambush on this most dangerous part of the trail, when he suddenly came around the last bend and saw half a dozen boys and girls and one elder man resting, looking completely worn out. They had managed to cut down eight trees from higher up the slope and maneuver them down to the trail. As Jason passed the barrier of trees, a devious thought entered his mind, and he looked around for a perch to use his Spencer.

Captain Taylor halted his men where the trail began to weave up the side of the hills that paralleled the West Fork. His sixteen-man patrol now numbered only twelve, thanks to that half-breed outlaw. Taylor knew without a doubt he'd lose more men if he followed Jason and the Apaches into the canyon ahead. The terrain was an ambush waiting to happen.

"Sharps!" he called. A grizzled old soldier, stick-thin with a ruddy complexion, rode his horse up beside the captain. "What's your range, Soldier?"

"I can poke a hole in a snake's belly button at five hundred yards, sir."

Taylor grunted, unimpressed. "We're not hunting snakes, Soldier, and last I checked, the US Army didn't issue snakes any belly buttons." He paused as he considered the sharpshooter's serious face. "I'm short four good men, not counting that damned Black teacher who couldn't even shoot the outlaw in the back properly, and two of the dead are on account of Jason Peares's long rifle. And he uses a scope."

"I don't need no scope, Cap'n. I use a Sharps .54-caliber hunting rifle with a thirty-six-inch barrel. If I get him in my sights inside of a quarter mile, he's good as dead, sir."

"Good." Taylor smiled and nodded. He had no need for the soldier's bluster, but the man's tactical assessment gave him a bit more encouragement. "River runs fairly straight up yonder," Taylor said, pointing ahead. "See how the path weaves along the hills?" In his side vision, he saw the sharpshooter nod. "Great place for an ambush. I've seen a dozen mountain trails like this one. I expect he'll find a place on that north wall somewhere."

Taylor waved at the expanse of cliff wall on the north bank of the river. It looked sheer in most places, but he could see some rocky outcrops that the outlaw could use to shoot from if he found a way up.

"Yes, sir, that's what I would do if I were down there." Sharps nodded. "With all that narrow, hillside, single-track up in there, we'll be vulnerable." The sniper paused and scanned the territory ahead. "No worries, Cap'n. I'll pick a spot up on that hill." He pointed to the left at a hill that towered over the trail. "If he's lyin' in wait down there somewhere, I'll find him and put a hole in his head."

"What's your name, Soldier?"

"Hansen, sir."

"Well, get to it, Hansen. And watch your backside."

"Yes, sir."

Hansen peeled his horse away and rode around the hill towering over the trail the soldiers followed. He quickly found that the far side of the hill had a gentle slope and half an hour later, he found his shooting position on the hilltop. His overlook covered the entire river valley, and he gazed down at the meandering river. The ground in front of him dipped almost straight down, and he doubted a man could get enough purchase to climb down safely. He'd have to ride back around the way he came when he finished his business, and that would put him far behind the rest of the men.

The corporal lay prone as he prepared his rifle, his head and shoulders protected by the shade of the lone bush that grew among the wild grass on the hilltop. He saw the soldiers negotiating the narrow trail directly below him, but he ignored them. Instead, he searched the river valley below and the far cliff walls, searching all the places he would hide if he intended to snipe at the captain's soldiers.

Less than five minutes later, he found the outlaw below him, maybe six or seven hundred yards up the trail. Jason Peares waited, lying behind a boulder by the water's edge. He had a clear line of fire up the canyon at the bend the Sixth Cavalry soldiers would soon navigate. It would be a massacre.

Hansen centered his sights on the back of Jason's prone figure. While he breathed, he concentrated on his target and allowed his side vision to observe the movements of bushes and trees down in the valley so he'd have an estimate of wind speed. His target was at the extreme edge of his gun's range of accuracy, but the outlaw was lying still, sighting along his own long-range weapon, and there was very little wind.

Hanson knew he was regarded as one of the best snipers in the western regiments, maybe even in the whole army. Growing up in Texas, he'd been an excellent hunter, but now he didn't have much in the way of skills outside of soldiering. If only he hadn't let those other deserters talk him into leaving his post without permission to go on that manhunt down in Mexico, maybe he'd have had a chance for a decent military career.

Until this assignment, he'd spent most of his enlistment in the stockade. All for a measly one hundred dollars in gold nuggets for bagging their human target. The bounty was shared between the three of them, but that gold had been confiscated by his post commander in Arizona. Why he assumed the army wouldn't catch them was beyond his current understanding. They seemed to have had it all figured out at the time.

He brought his attention back to his task at hand. He felt a twinge of respect for the outlaw and his long-barrel weapon. At any distance greater than, say, five hundred yards the outlaw would have the clear advantage. But right now, the outlaw wasn't aiming at him.

Hansen took a deep breath and let half out. Then he pulled the trigger.

Jason watched a single soldier creep along the trail. The man's posture indicated he expected an ambush. Suddenly, Jason felt foolish thinking he could easily outwit Captain Taylor. The man wasn't simply a murderer bent on revenge. He was a military commander trained in tactical maneuvers. He'd seen through Jason's expectation of catching the soldiers by surprise on the narrow track in the canyon.

The soldier stopped at the tree trap. Where the trail widened a bit, the Apaches had piled the trees in a fashion like an arrow with the trunk of one tree lying on top of the limbs of the tree before it. The eight felled trees formed an interlocking barrier of limbs and branches. The soldier couldn't move the first tree because of the weight of the next few trees.

The foot soldier walked back to the still-hidden column and returned with four more men. They struggled to the far side of the barrier, but still couldn't budge the trees. The branches of the last tree caught on the other trees and the soldiers couldn't get good footing on the steep sides of the trail.

They'd be busy for an hour or two, Jason thought as he sighted through his scope. He aimed at one of the four men working at the tree trap. Jason first thought to shoot their horses. He'd spare the men's lives but set them afoot so they'd have no choice but to retreat back to the fort, where perhaps they'd face some kind of justice. Unfortunately, Captain Taylor kept most of his men and the horses out of sight around the bend of an outcrop.

Jason picked a cartridge from his box of shells that lay on the ground beside his Spencer. He locked the round into the chamber. He took aim and controlled his breathing. He was just about to squeeze the trigger when he heard the busy chirping of some kind of bird. It was an angry, panicked sound close by. It was a signal!

Jason looked across the water and saw the gutsy kid frantically beckoning at him. The kid had followed him down from the high trail to his ambush spot. The kid pointed to the hilltop high across the river and Jason followed his gesture. He saw nothing of consequence on the hill the kid indicated, until he saw the flash of light.

Jason's mind worked in that expanded zone of panic, where time seemed to stand still, and the brain functioned at super speed. With the sniper on the distant hilltop, Jason knew he had less than half a second to get his body out of the path of the sniper's first bullet, maybe two seconds more before the shooter could reload and fire again.

Jason rolled and jack-knifed his body, using his rump as a pivot. Even as he moved, he heard the bullet zip past his ear and saw a flash as the ball of metal ricocheted off a boulder beside him. He completed his roll, scrambled to his knees, and grabbed the precious box of shells. Then he spun, looking in vain for the Spencer he must've tossed in his panic move.

A second bullet tugged at the back of his shirt collar even as the boom of the first shot echoed in from the distance. At that instant, Jason realized the hopelessness of his situation. The shooter wasn't using a single-shot sniper rifle, but something like a Remington or maybe a Sharps that had a magazine holding up to a dozen shots. The sniper didn't have to reload, but simply work his lever, sight, and shoot.

Jason scrambled to his feet, but lost purchase in the sand and pebbles of the riverbank. He slipped and fell to his knees as a third shot bounced off the same boulder he'd just been hiding behind. Finally, he dug in the toes of his boots and took off running. Four more shots barely missed him as he changed course to grab the Spencer he must have tossed in his sudden roll. It was half laying in the water near the cliff wall. He wrapped his fingers around the barrel, intent on running across the stream to hide in the trees. He had just lifted the weapon out of the water when his head exploded in pain. .

CHAPTER 26

AN HOUR AFTER THE ECHO of the shots died, Corporal Hansen reported to Captain Taylor.

"I got him, sir. In the head."

"Good. Where's his body?"

Hansen pointed up the canyon. "Last I saw, he was layin' face down in the stream."

Taylor nodded and called for his spyglass. A private ran back around the path to retrieve the glass from Taylor's saddle pocket. The captain examined the river, then turned to face Hansen.

"I see a lot of blood, Corporal, but I don't see a body." He handed the glass to Hansen who peered through it for a moment. When the corporal lowered the glass, Captain Taylor saw an embarrassed look on the man's face.

"Request permission to take a detail to find his body. He probably crawled in the brush and bled to death."

"Take one man," Taylor replied. "I can't afford to lose any more than that." He added, almost as an afterthought, "Just in case he's not as dead as you think he is."

Taylor turned away from Hansen, dismissing the man from his presence. He caught the gaze of Sergeant Stevenson and motioned him over from his task of supervising the men he was sending out to dismantle the tree trap. Taylor spoke quietly when the sergeant arrived.

"I want Jason Peares dead, Sergeant. Whatever it takes. Understood?" He paused. "He's a witness."

"Witness, sir? He didn't see our attack."

"He didn't have to. But you read the sign back at the trailhead. Jason Peares killed Hicks and Burdine, probably because they fired into a crowd of unarmed Indians. That bit of information, taken with the word of First Sergeant Crawford, can earn us a court-martial. You'll never get to enjoy your gold, Sergeant."

The sergeant still looked like he didn't fully understand, so Taylor explained further.

"Corporal Hansen killed Lieutenant Henry on *my* orders, but all I have against me is the word of First Sergeant Crawford, a Black man." Taylor paused. "Do you understand politics, Sergeant?"

"Never had much use for it, sir."

"It works like this. Even if Major Clark or Colonel Hatch believes the first sergeant, a Black soldier's word is never going to be enough to convict a White officer. I can say anything I want, make up any excuse I think might justify my actions."

"Unless the scout talks," Stevenson said. Taylor nodded. "But he's Black too, sir. No one will listen to him either, will they?"

"Separately, maybe not," Taylor said. "But I suspect Jason Peares is an expert tracker if he survived all those outlaw years eluding or even tracking professional posses, and that makes him what the courts call an expert witness. With the two of 'em making the same kind of allegations, the major might decide there's enough cause to investigate." Taylor focused his most serious gaze on his sergeant. "Continue your efforts to get us back on the trail until I know for certain Jason Peares is dead. It concerns me greatly that he's chosen to travel with the Indians. That's a development I didn't anticipate."

"All the same, sir. Gives us another opportunity to kill more savages along with him."

"I agree that's an added bonus, but make sure your men understand clearly what our priority is now. It's no longer the Indians. It's that goddamn outlaw Jason Peares. No one gets paid or discharged until he's dead."

Jason awoke trying to breathe, but he couldn't seem to make his lungs work. Panic set in quickly, then he realized someone was covering his nose and mouth. Someone was trying to kill him!

He grabbed weakly at the hand, such a tiny hand, then he opened his eyes and focused on the gun right in front of his face. A .45-caliber Colt pistol, one of the two that he usually kept stuck in his belt as backup weapons in case the Schofields in his double holsters weren't enough to handle whatever frontier trouble he occasionally found himself in. It was the gun he'd given to the Apache boy.

Jason realized he lay on his back. The boy lay next to him diagonally, covering Jason's mouth and nose with his free hand to keep him from uttering a sound as he regained consciousness. Pointing the cocked pistol, the boy gazed toward sounds Jason began to hear. He forced himself to relax and the boy looked down, his face only inches from Jason's. The boy removed his hand and Jason slowly and quietly sucked in a lungful of air. When he tried to move, an intense pain erupted on the right side of his head and the world swam into darkness again. He heard voices, sometimes far away, sometimes near.

"Here. Someone dragged him into the water," a raspy, older voice announced.

"Look at all that blood," a youthful voice said. "You must've split his head wide open."

"Naw. If I'd have hit him even with a grazing shot at that distance, there wouldn't be nothing left of his head." The raspy voice paused. "See the pit in that there boulder? I got him with a ricochet chunk of stone."

"He could be anywhere if they stuck to the water."

"Yeah," the raspy voice agreed. "You check those trees. I'll scout ahead. He can't stay in the water all day, especially if he's wounded. He's got to come out and lie up somewhere to mend his wounds."

Jason heard sounds of boot heels grinding into the river rock, a rider mounting up. The horse moved away, but other steps approached. They were careful steps, like a soldier picking his way through the brush, pausing every now and again to check the ground for tracks.

The steps seemed so loud, so close. The soldier had to be right on top of them. He'd see them any second. Jason reached to his holster, wrapped his hand around the butt of his gun, but couldn't find the strength to thumb off the leather loop from the hammer and pull the gun free. The effort only increased the pain in his head. Nausea boiled in his throat.

As the footsteps approached, Jason held his breath and tried to control the urge to be sick. Pain throbbed inside his skull. All he wanted to do was roll onto his side and curl up like a baby—maybe grab his head and try to press the pain away. But he didn't move, aware that any sound would betray them. He fought the pain like the Chinese immigrant railroad worker, Liu Wang, had taught him years before.

Control the pain, the man was always fond of saying. *Pain is merely a message that your body needs to heal. Once you have received the message, channel it into the healing process.*

Liu Wang lectured him on pain the first time he got shot in the shoulder. Just nineteen years old, he thought he was going to die. Liu Wang's words had sounded like so much gibberish, like Chinese riddles. But his teachings helped Jason fight through the pain many times in his life. If he lived until tomorrow, the pain would be gone, a ghost of a memory. Today, he had to feel it and live with it, even as his head hurt so bad he thought he might black out.

The darkness receded and the nausea faded. Again Jason heard the approaching steps. The boy lying across his chest began to tremble, but still he raised the gun and pointed it through the bush. With great effort, Jason raised his left hand and gave the boy a gentle pat of reassurance on the back. They made eye contact for a moment, and Jason wondered what atrocities the boy had seen in his short life that had brought him to the point that he was ready to kill a man. He could have fled and saved himself.

As he watched the boy's scared eyes, Jason tried to understand a life where women and children were chased through the mountains of their homeland, perpetually hunted like animals. He tried to imagine a life where an entire race of people seemed destined to be born into a war they could never hope to win. It was a life where they were always hunted for reasons they might never understand, by an enemy with inexhaustible weapons and supplies.

Jason always thought of his outlaw years as the darkest time of his life. Constantly running from bounty hunters, lawmen, and posses, he'd spent most of his adult life avoiding towns and people. He hid out nearly every day and traveled mostly at night, forever trying to avoid being seen or recognized, so he had at least some understanding of how the Apache had to live on the run.

The boy glanced down at him again briefly, and Jason found himself wondering if Apache children laughed and played games. At what age did they first begin learning how to kill soldiers? Did the Apache know another completely different world existed alongside their own, where women and children lived on ranches and in towns and didn't have to hide out in the mountains? Did they dream of a life where they wouldn't have to fear being raped or killed just because they looked different and lived a simpler life?

Jason knew the Apache fighting men were feared as vicious warriors. He found himself wondering how they lived twenty or thirty years ago, before the army declared war on them.

A few hours ago, Jason killed two soldiers he was certain intended to murder this particular boy. Now he lay helpless, trusting his life to the warrior-child. He listened to the sounds of the searching soldier getting closer.

The footsteps stopped and a distant voice ripped through the quiet air just the soldier yanked aside the bush hiding them from view.

CHAPTER 27

"**I** FOUND HIS TRACKS!" THE RASPY voice yelled from the distance.

Jason gazed upside down as the boy pointed the gun at the private's back. Thankfully, the soldier turned when he heard the voice, even as he pulled the bush aside. He stood there in plain view for a few seconds. The boy's gun wavered as he trembled in fear.

Then, without a backward glance, the private released the bush and ran back toward the water. Jason heard the distant man shouting his revelations, heard mention of a blood trail farther up the stream. Jason felt a new sense of respect for the boy. The lad had dragged Jason's hundred-sixty-pound, unconscious body across the river and hid him in the trees. Then, he'd erased their tracks and taken some of Jason's blood upstream and laid false tracks to confuse the soldiers.

The boy sagged his head on Jason's chest after the close encounter. Eventually, his trembling subsided and when he raised his head, Jason noticed his red headband was missing. Instinctively, Jason felt to his own head and realized the boy's headband held some kind of moist leaf poultice against the right side of his head.

"Thank you," he said. The boy sat up on his haunches and looked at him like he was trying to figure out what Jason just said. *Good-looking kid,* Jason thought. His face was oval with smooth skin and gentle features not yet hardened by manhood, his skin darkened by the sun. He had dark brown eyes that were soft and friendly. Jason remembered the boy stood as tall as his shoulder and was fairly scrawny.

The boy spoke a single word. "Daklugie."

Jason tried to shrug his shoulder but grimaced with the effort. "Sorry, but I have no idea what that means."

"Daklugie," the boy said again and pointed to his nose.

"Is that your name?" Jason pointed at him. "Daklugie?"

The kid nodded, his long, black hair framing his face. "Daklugie." He pointed at his nose again.

Jason pointed at his own nose and answered. "Jason Peares."

Daklugie gasped, eyes wide in recognition. He repeated something that sounded like *Jay-sone Peer*, the way some of the French-speaking Plains natives pronounced his name.

"Close enough," Jason replied. Apparently, his reputation had reached the mountain Apache of southern New Mexico. He wasn't sure why that revelation surprised him. Seemed like everyone else across the frontier knew his name. Why not the Apache?

They remained hidden until shadows from the declining sun darkened the canyon. Slowly, the pain in Jason's head subsided and he regained some of his strength. They ate venison and bread that tasted like corn meal from one of the two bags Daklugie carried on his belt. As the sky began to darken, they heard the captain and his soldiers ride past their hiding place and head upriver. Jason figured the soldiers either became frustrated with the interlocked tree trap they'd encountered and sought an easier path following the river, or they were trying to follow the boy's false trail.

Either way, the Apache survivors would gain a precious few hours in their escape to freedom. Fairly soon, the soldiers would likely camp on the river for the night. If the survivors were smart—and Jason knew they were—they'd travel familiar, high mountain trails in the dark and as late as possible, then rest only briefly before continuing in the morning.

Throughout the next day, Jason endured a throbbing headache and several bouts of dizziness as he and Daklugie struck a path up through the hills and continued on the high trail to the west. They came upon another barrier set by the fleeing Indians. A similar interwoven set of six trees only partially blocked the trail. When Jason moved to walk around the downhill side of the tree trap, Daklugie held him back and pointed at the trail.

As he studied the trail closer, Jason recognized what a gambler had once referred to as a head fake. That dealer was notorious for attempting an obvious misdeal with one hand while pulling an unseen deception with his other.

The poorly made trap of trees allowed a narrow space to pass on the downhill side, and it diverted one's attention away from a section of the trail that was dug out and camouflaged. The loosely packed trail would collapse under the weight of the first man or horse that stepped on it and the intruder would plummet to his death far below. While the soldiers might lose only one man to the trap, the loss would instill a measure of fear and anger in the men, two emotions that might be used against them later.

Past the trap, the trail leveled back down to the river, bringing a feeling of dread to Jason. Though the river wound back and forth across the relatively straight footpath, the soldiers would come across their trail early in the morning. On horseback, they'd make up time on Jason.

After dark, Jason discovered the river wound through another canyon with five-hundred-foot-high cliff walls. Initially, the sight was spectacular by moonlight, but after four hours on that part of the trail, Jason no longer felt impressed by the natural, cathedral-like spires carved by wind and rain over the centuries. Toward dawn, all he noticed was the constant throbbing pain in his head pounding in time with his heartbeat.

At times, the path was hardpacked dirt. Other times, it turned into loose sand and pebbles as it crossed the river dozens of times. In the water, Jason's boots slid across slime-covered river rock and more than once he came close to spraining an ankle.

They came across a long stretch of rocky trail made even more treacherous by the dark remaining after the moon passed behind the high cliff walls. Jason could barely see the ground beneath his feet and found himself stumbling and banging his ankles against sharp rocks. Even through the leather of his boots, the pain stung. Still, he followed Daklugie through the darkness, resting only briefly throughout the night.

They slept for an hour just before sunrise. As they ate another small portion from the boy's food bag, Jason realized Daklugie was barefoot. The boy looked as tired as Jason felt but had endured the hike across the gravel trail and sharp rocks without complaint. Obviously, his short lifetime of trail walking had given him stamina and tough feet.

After more than ten years of outlaw life, Jason considered himself a survivor of the worst that man and nature could throw at him. Yet, he knew he could never have survived a barefoot hike on the trail they had taken, certainly not in the dark.

The heat of the rising sun reflected off the walls of the canyon and they drank every time the trail crossed the river. At midday, the north cliff wall suddenly dropped away, and the path crossed the river one last time, then stretched into the distance up the steep side of the mountain on the south side.

Jason and Daklugie relieved themselves in the brush, then drank from the river as much as their bellies would hold. Jason filled his canteen, realizing the quart of water would have to carry them to the top of the distant ridge and beyond. Through the early morning heat waves shimmering in the distance, he could see the progression of survivors. They looked like tiny, antlike specks moving four or five miles ahead up the high trail.

Jason took a deep breath to strengthen his resolve. They were faced with a hard walk. Already the sun beat down and the temperature rose quickly to over a hundred degrees. They had little water and only the food Daklugie carried in his two small food sacks. Jason had no idea where his own ration kit was, though he thought he remembered setting it beside the boulder when he tried to get comfortable at his ambush. He was just thankful he hadn't also removed his canteen.

Fortunately, Daklugie had kept Jason's hat while hiding him from the soldiers. It fit tightly over the cloth the boy had wrapped over his head wound. Unlike the dark-skinned Apaches, Jason knew his light skin would have suffered severely in the harsh sun.

He couldn't remember where he'd lost the Winchester. Or did he give it to one of the Apache elders? Fortunately, Daklugie carried his Spencer and the box of shells.

As they topped the first ridge, Jason paused to look back over the trail. In the distance, the loose formation of soldiers began the long ascent up the trail, maybe two miles back. They'd have to travel slowly on the narrow trail, but they still closed the distance.

Jason knew how he would eliminate his enemy. He'd simply lie on the trail and wait until they rode to within a quarter mile. Through the shimmering heat waves rising off the ground, all the soldiers would see was the watery mirage the heat played on their eyes. They wouldn't see him until too late, and he could pick them off one by one with the Spencer, starting with their sharpshooter. When he opened up on them, he'd still be outside their rifle range. They'd have to turn and retreat back down the path, but he'd get most of them before they got too far away.

With a devious smile, Jason called to Daklugie and reached for the Spencer. He gestured for the box of shells so he'd have them when the time came to use them. When the boy handed him the box, Jason felt a sudden intense throbbing in his head. A dizzy spell grabbed him, and he wavered. He fumbled the box and dropped it, then watched helplessly as it tumbled down the steep slope, almost in slow motion.

In desperation, Jason dropped the Spencer and dove for the box. He caught it but lost his footing and slid a dozen feet down the slope. Though he knew he faced death almost a thousand feet below him, he refused to let go of the box of cartridges. They were his only hope of defeating the soldiers.

With his right hand, he caught hold of a dried-up shrub that miraculously held his weight. In his left hand, he clenched the box of shells. With a sigh of relief, he started to scramble back up the slope. At the last second, he realized he held the cardboard container upside down. When he tightened his grip, the top squeezed open and the cartridges spilled into the air.

In a panic, Jason grabbed at the falling shells. He stuffed a handful into his pocket as he watched the rest fall away and regained his feet on the trail. Still not believing his stupidity, he watched the sun flash off the falling pieces of metal far below him. The torn paper of the empty box fluttered down the hill until it became lodged against a small shrub.

He willed the tumbling cartridges to defy gravity somehow, wished they could fall back *uphill* into his pocket. He closed his eyes in despair, but when he opened them again, no amount of willpower could reverse the disaster.

Daklugie looked at him, then picked up the Spencer rifle. Jason reached into his pocket and retrieved the cartridges. He counted the shells as he mentally cursed his carelessness and the turn of events.

Eight shells, thirteen soldiers, and no Winchester.

CHAPTER 28

J UH AND HIS NINETEEN WARRIORS jogged toward the camp
from the north, down the Middle Fork. Poncé and two
others had ambushed an army patrol, firing their rifles and
making enough noise to get most of the patrolling soldiers to
follow them. Juh and his warriors proceeded west undetected.

Nearing the camp, no sentries challenged them, so Juh knew
they were too late. Anxiety clawed at his gut as he rounded the
last bend in the river. He recklessly splashed across the shallow creek and jogged a short cut through a small stand of trees.
Relief replaced dread.

"They escaped," he exalted as he realized the camp was gone.
"The lookouts warned them in time and—"

In the bright moonlight, he saw the first mound of earth.
Then he saw the second and third. Then he saw thirteen more.
They were huge mounds that Juh knew held many bodies.
Beyond the mounds, a pile of rubble stood.

Like a mindless man drunk on whiskey, Juh stumbled forward until his legs simply quit functioning. He fell to his knees
by the first mound of earth and wept.

Vaguely, he heard his men uttering their death chants. One
young man wailed in agony. When Juh was able to look up, he
saw his men wandering around aimlessly, all as grief-stricken as
he. He hauled himself to his feet, knowing he had to be strong
for his men. He would allow himself more time to grieve later.

Juh walked over to the young man who shamelessly cried

aloud. Only seventeen summers old, the warrior had just wed three days before leaving on the raid. Juh recalled the young man bragging about how much food he would steal from the soldiers to feed his new bride.

As Juh reached for the young man's shoulder, the warrior spun, knife in hand.

"I'll kill them all!" the young man screamed. "Everywhere, the bluecoats will fall under my knife until there are no more left to kill."

The young warrior turned and ran into the darkness. Juh turned to face his men as they gathered around him. He tried to talk, but the stuttering that affected him especially hard when he was nervous or angry choked him until he could only croak an unintelligible noise. He paused until his trembling subsided, then tried to work through his stutter.

"I don't understand this," Juh said to no one in particular. "The Buffalo Soldiers have always been honorable in war. They've never made war on our women and children."

Another warrior nodded toward the pile of debris. "They scraped all our belongings together like garbage and burned all that we are. Then they piled our people's dead bodies in their neat little holes without respect."

Juh nodded. The soldiers had piled river rocks on top of each grave—probably to keep animals from digging up the bodies. He was about to speak when he saw Brown Hair approaching from the West Fork junction. He appreciated that the young warrior had kept his wits about him and studied the area while the rest of the warriors were stricken. Brown Hair had no kin to mourn and as Juh looked into his hard, empty eyes, he truly believed Brown Hair had no emotion but hatred left in his heart.

"Some of our people escaped to the west," Brown Hair reported. "I found the tracks of the soldiers in pursuit. They left early in the day. Other soldiers buried our people, then headed toward the east, to their fort, but they left late."

Brown Hair's words hung in the darkness and Juh narrowed his eyes. If the soldiers left late, they probably traveled only a couple of hours before camping for the night. Brown Hair seemed to read his thoughts.

"Let me go after them. I'll cut their throats while they sleep."

As much as Juh wanted to allow it, he had to consider the best use of his men so they could rescue the survivors of the massacre.

"No." He shook his head and looked around at the warriors. "Our people need us. We will sleep until the sky lightens—"

"We should go after them now!" Brown Hair countered.

"Yes," another offered. "Punish the soldiers." He stepped to Brown Hair's side—a clear show of loyalty.

The two men turned to leave, but Juh reached out and grabbed Brown Hair's arm. The young warrior spun, and for a moment Juh thought the man was going to challenge him. The fire of revenge burned in Brown Hair's eyes, but Juh also saw the young man's respect for the Apache way of life. The years of Apache training held the young warrior in check. Around them, the warriors fell silent. Juh could almost feel them holding their breath, waiting to see what he and Brown Hair would do.

"Our people need us," Juh said. "Together. This isn't the time to let your own individual needs guide you. And we can't fight our enemy and fight sleep at the same time." He paused and placed a gentle hand on Brown Hair's shoulder, hoping to impart concern and respect in the gesture. "I want the soldiers to die also, but we must think of the survivors first. Our people are resourceful. If they still live, a few hours of rest for us will not hurt them. Yet, it will make us stronger."

The young warrior nodded, somewhat reluctantly Juh thought, and turned away. The rest of the men drifted apart to find a place to sleep, probably to be alone with their pain. For the time being, Juh had Brown Hair's support, but he knew it might not last long. If the young man left, Juh knew some of the younger warriors would follow.

No doubt, some of the more seasoned warriors also blamed him for the mistake of trusting Lives With The Enemy and for allowing the massacre of their families. Never in his wildest imagination would he have suspected an Apache, even one who lived and worked with the bluecoats, would invite a massacre on his own people.

On the journey back from the river, the warriors had jogged the entire previous night and the entire day and late into the night again. Juh recalled with pride that all of his warriors had endured the torturous run despite the extreme daytime heat. None had quit. Now Juh felt tired deep in his muscles, a fatigue from the hours-long run. He knew his body required several hours of rest to recover. Fortunately, they'd killed venison to eat on the way, but still they'd depleted half of their ration bags.

With their camp destroyed and everything burned, they had no way to quickly resupply their rations. Unless they found more food, they had to make do with what meager supplies they carried with them. Juh remembered times when he had done more with less, but he knew they still had a long journey and possibly a hard battle ahead of them.

"When we wake, you two will hunt us venison." He pointed out a couple of warriors. Then he indicated four other warriors. "You will pursue the soldiers. They'll follow the river until they find the valley that leads past the mining camp to the fort."

Juh studied his men. His gaze passed over Brown Hair and he knew the young man wanted to challenge him, wanted to fulfill his own thirst for blood. After a moment, Juh continued.

"Find a path over the south cliffs and get ahead of them. Make their journey difficult and kill as many of them as you can." Juh was greeted by a murmur of approval. He looked at Brown Hair next and said, "The rest of us will go after the soldiers that pursue our people."

"Let's light a fire and perform the war dance," shouted an exuberant voice from the fringe of the group.

Again, Juh countered with a gentle shake of his head. "Tonight we'll sing the death song, then honor our dead in silence. Rest among the spirits of our dead. When the survivors are safe, then we'll celebrate."

Lookouts were appointed and the warriors lay down to nap.

But even four hours later as the sky began to lighten, Juh still could not find sleep. The faces of his wives filled his mind. He formed a vision of his favorite wife and concentrated on Ishton's beautiful smile. Was she among the dead? What of his last surviving son, Daklugie?

He'd lost his two other sons in Mexico. They went into town with several others to trade for supplies, and they'd disappeared. Juh believed they fell victim to well-organized slave traders from the southern mountains of Mexico. Now his anxiety mounted as he wondered if Daklugie was among those massacred. If his son had died, his family bloodline would also end. There would be no more sons of Juh.

He sat up and found Brown Hair sitting also. He stood and walked past the young warrior, motioning him to follow. He led the way into the wide valley the West Fork flowed through and gazed to the east. Brown Hair stood beside him. As the sky brightened, the two men performed their silent tribute to *Ussen*, Creator of all things. When he finished, Juh turned to find Brown Hair looking at him impatiently.

The younger man said, "Now you understand why I will never be complete until I have killed every *White-Eye* who breathes."

"I have always understood," Juh responded. "In the years past, I lost two sons, and now I fear I'll never see my last again."

Juh paused and tried to suppress a shudder of hatred. "If the soldiers want a war, we will give them one they will never forget."

CHAPTER 29

FIRST SERGEANT LAFAYETTE CRAWFORD LAY on his back. He folded his hands together across his massive chest and gazed at the stars. The moon was only a distant memory behind the western mountains, but the tops of some low clouds were still edge-lit. Amidst all the war he'd seen over the years, the serene beauty of a moonlit, cloud-filled sky still filled him with awe.

He'd ordered camp made at the same junction of the West and East Forks where they'd camped the previous night. For reasons of hygiene, he and his men lay a hundred yards upstream from where the horses were picketed in the tall reeds at the junction of the streams.

Thankfully, Crawford could neither hear nor smell the animals. For a moment, he pretended he lay near a peaceful stream, the soothing sound of water tumbling over river rock seducing him into believing the war was a thousand miles away.

Crawford tried to recall when he started sleeping only on his back. He thought back to his childhood but couldn't remember the night he started the habit. Mostly, he figured he did it for safety. If attacked, he could roll quickly to his feet without scrambling around, making noise. The habit saved his life more than once when he finally became bold enough to run away from his master at the young age of fifteen.

As the eastern sky began to lighten, Crawford sat up, accepting sleep was gone for that night. Something had awakened him around midnight, he guessed, some kind of dream or drifting thought. Whatever it was, it kept him awake. He looked around and smiled in the darkness as he recognized Corporal Shelton's upright form. He'd been awake too, probably just waiting for Crawford to stir.

Crawford rolled up his blanket, stood, and pulled his sweat-soaked blouse away from his chest, for all the good it did him. When he let go, it just stuck to his skin again. He walked over to the creek and splashed water over his face and head. It cooled him, but he found himself dreading the heat of the coming day. He wondered if they could find a tree-covered trail to march home along. His closest friend, Levi Shelton, walked up beside him and put a hand on his shoulder.

"I hate this war, L.C."

Crawford nodded and splashed more water on his face, then ruffled his big hand through his tight-curled hair. "Ever think about quittin', Levi?"

"You mean, like deserting?"

Crawford punched his friend lightly on the thigh and shot him a look that called him stupid.

"I mean, when our time's up." He sat back on his butt, braced his elbows across his knees, and locked his fingers together. "Take all that money we've saved up and start a farm or ranch somewhere."

Shelton fidgeted, then sat down beside him and rubbed his leg. He glanced over sheepishly.

"Aw, Levi. You done spent all your money again?" Crawford said. The corporal just shrugged. "On that whore over in Central City?"

"Where else is a Black man gonna get laid around here if he don't buy it?" Shelton gestured, palms up. "Ain't no Black women out here. None that ain't already spoken for anyways."

"Well, you didn't have to give her *all* your money, did you?"

Shelton chuckled. "Spend a night with Mona and you'll be givin' her all your money too." He paused a moment. "Besides, where'd we start a ranch anyway? Here in New Mexico? I heard they got laws that force Black people to leave New Mexico Territory."

Crawford shook his head. "That was twenty years ago."

"Same difference. They still enforce 'em." Shelton shrugged and glanced behind him. Crawford heard the men start to stir. Through months of military habit, he knew they'd all awaken shortly before dawn.

"Besides," Shelton said. "You've seen the way they greet us in towns all over the territory. We save their lives, and they still won't even give us a damn drink."

"That's just the way things are," Crawford argued. "It isn't going to change in our lifetime; so we just gotta live with it." He paused for a moment. "But I was thinking maybe we could start somewhere like Texas or Oklahoma. Private Tucker's from Texas. He says there's lots of Black cowboys out there. Some even own ranches."

"I wonder how he's doin'."

"If he sticks close to Jason Peares, he'll be all right." Crawford paused and gazed over at the corporal. He always felt the warmth and comfort of friendship in Shelton's light blue eyes. He could speak his true thoughts without losing his command presence. "Levi, I swear to God above, I've never seen anything like this before."

Shelton looked away and Crawford imagined his friend was reliving the massacre. Crawford saw the scene clearly in his mind's eye. Bodies lay piled on top of each other, women and children shot down as they ran every which way, trying to leap over their fallen kin to escape.

"L.C., I'll be the first to admit that Apache warriors need killin'. There's just no makin' peace with 'em. But not unarmed women and children." He thumbed up the river. "Not slaughtered like that."

"They're gonna be on the warpath after this," Crawford said. "And I can't say I blame 'em." He stood.

Shelton stood also. "But it's our job to stop them, right?"

"Yeah." He paused. "That's right."

Crawford glanced behind him at the waking camp, watched the men wander to the water to wash their faces and gargle. He was about to say more but was distracted by shouting from the trees where the horses were picketed.

"First Sergeant!" came the warning from the darkness. "Private Andrews is dead, and the horses are gone!"

Crawford had just started to move toward the commotion when Shelton screamed and stumbled forward. Crawford reached out as his friend fell into his arms, an arrow shaft protruding from his back.

The first sergeant yelled, "Ambush!"

CHAPTER 30

C APTAIN TAYLOR PAUSED AS HE topped the ridgeline and gazed south into the distance. Mountain brush covered the peak where he sat, but no trees blocked his view of the wilderness in front of him. Hills and valleys marched into the distance as far as he could see in all directions. For a moment, he absorbed the marvelous panorama and forgot how much he hated New Mexico. Then he looked behind him to the north and saw the desolate system of rugged canyons and barren valleys.

Taylor glanced over at Mogollon Peak. Locating the landmark to the northwest gave him his bearings. None of what he saw appeared on the map he carried with him, and he and his men were not prepared for an extended campaign through such desolate landscape. He certainly hadn't intended to deal with any survivors, much less chase them into the hills. His men needed to resupply for an extended patrol. Sergeant Stevenson echoed his thoughts.

"Captain, sir," the man called.

Taylor looked over his shoulder as Stevenson topped the ridge, followed closely by the single column of troops. He faced front again and whistled at the point rider, then made a hand signal to halt for a rest.

"Yes, Sergeant," Taylor said as Stevenson reined up beside him.

"If we're going to follow them Injuns, we're gonna have to

stock up on some supplies. We've got water for a day, maybe two if we're—"

Taylor heard the man's words, but his mind drifted while he mentally calculated how many times a day he could sip from his canteen in this oppressive heat before he consumed all his water. By the time he realized the sergeant had stopped talking in mid-sentence, the man and one other soldier were already dead.

Captain Taylor had seen death on the battlefield many times and he'd seen the terrible wounds inflicted by war. Never had he seen the devastation from arm's reach. The sergeant's body literally exploded as the long-distance shot ripped through Stevenson and the man who had pulled up directly behind him. The two men were thrown from their saddles by the sniper bullet's impact. A third man screamed as the same bullet creased his right arm above the elbow. Blood and gore from Stevenson and the second man showered the third as that man grabbed his arm.

In the brief second Taylor took to recover from the shocking sight and to react, his ears registered a flash of sound as another bullet cut through the air behind him. The shot tugged at his hair, and another soldier just coming into sight over the ridge disappeared from his horse with a shout of pain.

"Ambush!" Taylor shouted. "Get off the trail!"

Taylor yanked his reins to the right and fled down the hill, zigzagging until he entered the trees. When he glanced back, he saw his men following, racing back and forth down the hill to make another long shot impossible. He pulled up and took a deep breath, finally realizing death had missed him by a fraction of an inch. He cursed his carelessness, should have seen the potential trap riding over the treeless ridge. Now he had three more men dead and a fourth wounded.

Captain Taylor took longer than he liked to organize his men. Still, he appreciated the fact that, although the men were army prisoners, they had some modicum of training. They were more or less controllable, either through the prospect of receiving gold and an honorable discharge, or through the fear each man held that Taylor would shoot them in the back if they tried to desert. When all his men gathered around, he voiced his concern for supplies, concluding they'd have to find and raid a mining camp.

"No need for that, sir," a man said from the fringe of the mounted group. "I got me a cousin mining gold and silver about half a day's ride west of here. He'll supply us."

"Very well," Taylor said. "Prepare to move out." He looked around and caught Corporal Hansen's eye. "Sharps!"

"Sir!" Hansen nudged his horse forward.

"Take one man and keep on Jason Peares's trail. If you get a shot—"

"I don't reckon he's gonna let me get close enough. This here's mostly open land," he said waving an arm around. "Ain't no canyon, Cap'n. I'm guessin' he took those shots from almost a mile away. I can't touch him."

"You have your orders, Corporal." Taylor searched the rest of his men, resting his gaze on a sharp-eyed corporal who looked like he knew how to lead men.

"You, there. What's your name?"

The man narrowed his eyes suspiciously before he answered. "Smith."

"Form a detail to bury those men up yonder. Then get everyone ready to ride out. We'll resupply, then pick up the trail again. Corporal Hansen will make sure we don't ride into another ambush. Isn't that right, Corporal?"

Hansen hesitated a moment, then nodded, apparently accepting the veiled threat in Taylor's words.

"That's right, Cap'n."

Six hours later, Taylor rode into the mining camp with the private who claimed kin there. He still hadn't bothered to learn the young man's name. His cousin, a big burly man with unkempt, black hair and beard and a holey undershirt greeted him with a friendly, toothy smile.

"Hi thar," he said, holding out his hand to Taylor. "Name's Lawrence."

"I don't care what your name is," Taylor answered. He reached into his blouse pocket and produced a small cloth sack. Then he shook the cloth bag so Lawrence could hear the jingle of metal and tossed it to the miner.

Lawrence deftly snatched the gold from the air with his extended hand.

"There's more where that came from," Taylor said, then paused a bit to let the offer sink in. "We need supplies."

The miner opened the bag and poured six nuggets into his left palm. He eyed Captain Taylor for a moment, then smiled. "We got supplies to keep us up here six months. What do you need?"

"Equipage for ten men for two weeks. Food, ammunition, extra water canteens," Taylor said while he summoned Corporal Smith forward. "The corporal will give you the specifics." He hesitated, watching the growing crowd of men gather behind Lawrence. He quickly counted eighteen men. "And I need volunteers."

"What for?"

Taylor paused and cocked his mouth in a half-smile that crinkled his hawk nose but didn't quite reach his close-set eyes. "For two hundred dollars in gold."

Lawrence looked at the ground and opened his mouth to speak.

Taylor thought the man was about to shake his head, so he interrupted the miner. "Two hundred *each.*"

A sudden chorus of voices confirmed the agreement. Most of the men complained they hadn't seen so much as a nugget of gold in the last three months from their played out claim.

Lawrence shrugged. "I guess you got yourself a posse. Who're we goin' after?"

"Renegade Indians on the warpath," Taylor lied. "They escaped from Fort Bayard and made it clear they're not comin' in peaceably. We'll have to kill 'em. And that half-Black traitor who set 'em free."

"Set 'em free?" a man beside Lawrence said. "What's his other half? Stupid?" He was rewarded with guttural laughter.

"So where's the rest of the gold?" Lawrence said, calming down from the melee.

"In the bank in Silver City."

"Now wait a minute. I—"

"Suit yourself," Taylor said, reining his horse around. "Corporal, gather up the supplies, and we'll be on our way."

"Hold on now!" Lawrence and several other men shuffled quickly alongside Taylor's horse. As the captain stopped, Lawrence said, "I didn't say we wasn't goin'."

"Very well," Taylor said, turning in his saddle. "Everyone who's volunteering be ready to move out in five minutes."

An old man detached himself from the group and moved over to Taylor. "I know a fair bit about the Injuns in these parts. Is it Victorio we're after?"

Taylor shook his head. "We're chasing a chief named *Hoe*."

The man nodded. "I don't know where they are now, but I figure they'll be headin' down Mexico way."

The captain studied the old man. He didn't look like he knew much about anything. A mop of dirty red hair draped over the top of his head behind a receding hairline. His face showed he was about sixty, and he had brilliant blue eyes, but they were spaced wide apart.

Taylor said, "I thought all the Indians stuck to the mountains of New Mexico and Arizona."

The redhead nodded. "I know Geronimo and Victorio both got hideouts down in Mexico. But them and most of the other chiefs tend to stay around these here parts, especially if they got kin over on that big reservation."

"You mean San Carlos?"

"Yeah. But Juh's got hisself a mountain fortress down there in northern Mexico. I know it's true 'cause I use to trade with some of 'em. Whiskey and skins and such. And I still got my hair to prove it."

Taylor nodded, still considering the information. "And?"

"Well, they'll probably head down out of the hills and strike a trail along the Gila River until it turns west. Then they'll hightail it across the flats and back up into the Big Burro Mountains. They got horses?" Taylor shook his head. "Then they'll keep to the high ground. I hear them Injuns can make fifty, sixty miles a day afoot as the crow flies, when they've a mind to."

"In the mountains?" Taylor immediately cursed himself for blurting out his surprise. A well-equipped mounted cavalry company barely made that distance on open land.

"*Especially* in the mountains, Cap'n. Even in this heat."

Captain Taylor called Corporal Smith over. "Take four men and the old-timer," he gestured at the redhead. "And take half the miners too. Get down to the turn in the river and start a patrol. Wait for Jason Peares and the Indians to show.

"Ride hard and don't stop until you get there. I want you in position before they get down out of the mountains. We'll pick their trail along that footpath back yonder," Taylor knew he didn't need to mention the path where they were ambushed. "And make sure they don't backtrack."

The redhead spoke up. "Them Injuns keep hidden stashes of food and weapons all over the mountains, you know. I heard that from one Apache while he was drunk on some of my whiskey."

Taylor nodded. "If we ride herd on 'em hard enough, they won't have time to get to their stashes. All they'll be able to do is keep running. Maybe not even sleep. Get moving, Corporal." Taylor raised his voice to the rest of his men and his half of the miners. "The rest of you are with me. Let's move out."

Captain Taylor called after Corporal Smith. "If you find that outlaw and his Indians, I want them all killed. Is that clear?"

"Very clear, Captain."

CHAPTER 31

"THEY DONE KILLED ME," SHELTON said.
"That's a fact, my friend."

Corporal Levi Shelton stared upward, his blue eyes glazed and unfocused. Crawford held his best friend in his lap and gently stroked the side of Shelton's face with a huge hand. The man's skin felt clammy and cold.

"I can't feel my legs." Shelton trembled again. An hour ago, he'd clenched Crawford's arm so hard, the big man almost cried out in pain. Now Shelton's hands hung limp by his side. "It hurts so much, L.C. My chest feels like it's on fire."

Crawford nodded even though he knew his friend could no longer see him. "I know. They used poison on that arrow." Crawford paused. "Ran off all our horses and stole what little supplies we had left too. Got no medicine left. There's nothing I can do."

Shelton nodded his head with jerky movements. "Yes, there is." His eyes closed. "Don't let me suffer. You know I'd do the same for you."

Crawford hadn't shed a tear since he was fourteen. Now he did. He gently laid his friend's head on the ground and unfastened his holster flap. As he pulled his Remington, Shelton spoke. Crawford leaned down to hear his friend's last words.

"I wish I could have been more like you, L.C. I wish I had saved up my money instead of spending it whoring around. I could've left it to you for your ranch."

Shelton coughed and tears brimmed in Crawford's eyes.

"You think where I'm goin', they never even seen an Apache or a White man?"

Crawford placed his forehead against Shelton's. "You rest easy, my friend."

Private Nance handed the first sergeant a kerchief. Crawford placed the rag over Shelton's face so he'd remember his friend properly, then pressed the barrel of his gun against Shelton's temple. He hesitated and glanced at the men standing around him. Several pulled off their hats. Crawford closed his eyes and pulled the trigger. He stood, then unashamedly wiped the tears from his eyes.

"All right, two of you," he arbitrarily pointed out two privates. "Grab your knives and help me get him buried. Then we're movin' outa here on the double. The rest of you pair up and keep your eyes open. Those Indians are around here somewhere, and they ain't happy. At least we got our rifles and the canteens and the ration kits we sleep with."

Crawford gestured toward Shelton's body. "This here's the last man I want to lose."

With no shovels, it took an hour to get a hole deep enough for Shelton's body. The first sergeant said a few words most of his men didn't hear as they were busy scanning the trees on the opposite side of the river. Crawford was pleased all his men were at a battle-ready posture, holsters unsnapped and rifles at the ready.

After the burial, Crawford marched his men in a single-file formation *at the double*, a jog faster than a normal march, but slower than a full-out run. They'd only made half a mile downstream when they saw their next problem.

Crawford figured to outpace the Apaches, hoping his enemy couldn't travel as fast over the tops of the rocky canyon as the soldiers could down in the valley. Within minutes, he realized the error of his thinking, and he halted the column under a sheer cliff wall. Private Silas Nance squatted beside Crawford.

"Sergeant, we got us a bit of a problem here."

Crawford nodded. "Yeah, don't I know it." He paused, looking around. "We have no food but our emergency stash and not enough ammunition."

"And this trail, Sarge." Nance waved his hand around at the shadows cast by the trees and cliffs. "These devils are gonna hound us all day and into the night. Normally, Apache don't travel at night, much less make war, but these will. I guarantee you we won't get much sleep tonight."

"You ain't tellin' me anything I don't already know, Corporal. Right now, I'm more concerned with surviving twelve more hours of daylight." Crawford pointed at the portion of the winding trail he could see through the brush. "The river keeps winding all over creation down here in this canyon."

"And the trail keeps crossing it," Nance added. "Puts us in the open two or three times an hour."

"Makes for good target practice," Crawford agreed. "See those walls up yonder?"

Nance followed Crawford's gaze through the trees ahead and nodded. Because of the intense summer heat, the Gila River was barely a trickling stream. It wound back and forth through the canyon, often flowing right up next to sheer rock walls. The canyon wall opposite the sheer rock was less steep and was tree-covered, offering plenty of ambush spots where the trail followed or crossed the stream.

Crawford knew they'd never outrun the Indians on the winding trail. Worse, if they stayed in the canyon, his men were asking to be ambushed. To be effective as a warning against ambush, the point guard would have to stay within sight of the jogging troops because of the winding trail. That soldier would, therefore, offer little advance warning of an attack.

Nance continued. "These cliffs get any closer together, those Injuns'll be able to throw rocks at us. After what got done to their people, they ain't gonna rest until every last one of us is dead."

"And?" Crawford looked at the soldier impatiently.

"Let's backtrack and get off this river, pronto. Otherwise,

they're gonna pick us off one by one down there. Probably a dozen o' them devils out there."

Crawford considered the man's reasoning. "All our spare canteens were with the horses. Without the river, we'll have no water and no game for food."

"True," Private Nance agreed and pointed along the canyon river. "But this way here is gonna take us almost four days without horses, with them pickin' at us the whole way. We were only equipped for a four-day patrol, Sarge, and that started three days ago. We got less than fifty shells apiece on our belts and that's not enough to fight a running battle."

Crawford got the feeling Private Nance paused so he could absorb the logic of his argument. In a moment, Nance continued.

"If we march over that ridge," Nance pointed to the south, "we'll be back into the pines by midday tomorrow and in the shade. By nightfall tomorrow, we can drop in on one of those mining camps south of here and maybe borrow some food or horses."

Crawford always respected Private Nance for his frontier smarts. "That high trail is gonna be mighty tough on the men, Silas."

"No tougher than this one, Sarge."

"Well, we just might be able to keep ahead of the Apaches. It'll be just as hard for them."

"I doubt that, Sarge. They're born and raised out here in these godforsaken mountains. They'll find a way to get ahead of us, but not before noon, I'm guessin'. And going that way we'll only have to put up with 'em for one more day, not four."

"All right," Crawford said. "Inform the men. Refill what canteens we have, then we'll backtrack and strike due south." As an afterthought, he added, "God help us if they get us hemmed in out there somewhere with no water or food."

CHAPTER 32

J UH LED THE WARRIORS UP the steep trail and paused as the trail veered to the south over the ridge. They'd be framed against the sky, so Juh proceeded alone to study the tracks and draw any ambush that might be waiting for them. As he studied the darkening panorama around him, Brown Hair jogged up from the end of the line of warriors. The young man had disappeared down a steep hill a while back, saying only that he wanted to explore something unusual.

"What did you find?" Juh said.

In response, Brown Hair untied a small skin sack from his belt and held it open. Juh saw cartridges reflecting the dim evening light. He shrugged and Brown Hair explained.

"These are larger than what we use for our Winchesters, but slightly smaller than what the soldiers use."

Juh considered the news. "The long rifle?"

"That's what I thought. But he's not much of a warrior if he can't take care of his ammunition."

They continued to study the tracks. Brown Hair pointed to the dried blood splattered around the brown grass.

Juh nodded, then gazed into the distance. The trail led down the hill, curving back and forth around rocky outcrops and boulders. It disappeared into the tree line about four or five hundred paces away and then crested over a bald knobby ridge almost a mile away.

"This one with the long rifle has the eye of an eagle to ambush the soldiers from such a great distance," Juh said.

"Are you sure he's the same one who killed the soldiers below?"

"Must be," Juh said, recalling the tracks he'd studied the day before. "We know he shot from the trees by the river, a great distance from the trail where the tracks of my son and the others were. The tracks clearly showed he approached them. After that, there were no more tracks of Grandmother and the others. He voluntarily gave his horse and the army animal to our people, and his boot tracks then proceed beside Daklugie. They are not his captives."

Brown Hair stood. "Someday Daklugie will be leader of our people. He is brave to walk without fear beside his enemy."

"No," Juh said, shaking his head. "This man is no enemy."

"But he rode with the soldiers! You saw his tracks with your own eyes. That's how he came to be at the river."

"Your mind is blinded by hatred, Brown Hair," Juh said, looking at the tracks on the ground. They were a day behind the survivors. "The soldiers hate us because we're different, and it's true we must fight or die. But not all the *White-Eyes* are our enemy. This one with the long rifle is a man of honor."

"Honor!" Brown Hair spat out the word with contempt. "The *White-Eyes* will honor my blade with their blood! This one is no different."

Juh turned to face the angry young man. "Look at the ground beneath your feet, darkened with the blood of our enemy. They are weaker because of the long rifle of this warrior. Surely, even you can see that, can't you?"

Grudgingly, Brown Hair turned away and nodded. "True."

"Then let this one live. He saved my last son. He may be our only ally."

Brown Hair hesitated for a moment, and Juh thought he might have reached the young man. Then Brown Hair fixed him with a dead stare, and Juh knew hatred had won the battle over reason.

"He's *your* ally, not mine." Brown Hair walked ahead down the trail, calling back over his shoulder. "He's one of the *White-Eyes*. If he crosses my path, I'll cut his heart out. Then I'll possess his long rifle."

Captain Taylor halted his column just before they rode out of the trees and onto the trail. He'd seen a movement in his side vision and looked in surprise as several figures walked over the ridgeline where he had suffered his own humiliating ambush. He started to call for his sharpshooter, then remembered he'd sent Corporal Hansen ahead yesterday. Instead, Taylor called for a dismount.

For the past day, he'd kept his men in the trees. They couldn't make very good time riding around all the trees and brush, and the horses had to be fairly uncomfortable maneuvering on the slant of the hill. He'd given Jason Peares his last opportunity for a long-range shot. When he saw the Indians walking over the ridgeline, Taylor knew they couldn't see his men hidden in the dense trees. He held another advantage also. The tree line sat in the deep shadows of late evening, far below the ridge.

Quickly, Taylor organized his men into a firing line. The horses were led far back into the trees so their noise wouldn't betray the soldiers to the approaching Indians. This was going to be too easy.

"Who are they, Captain?" Lawrence said beside him as they crouched at the base of a tree.

"How the hell should I know?" Taylor threw a withering glance at the big man and added, "They're Indians. Isn't that enough?" Lawrence didn't answer.

Taylor could tell by their careful demeanor the Indians were scouting, watching for tracks as they moved. Their line spread long and scattered wide across the trail as they advanced quickly, but cautiously. Clearly, they were uncomfortable out in the open and made quick progress toward the trees. Most of them would pass within a hundred yards of his waiting men.

Taylor assumed they were Apache only because this was Apache land, but he'd never learned how to tell one Indian from another, and he didn't care to start learning. He studied the one in front. With long, black hair and wide shoulders that tapered to a narrow waist, the warrior looked like a fierce fighting man. Like the rest of the warriors, the man moved quickly down the hill, Winchester held at the ready. *He looks like a predator,* Taylor thought. He recalled what an officer had told him over in Arizona. He'd referred to the Apache as the tigers of the human species. Now Taylor understood what the officer meant.

The warrior's gaze darted quickly from side to side as he scanned the trees and terrain ahead of him. He spaced each footstep wide apart, legs bowed outward for stability, and he hunched forward a bit at the waist. The man looked like he expected danger and seemed ready to react instantly to any trouble.

Even from the distance, the dark-skinned Indian looked like someone accustomed to leadership. Something in Taylor's gut told him he was looking at Chief Juh. It couldn't be a coincidence these Indians happened to be scouting on the same trail the runaways had taken. Somehow, the Apache chief escaped the army trap at the Rio Grande River, eluding almost a hundred patrolling soldiers.

If the warrior chief straightened from his predator-like posture, Taylor realized the man would stand tall and lanky. He lacked the thick-muscled definition of the brown-haired warrior stalking beside him. That one was young and thick in the chest and had shoulders with sinewy muscles bulging from his arms and legs. His dark face was narrow with high cheekbones and hard features.

The brown-haired warrior frightened Taylor the way a mountain lion would frighten even a heavily armed hunter. *Make one mistake and the savage animal would rip you apart,*

Taylor thought. He appreciated the comparison and as they approached, he understood why he felt the knot of fear in his gut.

The Indians wore paint on their bare chests and faces in shades of red and brown like no civilized man would ever wear. Dark eyes, and what looked to Taylor like a snarling scowl, made the warriors look even fiercer. The sight invoked a deep primal fear in Taylor, despite the fact that he and his men held a superior ambush position. He smelled the sweat of his own fear, and he felt it dripping from his armpits, sliding down the insides of his arms. He knew his men couldn't sense his fear, but still he hated himself for it.

Taylor held his fire. He wanted to let the warriors get so close none of his men would miss. He wanted to savor the moment of his victory. These Indians were his enemy, savages trying to prevent the spread of civilization across the land. They were murderers and butchers of helpless farmers and ranchers and miners. They deserved to die.

His fear and excitement built as he watched the Indians approach their deaths. He found it hard to imagine these people engaging sympathy or political support, even from the most soft-hearted easterners. Senator Bennington had to be wrong.

Captain Taylor hated to even think of the Indians as people. They were too barbaric to understand the concepts of politics, business, economics, and all the other notions that defined civilization.

No matter, he thought. He squeezed his arms against his side to let his uniform soak up the sweat then aimed his rifle at the warrior chief. He wiped sweat from the tip of his nose. Goddamn desert heat. High up in the mountains at sundown and it still felt like a hundred degrees. Taylor hated this land and everything in it.

He stared down his rifle sights at Chief Juh and thought again about Senator Bennington as he had many times since the attack on the Apache village. The senator said he wanted Chief Juh alive to continue the war. Taylor had protested in the hotel in Silver City, but Bennington had simply brushed aside his objections with a wave of his cane.

"After you attack his village, Chief Juh will have no choice but to go on the warpath. Then any hope among the Apache tribes of forming a unified army will fade away. The army will hunt down Apache everywhere, like dogs, until they're all dead."

As each hour passed, Captain Taylor's hatred of the half-breed outlaw and the Apache grew stronger. He didn't care about the strategic implications of the senator's political plan nor of his own orders. The call of what seemed right was too strong. These Indians were here now, in his sights. If allowed to live, this handful of savages would continue to engage whole companies of trained soldiers, evading them with their high mountain, hit-and-run tactics.

No, Taylor thought. *To hell with the senator's plans.*

He sighted on Chief Juh's chest and when the warrior moved too close to miss, Taylor pulled his trigger.

CHAPTER 33

J UH MOVED QUICKLY DOWN THE hill. The tracks he had studied were a day old, so he felt no danger from a lingering enemy. Still he felt an increasing discomfort, but he couldn't discover its origin. He uttered a single command in the Apache warrior language, and Brown Hair moved several paces away to Juh's right as a precaution. As he continued to scan the darkening land, he realized he'd feel a lot more comfortable once he and his warriors moved out of the open.

The day-old tracks of the Apache survivors followed the trail almost straight across the wild grass before dropping steeply into boulders, shrubbery, and tall brush. The disorganized tracks of running army horses veered off the trail to the west. In his mind, Juh could see the soldiers scattering to avoid the ambush from the long rifle.

Ahead of him and to the right, a huge stand of trees covered the sloped land, sweeping off to the west and to the south, down the hill to merge with the brush in the lower elevations. The trail he followed meandered back and forth across the rocky terrain, finally entering the trees farther downhill.

Juh continued forward, and his sense of danger increased. He made a brief motion with his left hand and knew without looking that his men immediately scattered off the trail and away from each other. If ambushed, they wouldn't get caught in a bunch that would make for easy targets. Juh wondered why he suddenly thought about an ambush.

From the earliest day of warrior training, all Apache warriors practiced relentlessly how to organize and conduct an ambush. They also practiced how to escape one. Like the well-trained soldiers that hunted them, all warriors knew without thinking exactly what to do when attacked or when attacking.

Suddenly, Juh realized what bothered him. He'd briefly caught a whiff of a strange yet familiar odor that didn't belong in the still hot, evening air. He recognized the faint scent that Lives With The Enemy always seemed to carry with him—the smell of the soldiers and their animals. For a moment, Juh hesitated. When he started forward again, his movement startled a jackrabbit into a run. The little animal ran toward the trees, then stopped all of a sudden and sniffed the air. After a brief pause, it ran again.

Away from the trees!

When the realization of danger hit him, Juh instantly dropped to the ground. Even as he moved, he felt the wind of a bullet pass close by the side of his head. The familiar deep boom of an army Springfield rifle reached Juh's ears almost instantly. Many more shots followed the first, but Juh knew the rest of his warriors had hit the ground the instant they heard the first report. In the slight delay after the first army barrage, Juh prepared to return fire.

Over the years, the Apache learned well how the army made war. When the soldiers predictably fired from a line, the flashes in the deepening shadows betrayed their positions. Juh knew precisely where his men were behind him and knew that each would target the closest section of the line of soldiers. The Apache never fired randomly.

Juh fired four times in quick succession into the left end of the line of soldiers. He couldn't tell in the deepening shadows if he struck any targets, and he didn't wait to find out. While he and half his men fired at the soldiers, the other warriors jumped up and sprinted toward concealment.

After firing his shots, Juh jumped up and headed toward cover while the first group of warriors took to ground to provide cover fire. Around him, he saw his men zigzagging across the open land while the first group exchanged gunfire with the hidden soldiers. Within two minutes, all the warriors made it to the safety of the boulders without a single casualty. They continued to pick their way downhill until safely hidden among the trees on the gentle, lower slope. The warriors gathered silently around Juh.

"These are the same soldiers pursuing our people."

"Let's go back and kill them!" one warrior said. A few others agreed hesitantly.

The last warrior ran in from the direction of the trail. He had the duty to run interference with any pursuing soldiers or to spy on them and discover their next move while the other warriors escaped. "The soldiers are regrouping deep in the trees. I think they're setting up a defensive camp."

Juh nodded. "They're probably afraid we'll attack after dark."

Another warrior shook his fist. "They think we're stupid! Only a fool would attack in the trees at night."

"Better for us they stay put, cowering in fear," Juh said. "The tracks showed two other soldiers are ahead of us by nearly half a day. Our people need us. At least most of the soldiers are behind us now." He pointed out a warrior to take the point position.

"Let's move fast. We'll follow the next ridgeline to the east, then we'll travel south until the high moon, then we'll rest until sunrise and continue down to the Gila River. We'll try to meet our people before they cross."

Juh scanned his warriors' faces. "Where's Brown Hair?" No one answered. Juh nodded and pointed out two warriors. "Return for him after the soldiers are gone. If he's dead, sing the death song, and bury him where no *White-Eyes* will ever find his body."

The two warriors just turned away and then froze at the familiar, brief call of a coyote. A dark figure walked toward the group, almost appearing like a spirit out of the shadows. Brown Hair stepped forward, carrying a thick mop of black hair in his left hand.

"One less enemy to fight," he said triumphantly, holding up the shaggy scalp.

"It stinks," one of the warriors said, taking a step back.

"That's because the *White-Eyes* never bathe," Brown Hair returned. "This one will journey forever in the next life without his hair or his eyesight."

Brown Hair tossed the filthy mess aside and looked defiantly at Juh, his chin held high. Juh stepped forward and faced him from arm's length.

"We've had this conversation many times now. The Apache do not take scalps," Juh said. Brown Hair remained silent, and Juh turned his head to address all the warriors. "I gave my promise to my father and to my wife, Ishton, that I would never take scalps. Nor will I ever allow any man who follows me to take them."

"Are you telling me to leave?"

Juh shook his head. "You're a skilled fighter, Brown Hair, and I need you. Our people need you." Juh addressed the group again. "Those who choose to follow me willingly refuse to take scalps." To Brown Hair, he said, "When we see to the safety of our people, you may follow another leader." Juh addressed the group again.

"Any man who chooses to follow Brown Hair has my respect. I think he'll make an excellent leader." He reached out, gripped Brown Hair's shoulder, and smiled. The young man inclined his head slightly as he grasped Juh's shoulder in return.

Juh nodded and followed the point man into the darkness. Brown Hair walked beside him.

"There are more men with the soldiers," Brown Hair said. "They brought hill-diggers along to fight. The ones who destroy the earth digging for the yellow rock that holds so much value to the *White-Eyes*. I only saw White men. There were no Black soldiers with them."

Juh nodded. Regardless of his feelings about the young man's scalping, he knew very few warriors could have attacked the soldiers in their own camp and lived to tell about it. Still,

Brown Hair's news was both good and bad. Juh felt relieved knowing exactly how many of the enemy he might have to fight. Yet, he and his men were now outnumbered almost two to one. He thought there would be more soldiers. Maybe the others had gone back to the fort for reinforcements or for more supplies. He didn't like not knowing where the Black soldiers were.

The warriors jogged into the darkness. Late the next day, they descended the steep southern edge of the Mogollon Range into the rugged foothills that separated the mountain range from the hot desert flats to the south. Juh and Brown Hair paused atop one hill and gazed down into the winding valley that caressed the river, guiding it gently to the west.

"This is bad," Juh said as they studied the distant army encampment.

"Looks like two, maybe three soldiers. A small patrol."

"This commander knows where our people are headed. He must have sent soldiers down the west side of the mountains to patrol the river before we ran into them yesterday."

Brown Hair nodded. "If our people have not crossed yet, they may be trapped. This won't be the only patrol. The survivors will have to go far to the west to avoid being seen."

"Agreed." Juh led the warriors through the foothills to the west, paralleling the winding river. They spotted four more two-man camps. Juh knew the survivors had a few older warriors among them. He'd recognized their moccasin tracks along the trail. The old warriors could easily have quietly disposed of a single camp so the rest of the people could cross the river and head south. If they did, the soldiers would soon be missed, and the army would then converge on the fleeing Apache survivors.

Juh looked toward the Big Burro Mountains to the south. If his people could find a way across the river undetected, they'd try to keep to the high ground. If successful, they'd be safe for a while. He made his decision quickly.

"Brown Hair, take six men and continue over the mountains to the west. Find the soldiers. Distract them, make them follow you. Lead them away from our people."

The young man nodded. "What will you do?"

"I'll take the rest of the men and circle around to the east of the mountains." He indicated the Big Burro Mountains in the Apache way, pointing with his nose. "We'll try to meet the survivors at the southern tip before they head south across the plains to the Animas Mountains."

Juh and Brown Hair stood at the same time and turned. The point man stood a second later, and Juh heard him start to speak. Suddenly, the warrior and Brown Hair lurched forward and fell to the ground, a tangled mass of blood and gore. Juh instinctively dropped to a crouch and rolled, seeking cover behind an outcrop of boulders. He watched both of his warriors tumble a short distance down the hill. The boom of the long-distance army rifle exploded in from the west.

After a moment, another shot chipped a piece of rock from the boulder and Juh knew the hidden army sniper was trying to scare him into motion. Several of his warriors crept into his view down the hill, but Juh motioned them back and signed to them the same instructions he'd given Brown Hair. With satisfaction, he watched his warriors hurry away without hesitation. Sadness touched his heart as he gazed downhill at the two bloody warriors. He'd underestimated his enemy and a single shot had killed two of his best fighters.

Juh was trapped—pinned down by an army sniper with a higher vantage point. He settled back against the boulder, wondering if darkness or the soldiers would arrive first.

CHAPTER 34

A T PRIVATE NANCE'S SUGGESTION, CRAWFORD ordered his men to keep to the ridge lines. With few exceptions, the ridges were barren of trees, making an ambush nearly impossible. The plan worked. He'd only lost one more man, a private named Thaddeus Irving, to the enemy under the most improbable circumstance. If someone had told Crawford about the attack, he wouldn't have believed it. He still couldn't believe an Apache a hundred yards distant could shoot an arrow with enough force to completely pierce a man's chest and exit his back.

Fortunately, Private Irving didn't have to suffer the same long and painful death from poison as Shelton. He died instantly as the arrow severed critical organs within his body. The soldiers caught the attacking warrior in a hail of bullets, but the detail Crawford detached to retrieve the weapons and ammunition of the dead warrior found only smeared blood.

"Apache devils are like ghosts," Nance said as he flopped down on the ground beside Crawford. "Got up there and dragged their dead away."

"Doesn't surprise me," Crawford said, nodding. Many times, his Company B engaged Apache warriors in battle, but the Indians never left their wounded or dead behind.

Around him, four men napped in awkward positions among the scattering of boulders that formed a natural fortification on the hilltop. Four others stood guard in the late evening. Crawford noted the sparse ground cover with satisfaction.

"We ought to be safe here for the night."

Nance agreed. "Devils can't get within a hundred yards without being seen. Nothin' for them to hide behind. And the moon will be bright tonight. They won't try to sneak up until early in the morning."

Crawford understood the private's message. He called in two of the guards and told them to get four hours sleep. Then he and Nance climbed up onto their boulders and peeked over the top, rifles ready. They saw no movement on the gentle, downhill slope before them.

Crawford faced south. The last ridge between them and the Piños Altos mining camp lay two miles distant and about a thousand feet lower. Eight miles farther sat Fort Bayard and home and safety. It was eight long miles through dense tree-covered slopes offering many opportunities for the Apache war party to pick off more of his soldiers.

Private Nance seemed to sense his concern. "Ain't gonna be no picnic, Sarge. We'll lose some more men."

Crawford nodded. Traveling along the ridge line kept most of his men alive, but more than tripled the length of their return trip. So far, they'd endured two nights and two days afoot on a trail that would ordinarily be a fourteen-hour horse ride. They had another long night and day to come. They'd stretched their water and rations thin. No one ate since yesterday and each man drank only a sip of water that morning. Burning heat and the thin air sapped the strength of even the strongest soldiers. The dark blue color of their uniforms soaked in the heat and the heavy wool material held it in.

Looking at Nance, Crawford understood the desperation of their situation. The man's dark face showed heat blisters, and his lips were dried and cracked. Instinctively, Crawford licked his own cracked lips with a dry tongue.

"You know, Sarge. A single runner could get through to the fort and bring back reinforcements by sunup."

Crawford shook his head. "Them Apache know where we're tryin' to get to. If I was them, I'd be sitting right down yonder, waitin'." He nodded down the hill. "You wouldn't get a mile."

"If I went thataway, maybe. But I figure to backtrack a ways." He thumbed over his shoulder. "Then I'll cut downhill and hightail it around that ridge. Ain't but ten miles, tops. I'll be at the fort in three hours. Be back up here before y'all even get to sleep."

"I doubt if anybody'll get any sleep after the sun goes down." Crawford considered the plan, realizing quickly they didn't have much choice. "Take all the water you need. I don't want you fainting from thirst."

"And I'll be needin' someone's boots. I plumb wore a hole in my left boot. And the right one, well...." Nance looked down. The sole of his right boot was mostly torn away from the upper leather.

"Okay," Crawford said. "If you aren't back by sunrise, we'll have to take our chances down in the trees with those Indians. We won't survive up here another day without water."

The contents of all nine canteens added up to only two mouthfuls of water. Nance drank it all, changed boots, and departed without farewell. After the private vanished into the darkness, Crawford crouched behind a boulder with his men and waited. He gained little comfort from the knowledge that the Apache didn't like to travel or make war at night. He'd learned the hard way the Indians were as effective at night as during the day, though now he suspected the warriors slept at night while his men jumped at shadows and night sounds.

He and his men were fairly safe in the boulders, but if Private Nance didn't return, they couldn't wait for a nonexistent rescue. Besides, Crawford figured their chances in the trees were better in daylight. At least they might have an opportunity to shoot back. Army training seemed woefully inadequate for this kind of hit-and-run, mountain warfare against an invisible enemy.

Half an hour after Nance left, a single gunshot echoed through the night air.

CHAPTER 35

JUH WAITED UNTIL DARKNESS GAVE him the freedom to move unseen. No soldiers raced to his hill. The sniper had probably been satisfied about killing two warriors with a single bullet. He left Juh to sweat. Most likely, the shooter was off somewhere eating or bragging on his shooting skills to his fellow soldiers.

A dozen paces down the hill, Juh knelt beside the tangled bodies of his warriors. His first duty was to bury them so their bodies could never be found. He sat for a moment, reflecting on the lives of his men. Brown Hair had no living kin. His hatred for the *White-Eyes* burned so intense, he knew no other purpose than to hunt and kill them. He had never married.

The other warrior left behind four children from his two wives. Juh found himself wondering if the man's family had been sent to the eternal resting place by the soldiers, or if they still lived among the survivors of the massacre. With nearly three-fourths of his village murdered, Juh accepted the sad truth that the warrior had most likely gone to join his family.

Juh was so involved with his own thoughts he didn't realize Brown Hair was moving until the young man touched his shoulder. Juh nearly fell backward in his surprise.

Brown Hair explained. "I felt that bullet pass just under my arm, so I had to play dead or that shooter would've killed me before I got to cover."

Juh and Brown Hair buried the warrior and sang the death song for him and his family.

"As is our custom, their names will never again be spoken by the Apache," Juh said.

They reviewed the plans Juh had communicated with the other warriors and went their separate ways. As a young man, Juh remembered the thrill and freedom of running day and night. During training or hunting forays, he loved the adventure of traveling dozens of miles in a single day or night and returning to camp with venison or supplies. The runs always made him feel alive, as though the life of the land flowed through his veins.

He acknowledged that age had softened him somewhat and slowed him so that he could no longer compete with the young warriors. Accepting the role of leader left him with few opportunities to hunt or forage with the younger men. Tonight he felt the life return to his body. He followed the tracks of his warriors in the moonlight and caught up with them as the eastern sky began to brighten outside a horse ranch in the lower foothills of the Big Burro range.

Juh approached the ranch from the east and called out to his band in the predawn darkness, using well-practiced animal calls. Every warrior had his own unique call, and all warriors recognized the calls of every other warrior.

With all his men gathered around him, Juh complimented a warrior with gray hair who had the reputation of stalking his enemy with the cunning of the wolf. Gray Wolf had assumed leadership in Juh's absence.

"This is exactly what I would have done."

Gray Wolf accepted the compliment with a nod. A few years Juh's senior, he walked with a noticeable limp that never seemed to affect his ability to run or fight.

"We can take some of their horses," Gray Wolf said. "And maybe a few extra animals for food. Two of the warriors can shoot at the house, keep the *White-Eyes* inside until we escape."

Juh looked around at his men. They all squatted close

enough so he could see the emotions on their faces. He thought he could read anticipation in their expressions. They'd be able to fill their bellies with tasty horse meat instead of sparingly eating tiny bits of venison and corn meal from their ration bags. But in more than one set of eyes, Juh saw a hunger for revenge. He felt it himself and knew his next decision would satisfy that need and help his people at the same time.

"No," he said simply. "We won't cower around and steal like dogs." Juh pointed out two warriors. "Set fire to the house. Drive those inside out the front. Then we'll do the same to them as their soldiers did to our people."

Gray Wolf protested hesitantly. "But what is to be gained by killing women and children? That'll only set the soldiers on our trail again."

"Exactly," Juh said, nodding. "The soldiers are already pursuing our people who survived the massacre. If we only steal horses, few will take notice. But if we kill everyone here, the army will know we're a war party. They'll have to deploy more soldiers to protect the other settlers and ranchers in this area."

Gray Wolf nodded in understanding and Juh continued. "The more soldiers protecting ranches or hunting after us, the fewer there will be to chase our people." He looked at each of his men. "Between our efforts and Brown Hair's, maybe we can still save the last of the Nednhi Apache."

"I understand," Gray Wolf said.

The unpleasant task took only a few minutes after two warriors set fire to the roof and the south wall. The men of the ranch ran straight toward the water trough, while the women shepherded their small children into a group in front of the house. They were quickly surrounded by Juh's warriors.

Juh studied two boys that stood with one of the two Mexican families. For a moment, Juh thought about his own sons, Daklegon and Delzhinne, both about the same age as these boys last time he'd seen them. He picked out one of the young men and motioned him forward. Juh spoke again, and a warrior brought an unsaddled horse from the corral and gestured for the boy to ride away to the east.

The boy hesitated, and the warrior smacked him lightly on the side of the head with the stock of his rifle. Stunned, the young man fell to his knees and the Indian dumped him across the horse's back, then slapped the horse on the rump. The boy gripped the mane and struggled into a riding position on the racing animal.

When the horse passed through the front gate of the ranch, Juh turned his attention back to his captives. He'd wanted a White family to kill, but the Mexicans would serve his purpose just the same. They hated the Apache just as much as the whites and Juh knew they took every opportunity to kill Indians. Besides, it was well known that the Mexicans had started the practice of scalping by putting a bounty on Apache hair.

Juh studied his prisoners and decided not to let them suffer by wondering what would happen to them. There was no need to torture them or for them to watch their loved ones die. He would not make them beg for mercy for the children. These people weren't his enemy. They were casualties of war. He decided to grant them a quick death. He spoke briefly in Spanish.

"You die today so that my people may live."

Several minutes later, as his warriors cooked a horse for food, Juh still stood over the bodies of the ranchers. In his heart, he hated killing people who were neither warriors nor soldiers, but he had to follow the same rules as the soldiers who declared war against not only his warriors, but against his entire race. He recalled his vision of the extermination of his tribe and of the orderly row of burial mounds at his destroyed camp. Only with that memory could he justify what he'd just done.

For a moment, Juh closed his eyes and replayed the scene in his memory. He had expected to feel some sort of relief. He'd hoped revenge would wipe away at least some of the pain of what had happened to his own village. Unfortunately, the knot in his gut only grew. He'd killed many times before, but only in battle.

Never like this. He couldn't bring himself to feel the pleasure he knew the soldiers felt as they annihilated the Apache village.

After long moments of consideration, Juh joined his warriors and sat silently. He stared into the fire even after one of the others handed him a stick holding a huge chunk of well-cooked horsemeat. He met the stares of all his warriors.

"Revenge is never as satisfying as we imagine it might be." He paused. "These are the rules of war given to us by the soldiers. They kill our children, so we will kill theirs."

The warriors ate in silence, and Juh was pleased none of them asked for the victory celebration. For a moment, Juh wished he had Brown Hair's lack of compassion. That young warrior could have done this dreadful deed without any feeling of guilt at all. No doubt, he would have enjoyed it too.

Juh ate his fill of meat and vegetables scavenged from a small cellar beside the burning house. He and the warriors drank water from huge barrels beside the barn until they could hold no more, and then they refilled their water skins for the long ride.

Without a glance back, Juh led his warriors on stolen, unsaddled horses straight west toward the near mountain peaks. They pushed their animals hard and reached the top of the range two hours later. Some distance south, they found a hidden cave known to all the warriors.

In many caves and crevasses throughout the mountains of southern New Mexico, the Apache cached food and supplies for times when soldiers pursued the tribe. Often, the elderly or injured or new mothers of tiny babies remained at these secret places under the protection of young warriors, while the rest of the tribe continued south to the stronghold.

Juh knew his survivors would find their way to this particular cave since it was on the trail they'd normally take to Mexico, but only if they'd been able to sneak across the river without being detected. They wouldn't if they had been forced to detour to the west by the soldiers hunting them.

When the warriors arrived at the cave, Juh found the supplies intact. Now he faced a difficult decision. If they stayed and waited for the survivors, they risked confrontation from soldiers possibly dispatched to investigate the raid on the ranch. The soldiers would easily be able to track them when the sun rose. Yet, he knew the speed his people could make over desert mountain terrain. They should already be here.

Juh figured Brown Hair and his warriors would have reached the other side of the Mogollon Mountains, harassing the soldiers and distracting them from their pursuit. If Brown Hair was successful, the survivors could continue to the next storage place of supplies and ammunition far to the south. The Apache referred to the landmark in the Animas Mountains as Two Pointed Rocks Rising Above A Flat Boulder. The supplies were carefully concealed beneath the namesake flat boulder that formed the base for two rock spires towering above the ground.

Juh hated to travel away from his people. What if he made another mistake of judgment? How many more would die?

On the other hand, he couldn't split up his men and run them all over the desert looking for tracks. The best thing he could do was trust his own medicine, as his people did. He had to make a decision based only on what he knew to be true, not on guesses. He had to believe the survivors would do what they'd been taught all through the years. He had to trust Brown Hair to do what he'd trained for.

Juh turned to his men and announced his decision.

"We'll go south."

CHAPTER 36

FIRST SERGEANT LAFAYETTE CRAWFORD TOOK his four-hour sleep shift sitting propped against a smooth-sided boulder with the brim of his cap pulled low over his eyes. Just on the verge of waking, Crawford's subconscious mind became aware of the increasing heat of the morning. When he heard the whisper in his ear, he opened his eyes and tried to mentally catalog all the sounds around him before moving. Total silence greeted him, except for Private Hendricks' hushed voice. The man hesitated before speaking again. He seemed to know Crawford was awake, perhaps by the slow deep breath he took.

"Don't make no sounds, sir. I found me one. Seen a bush move out yonder, about a hundred yards away."

Crawford stayed still. "Wind?"

"No, sir. I don't mean wavin' in the wind," the private said. "I mean really movin'. Like it was tied to somebody's back and crawlin' real slow toward us, sir."

"Quit callin' me *sir*. I'm not an officer," Crawford said, angling his head to the left toward the private. He pushed his cap back so he could see the man. "And quit yappin' about the bush and shoot it."

From two feet away, the explosion of the Springfield rifle rang like a dynamite blast in Crawford's ear. He heard a distant scream of pain, heard Hendricks' victory shout through the ringing that echoed inside his skull.

"I got 'im!"

The private chambered another round and took aim again. Crawford swiveled on his butt and got to his knees. He stuck his head over his boulder and watched as the warrior rose from the ground and stumbled downhill, half bent over at the waist. The man ripped the bush from his back just before Hendricks' second shot propelled him into a tree. He bounced off, leaving a red patch of blood on the bark, then rolled a few more yards down the slope.

Both men dropped behind the boulder and Hendricks was grinning from ear to ear.

"Nice shooting, Private." Crawford noticed the rest of the men had jumped to battle readiness at the sound of the first shot. "All right, listen up," he said. "If Private Nance had reached the fort, he'd be back by now. So don't be expectin' reinforcements." He paused and looked each of his men in the eye. They all returned his gaze expectantly.

"We're gonna have to make a run for it." Crawford let his words soak in. "Leave all your equipage behind, 'cause we got ten full miles to run. Eat any food you have left and drink up the rest of your water. Then leave your sacks, canteen, anything else that'll weigh you down. Take only weapons and ammo. Any questions?"

Hendricks spoke up. "We ain't got no water, sir." Crawford cocked his head at the private. "I mean, *Sarge*. Silas drank it all. And he took my shoes."

Crawford looked down at the private's bare feet and shot him a look that asked why he didn't wear regulation stockings on his feet.

"So what do you want me to do? Carry you?"

"Gee, Sarge, would you?"

Private Willis chimed in. "How 'bout if I give 'im *my* shoes, Sarge? Then you can carry me instead."

The men shared a laugh, and Crawford chuckled with them for a moment. They needed a brief respite from the tension of their situation. It occurred to him that it might be the last laugh some of them would ever have if he didn't find a way to get them all back to the fort alive.

"All right, let's get serious." The men sobered quickly. "We leave in five minutes. Two groups of five on the double all the way back to the fort. No stoppin' and no restin'. First group runs a hundred yards, then stops and covers the trail to the sides and to our back. Second group runs a hundred yards past the first, total of two hundred a stretch, then drops and covers. We'll run-and-cover all the way. The runners shoot anything that sticks its head up in their path. Clear?"

Crawford knew there wouldn't be any questions. They'd trained for ambush evasion on the run many times. Reloading single-shot Springfields on the run was a chore, but they'd trained for that too.

Crawford pointed out Private Hendricks and four others to form the first group. All the soldiers checked their carbines and Remington handguns. They tossed everything but weapons and ammunition in a pile, and then looked at Crawford. He nodded.

"First group, go!"

Hendricks and his men double-timed down the hill at a controlled pace designed to conserve energy while Crawford's men took aim downhill beyond the running men, searching for an enemy. About a hundred yards down, the first group dropped to the ground to provide cover fire. Immediately, Crawford and his men jogged downhill and passed the first group.

Company B covered the first two miles downhill with little problem, and Crawford's group was the first to head up the next hill. The hill was steep, and by the time he'd covered his two hundred yards, Crawford was winded. When he flopped down on his belly to cover out to the side, he realized the flaw in his plan. Chest heaving for air in the high altitude, there was no way he or his men could accurately aim at a target more than a couple dozen yards away. He heard the other group coming up alongside and was just about to shout instructions for fifty-yard intervals instead of one hundred, when the attack came.

Crawford heard the dull thud of an arrow striking home, accompanied by a scream. He heard one of his group tumble to the ground behind him. If his plan of escape was to work, the rest of the runners had to keep moving. He hollered out the order to leave the wounded for the cover team and then tried to make sense of the shouts around him.

"Where'd that arrow come from?"

"Over here, Sarge." The shout came from behind him on the downhill side, amidst gunfire.

"Keep moving and watch your ammo!" Crawford warned. They'd run out of bullets real quick on a ten-mile retreat if they started shooting carelessly. "Everyone maintain your field of fire!"

The private a few yards to his right didn't listen. He got up on his knees, searching for the shooter. Crawford started to order him back down and saw a distant movement in his side vision, slightly uphill, maybe eighty yards out.

The first sergeant swung around and snapped off a quick shot without aiming. His bullet tore bark from the tree the Apache warrior crouched beside, but he saw a puff of smoke just before he heard the familiar crack of the distant Winchester. The private beside him grunted as his body was slammed to the ground. Crawford reloaded and fired again but missed the well-concealed Indian. Between the gunshots, he heard the call from above to advance.

"Second group, go! Grab the wounded."

Two privates grabbed the man with the arrow stuck in his thigh and Crawford lifted the injured private next to him over his shoulder. The group labored up the steep hill, grunting and gasping the entire way. The first group had two warriors pinned down as Crawford crested the hill. His heart thumped so loudly in his head, he didn't hear the thunder of hooves until the cavalry was almost upon him.

Company E, also of the Ninth Cavalry, he recognized with pride, was led by Sergeant Steven Wilcox and Private Nance. As if by some prearranged command, half the mounted troops charged downhill at the retreating warriors, while the rest dismounted to provide cover for Company B.

A half hour later, Crawford greeted Wilcox with a firm handshake. It seemed like weeks since he'd seen his friend, but in fact it had only been a few days. Wilcox and his detachment from Fort Cummings had escorted Senator Bennington's stage from El Paso to Deming where Crawford's detail met the stage. Wilcox's detachment had the duty to escort the next coach to Fort Bayard. Still, the first sergeant was never one to relax his military bearing in front of his men.

"Sure am glad to see you, Sergeant Wilcox."

"How can I help, First Sergeant?" Wilcox stood almost a head shorter than Crawford. A wide smile graced the lower half of his face, balanced against dark eyes and a wide nose, giving him a serious but friendly look.

"I'd be obliged if you could retrieve my best friend's body down by the river. And Private Andrews. Private Nance can show you the way."

"You mean Levi Shelton?" Wilcox said. Crawford nodded. "I'm sorry. He was a good man."

"The best. Private Irving is buried back along the ridge up yonder too."

"We'll bring them all home, First Sergeant."

The field medic cut open the wounded private's leg to get the barbed arrow shaft out and to make sure no poison was present. The man shot next to Crawford died a few minutes after Company E arrived.

Crawford's troops made good use of the extra water and rations, then doubled up on the spare horses and rode back to the fort. After giving his report to the major, Crawford requested and received permission for his men to have a full day of leave. As he expected, after baths, shaves, and fresh uniforms, most of the men opted to spend half a month's wage for whiskey and recreation with the saloon girls at Central City. He declined to go with them.

Normally, the men would have made a great show of heading west toward Silver City before turning south to the off-limits town of Central City. Today, Crawford had a feeling the major pretended not to notice the subdued soldiers riding out directly toward the forbidden town of gambling and ill repute.

Crawford watched the solemn procession of soldiers ride south. He knew it wasn't so much the difficulty of the mission or their near-death experience that weighed heavy on them, as much as the betrayal and ambush ordered by an army officer. He suspected the real reason the major ignored the soldiers' direction was that in a day or two, they'd be reassigned under a new officer with orders to pursue and arrest Captain Taylor and his men. In the meantime, morale had to be maintained even if strict discipline was relaxed.

At noon on the second day following Crawford's rescue and return to the fort, Sergeant Wilcox and his men rode in. Crawford stood in the center of the parade ground and watched Company E proceed straight toward the hospital where the three wrapped bodies would be stored until burial. He was so engrossed in the emotion of the moment, of seeing his friend alive again in his mind's eye even as his body passed by, he didn't notice Major Clark had walked up beside him until the man spoke.

"My condolences to you, First Sergeant."

Crawford snapped to attention by habit then relaxed when the major said, "Stand at ease." The officer took a deep breath as if pondering something, then added, "Walk with me to my office. I've got orders for you."

They covered almost the entire distance before the major spoke again.

"All the Ninth Cavalry officers are still in the field, so I don't have anyone else to track down Captain Taylor."

"So that's it, sir? He gets away with it?" Crawford sighed and looked back toward the hospital.

"Not exactly," Major Clark said. He stopped, and Crawford paused beside him several steps from the covered porch of the headquarters building. The major gave him a serious look. "I'm ordering you to find and arrest him."

"Sir?"

The major waved aside Crawford's surprised look. "He ordered his men to open fire on your company, and he ordered the murder of innocent women and children. He's a war criminal, First Sergeant. You'll have the eight able-bodied men you returned with, plus the eleven you sent back earlier with the casualties. This morning, I received a telegram from Colonel Hatch. He endorses my request to reassign Company E under your command." Major Clark paused again.

"By the way, the colonel tells me that wily rascal, Chief Juh, somehow escaped capture down by the Rio Grande. We think he's responsible for the massacre over at the Jimenez Ranch two days ago. So now we've got a band of mad Indians out there murdering civilized folk in revenge for Captain Taylor's massacre."

"Bringing the captain in isn't going to stop the raids now, sir."

"I'm aware of that. The colonel's already ordered two companies from Fort Cummings to ride up here, and I've recalled one of my companies from the field to help track down Chief Juh. You also have standing orders to round up and arrest the chief and his warriors and any other armed Apaches you come across. If they don't surrender, kill them. We can't have them raiding and terrorizing innocent folks."

Major Clark led Crawford into his office and handed him his orders. Crawford read his instructions quickly, noting that while Taylor was wanted for breaking several military regulations and for killing four soldiers and an officer, the document held no mention of the dozens of unarmed Apache he'd murdered.

"Captain Taylor is a disgrace to the United States Army, First Sergeant," Major Clark said formally. "You are authorized to use whatever means you believe are necessary to bring him back for trial." The major paused. "You're dismissed, First Sergeant."

Crawford snapped to attention. "Sir, he's not likely to respect the authority of a Black soldier to arrest him."

Major Clark looked up from the mound of other paperwork

he'd already turned his attention to. He gave Crawford a wry smile that Crawford could only interpret as devious.

"I supposed you'll have to find a way to convince him otherwise, First Sergeant."

CHAPTER 37

J ASON PEARES HAD SUFFERED THROUGH four days of blistering heat with not enough food or water or rest, and now
he had no idea where he was. As near as he could tell, he
was somewhere near the Arizona border. He'd given up caring
three days ago, after the group finally crossed the Gila River and
headed south in the low flats between mountain ranges.

Soon after crossing the river, his feet got so numb and cal-
lused he stopped feeling the burning heat through his moccasins. Fortunately, he'd been able to retrieve them during one of
the nighttime stops when he and the boy caught up with the
main group. His boots were a distant memory, torn up hiking
over the Mogollon Mountains. His head had been hurting every
day, a constant throbbing reminder of the army sharpshooter's
ricochet.

Jason stopped to look around, squinting severely. Daklugie,
also walking with his head down to avoid the glare of the bright
sun, bumped into him and fell back on his rump. Jason wavered
for a moment, dizzy from the heat, but steadied himself just
before he thought he'd fall over too. He shook both the canteens
hanging from his shoulder straps. One was empty, the other
half-full of precious liquid. Daklugie's water skin looked almost
flat.

When Jason offered the boy a sip from his canteen, Daklugie
simply shook his head, clawed his way back to his feet, and kept
walking. The boy pulled off the red bandanna Jason had re-

turned to him and draped his long hair over his face—probably in an attempt to shield his eyes against the sun's intense glare.

Jason watched him for a moment, then looked beyond to the next closest Apache. About a quarter-mile distant, that man or woman was only a vague shadow distorted by the heat waves shimmering off the barren land. He'd seen some harsh landscapes during his outlaw years on the run, but he'd never been anywhere as desolate as where he now stood.

The surface of the ground resembled a giant puzzle, like the ground tried to soak up a thunderstorm one moment and got heat-blasted by the sun the next. Cracks ran every which way across the topsoil, leaving chips of dirt with the edges turned up. They crunched as Jason walked over them.

For long stretches of time, Jason saw not a single blade of wild grass, not even a dried and burnt cactus. The arroyos and dry gulches he crossed were mere memories of creeks. When he did see a bush or a tuft of grass, it was usually dried and charred almost black.

The land even *smelled* dead. Dust and dirt was all he could smell. Missing was the ever-present hint of sage and other aromatic plants he'd come to associate with the southwestern desert. In fact, there was no breeze tickling through the branches of dead native plants. There were no birds singing and no insects buzzing or chirping. There was only the continual crunch of his moccasins on the burned and cracked dirt.

It was the ideal terrain to get lost in though, because the godforsaken land was absolutely the last place experienced soldiers would think of looking. If they ever wised up and considered the impossible, they'd find Jason and the survivors out in the open and slaughter them.

He looked around the shimmering landscape. The survivors had chosen a southern path through the center of a valley many miles wide. As he wavered on his feet, Jason tried to focus on mountain peaks rising above the horizon maybe twenty miles to the east and another set that rose an equal distance to the west. After a while, the path of the Apaches turned toward the southeast, but Jason could see nothing in the distance to indicate why they chose that direction. He simply trusted they knew where they were going and followed them.

Over the past few days, Jason had learned a tremendous respect for these desert people. They were incredibly resilient. He had always thought of himself as the ultimate survivor, never giving in to pain or despair no matter what the circumstances, but these people were far more skilled and resourceful than he had imagined.

Five days ago, he and Daklugie caught up to the main group of Apache as they stopped to rest for a few hours. The survivors were no longer weaponless, half-naked, and barefoot as they'd been when he'd first met them. He found all the boys had fashioned bows or lances, and some of the Apache had made moccasins from material salvaged from the soldiers' supplies. Others made sandals from the tough leaves of the agave plant. They ate on the move, and most of the Apache carried a water skin made from the stomach or intestines of small animals.

Jason quickly discovered he wasn't traveling with a bunch of helpless women and children. He wasn't leading fearful survivors to safety. They knew exactly where they were going, and they knew how to survive on the land. His only contribution would come if Captain Taylor and his men caught up with them. It occurred to him that these people had been outrunning soldiers for years. Except for Daklugie, *Ancient One*, and the others he saved from the first four soldiers, the rest of the tribe would have survived with or without his help.

Jason and the band of Apache came down out of the Mogollon Mountains intent on crossing the Gila River and heading straight south, back up into the Big Burro range. Soldiers from several army encampments patrolled along the river, so the band turned west for a while to keep their location a secret from the searching soldiers. Had they crossed into the Big Burro Mountains at night, the tracks of such a large number of people would certainly have been discovered the next day. Once the mounted soldiers knew where they were, the band wouldn't have been able to elude them for long, even up in the mountains.

The fact that the soldiers had set a picket line so far south in the path of the Apache disturbed Jason. Clearly, the army knew precisely where the band would try to cross the river. That meant the soldiers also knew where the Indians were headed and would probably have soldiers waiting there. Jason assumed the Apache realized this truth as well, and he wondered how they would avoid that reception. All he could do was trust them, even if he couldn't communicate with them. If the time came and they needed his help, he'd help. He'd already made his choice six days ago. Now he'd just have to live with the consequences.

The woman Jason came to regard as *Leader* made the decision to avoid crossing the river. They headed west for another whole day and night then crossed and headed south. While hiking in the foothills along the river, the survivors foraged continuously. The children plucked bugs and geckos from beneath rocks and brush. Adults stopped briefly to dig up prickly plants and cut off their bulb-like root. Then they replaced the bush exactly how they found it so no one would notice what they'd done.

Everyone accumulated edible plants and tiny critters in sacks made from shirts or skins. While Jason had no idea where they were going at the time, he realized now, six days later, the Apache had been preparing to head into the most desolate patch of land in the region. Fortunately, he had followed their example of foraging, and Daklugie seemed happy to carry his food sacks along with his own.

Over the days, Jason learned that bringing up the rear of the group was the most honorable and dangerous duty. He was the most experienced at handling firearms and the army would likely attack from the rear, so *Leader* assigned him through hand gestures to trail the survivors. Daklugie put up a brave and animated argument with his mother and ultimately prevailed, taking his place at Jason's side.

Jason wondered if Apache children had some kind of coming-of-age duty when they were old enough to assist or train with warriors. Traveling with Jason seemed to be Daklugie's honored duty, and he poured all of his energy into the task. Most days, however, they got the least amount of rest since they reached the gathering only after the slowest of the travelers.

Jason remembered the first time he caught up with the group. He'd counted twenty-eight survivors. Daklugie ran up to his mother, pointing at Jason and shouting a distorted version of his name.

Jay-sone Peer!

Ishton—*Leader's* name, Jason now knew thanks to a brief introduction by Daklugie—recognized his name, as did *Ancient One* and several of the elders. Some of the Apache nodded at him, but others just stared. They gave him food, far more than his fair share, like he was some kind of hero, and soon he had to pretend he was full just so others could eat. In years past, usually when someone recognized his name, they either cowered in fear or tried to kill him, like he was still an outlaw. Here, he enjoyed the feeling of respect these people bestowed on him.

Now as he plodded almost aimlessly across the scorched earth, almost faint with hunger and thirst, he tried hard to remember why he'd become involved with these people and how he came to be walking across a land even Crawford's God seemed to have forgotten about.

Late in the day, he passed the first body. An elder man carrying a small sack of supplies had fallen face down on the ground. Jason entertained the brief thought of stopping by the old man, but his feet wouldn't stop moving. He doubted he had enough strength to kneel down and stand up again. Just ahead of him, Daklugie spoke a single word without stopping.

Late in the evening, he found the entire Apache tribe standing beside Grady and the army mount. He immediately sensed this wasn't a rest stop and pushed his way through the crowd to see what the commotion was. Ishton knelt beside *Ancient One* and they spoke quietly. The young pregnant girl and an elder woman who had been riding on the army horse with *Ancient One* stood nearby. Jason saw the horse raise its head and try to take a step forward. Instead, it only shuddered and pawed the ground.

Other survivors had untied the stretcher from the army horse and now a woman attended to the boy's chest wound. Four days earlier, someone had built a canopy of shrubbery branches and leaves to protect him from the sun. Now the canopy was dried-up, crisp and brown, though it still provided some shade for the boy. He still breathed.

The army horse finally sat down on its haunches. Then its forelegs gave out, and it collapsed on its side. For a moment, Jason thought about easing the animal's pain, but he knew he couldn't spare a single bullet. If Captain Taylor and his men caught up with them, every shot would be needed.

In almost slow motion, two boys placed the travois behind Grady and tied it to the saddle. Jason wanted to say something to his horse, walk over and give the animal a friendly pat, just to let it know he cared. But he couldn't find strength to do more than think about it. Grady accepted the load and trudged forward, head hung low.

Ishton and an elder man grabbed *Ancient One* under her arms and helped her to her feet. Together they struggled a few steps before the elder woman's legs gave out. She sat on her knees and uttered some words. Ishton knelt silently beside her for a long time, then she stood and touched *Ancient One* on the shoulder. Ishton spoke a single word and turned away. One by one, the Apache people touched the old woman on the shoulder and uttered the same Apache word, then resumed their trek across the sun-scorched land.

Jason realized the people were saying goodbye.

CHAPTER 38

D AKLUGIE GAVE HIS SILENT FAREWELL, and finally Jason stood alone with the elder. He knelt beside her. She looked at him through narrow slits under her heavy eyebrows. She said something he couldn't understand, then nodded once and leaned over on the hot earth. She placed her arms under her head as if curling up to take a nap. He watched her for a moment, knowing her long life was coming to an end.

As he watched her, he couldn't tell if her eyes were still open or not. He wondered how it would feel to reach the end of such a long life and sort through all the memories and all the changes in the Apache way of life she'd seen. He was curious how old she truly was as he laid his palm against her forearm. Her skin felt dry and leathery and hung from her bones like an old and well-worn cloth. He heard her speaking softly in the singsong voice he had come to realize was unique to her alone. None of the rest of her people spoke that way.

Jason wondered how it would feel to simply lie down and die, watching his friends, what few he had, walk away. *It would be lonely and sad,* he figured. In that moment, he decided he would not leave the old woman to die alone. He'd stay with her, maybe hold her hand until she stopped breathing.

Hot air swirled around under the brim of his hat, and he closed his eyes for a moment as the dry breeze burned his eyes. Then he took a deep breath and hauled the elder into his lap, got his arms under her back and legs. Heaved his last ounce of strength and got up on one knee and a foot.

Then he fell over.

He tried a second time and managed to get to his rump but couldn't find the strength even to get to his knees. A third attempt a few minutes later was his last, he knew. He sat on his rump with the old woman lying in his arms. The heat almost made him pass out. If *Ancient One* died that instant, he had no strength to even roll her body off him. Death was standing right behind him, its hand on his shoulder, waiting. Jason felt his fear of death leave him, floating away on a breeze of acceptance.

A shadow fell over him, and he looked up at Daklugie. Beside the boy, Ishton and two others stood. They grabbed him under his armpits and hauled him to his feet. He stood shakily for a moment, holding his burden. He could hear the woman in his arms speaking softly in her language, almost singing to him. He tried to move his left foot.

Unseen hands pulled him forward, helping him bear the weight of the old woman. He squinted at the ground ahead of him. He sensed rather than saw Daklugie move behind him. The boy's small hands pressed against his lower back and shoved him forward.

Several of the Apache guided him for maybe an hour, or maybe a day. He couldn't tell how long for certain, but he remembered the hot darkness of night and the strain on his arms. The next day seemed even hotter than the one before. Eventually, the helping hands fell away. Once he heard a tumble behind him and wondered who had fallen. Maybe it was Daklugie or his mother. He dared not stop and look. If he lost his balance, he'd never regain his feet, with or without the burden of *Ancient One.*

Jason lost all awareness of the passage of time. The hours blended into a long trail of misery. He was vaguely aware of long stretches of light and sweltering heat, followed by darkness that was barely cooler than the daytime. He didn't even know if the old woman he carried still lived, though he imagined he heard her singsong whispering every now and again. He couldn't stop, not even to drink or eat or make water. Not that his body could manufacture any water to lose.

All he could do was continue to drag one foot in front of the next. He simply hoped they got somewhere safe before Captain Taylor found them.

CHAPTER 39

FIRST SERGEANT LAFAYETTE CRAWFORD PAUSED just over the same ridge where two other ambushes took place in the last few days. A sergeant of Company E, Solomon Howard, who hailed from South America, scouted the entire area for almost an hour, then gave an account of the tracks he read.

"Looks like the Sixth Cavalry unit rode off thataway in a big hurry, First Sergeant. Came back a day later and had themselves a skirmish with those Apache warriors over by them trees." The sergeant thumbed over his shoulder. "Looks like everybody's following everybody else down this here trail."

Crawford made his decision quickly. "Sergeant Wilcox."

"Yes, First Sergeant." He nudged his horse closer to Crawford's.

"Take twenty of your men and scout this trail. I'm guessing Captain Taylor's long gone, but you might run up on them, so look sharp. I'll take your other six men with Company B, and we'll follow these tracks to see where they went. Could be somebody out here knows something about where they might be headed. We might be able to get ahead of 'em or box 'em in somewheres."

Wilcox nodded and led Company E down the trail. Crawford kicked his horse into a walk and guided his company headed to the west. His thoughts drifted back over the last couple of days. He'd started this new mission with the burial of his best friend, Corporal Levi Shelton, along with seven other men of Company

B. Four of the men and their lieutenant had been killed during the first ambush by Captain Taylor's men. The fact that he and his men had to be rescued on the trail by another company still burned.

As it turned out, only four warriors had attacked them throughout the whole ordeal of their return march to the fort. They'd killed two that last morning. Private Nance chanced upon one the night before on his way back to the fort. He'd caught the warrior doing his private business, but a hastily aimed shot missed the man. The Apache ran off, and Nance gave chase briefly, but sprained his ankle real bad jumping over a log and had to practically limp the whole ten miles to Fort Bayard. The final two warriors were run down by Sergeant Wilcox's men.

Major Clark surprised Private Nance just before the company reported for the burial. Gave him his two stripes back and informed Nance he was nominating him for the army's highest decoration—the Medal of Honor. Crawford figured no one deserved it more. The major credited Nance with saving the lives of the men under Crawford's command who survived the Apache attacks. The first sergeant knew those last two warriors probably would have disappeared in the trees, come back around, and killed more of his men had the private not brought fresh troops from Company E to engage them.

Crawford always knew he and his soldiers wouldn't live forever. They were, after all, in the business of war and death. More likely than not, they'd get killed out in the desert or the mountains in battle with their elusive enemy. For some ridiculous reason, he always figured it would happen at some time in the distant future. Losing his friend and so many other men in a single campaign reminded Crawford of his own mortality. Closing his eyes briefly, he allowed himself the luxury of feeling the sorrow. He missed his friend terribly.

Despite the scorching morning temperature two days ago, Crawford and the men of Company B formed up on the parade ground in full dress military uniform, complete with swords. Major Phillip Clark and Lieutenant Stanley Reeves rode stiff-backed on their horses, while the men of Company B marched afoot in a two-column formation to honor their dead. Crawford marched at the rear, guiding the two-wheeled, horse-drawn cart containing the rough sawn caskets of the men. Tied to the back of the cart, their horses followed. Each animal was equipped with a dead soldier's saddle, boots, sword, and spurs. Those items represented the fighting man's most important possessions.

Major Clark said words for the dead soldiers, but Crawford didn't hear them. He could only think about what kind of an animal Captain Taylor was to have killed all those helpless people, then ordered his men to fire on other soldiers. Hatred simmered inside Crawford, an emotion he hadn't felt since his slave days.

The first night of their mission to arrest Captain Taylor, Crawford ordered his men to make camp at the same place they bivouacked with Taylor's men. Sentries found all the dead army horses quite a distance from the camp, and they discovered how the Indians managed to steal away the horses without a sound. They'd used leather thongs to muzzle them, then tied pieces of cloth over all the horses' hooves to lead them away quietly.

Crawford shook his head as if to toss away all the unpleasant thoughts as Company B rode down into a secluded valley where they came upon the mining camp. He signaled his men to halt and proceeded into the camp alone. Four men waited for him, and when he saw the sneers and looks of indifference on their faces, he knew immediately the conversation wouldn't go well. One of the men spat tobacco juice toward his horse.

"What can we do fer ya, Soldier?" the apparent leader said. He was a huge bear of a man with a head of shaggy, dirty blond hair. His full beard reached down to his belt.

One of his companions was almost as big and had a huge hole in the front of his filthy red undershirt. The two other men, both equally filthy from working in the mines, were slender—one tall, the other short. The leader held a double-barrel shotgun at his side. The shortest of the slender men had a pistol tucked in the front of his pants.

"I'm First Sergeant Lafayette Crawford, Company B, Ninth Cavalry. Tracks of the Sixth Cavalry horses came this way. Appears they left with more riders than they arrived with." Crawford paused and scanned the mining camp.

The valley floor was maybe fifty yards wide and was fairly flat. Beyond the four men facing him, he saw what looked like homemade hard-rock mining equipment sitting in the middle of the valley. The dried-up creek bed looked like it hadn't seen water in months.

A half-dozen shacks lined both sides of the valley floor and some stood on stilts at the base of the northern slope. Four huge cavern openings were dug into the south cliff wall and were shored up by timber from the pine trees cut from the nearby mountain slopes. Dozens of trees lay piled near the entrances to the mines for use in shoring up the holes as the miners dug farther into the hill.

"So," Crawford continued. "I was wondering if you could tell me where they were headed."

"Ain't seen no soldiers hereabouts."

Crawford ignored the lie. "They're commanded by a renegade captain who's wanted for murdering an entire village of Indians and ambushing my men."

The man with the holey undershirt laughed. "Always heard your kind made pretty stupid soldiers. I s'pose you shoulda been a bit more careful." The man guffawed laughter at Crawford. The guy to his right agreed.

"As far as the dead Injuns are concerned," he said, looking to both sides at his companions as if for approval. "That don't sound like a bad thing to me. They's just Injuns."

Crawford nodded. "Any men from this camp who joined them are outlaws and are subject to arrest by the US Army. If you withhold the information I need, that makes you outlaws also. Then I'd have to arrest you too."

Four other men crawled out of a mine and headed toward Crawford, two grabbing up rifles on the way.

"Well, you can't come in here and start threatening us. And you can't arrest no White men."

"That's right," the leader agreed. He waved the open end of his weapon at Crawford, though he hadn't yet stuck his fingers inside the trigger guard. "We ain't scared of you."

Crawford stared the man down for a moment, then he grunted at him. "You should be," he said quietly.

The first sergeant raised a gloved hand and made a forward motion with two fingers. Within seconds, his troop of twenty-five men rode into the camp and lined up on both sides of him.

"Sir, I'm going to give you another opportunity to assist the United States Army in bringing criminals to justice."

The four men looked at each other as the other miners approached. One of the unarmed men took a step back. The leader sneered and spat more juice at Crawford's horse.

"Ready weapons!" Crawford commanded.

In one coordinated movement, the soldiers withdrew their Springfields from their scabbards, barrels pointed skyward.

"You're fixin' to die, Soldier." The man in charge of the motley group took aim at Crawford with his shotgun.

"I suppose that makes two of us," Crawford answered. He looked to his left and right at his men. "Pick your targets!"

Twenty-five rifle barrels lowered and the eight miners fidgeted, glancing back and forth between them, clearly unprepared for more than a bluff. Two of the newcomers dropped their weapons and raised their hands.

Crawford said, "Sir, have you ever seen what a .58-caliber shell from an army Springfield rifle can do to a man?"

The leader grunted and spat tobacco juice to the side. "I reckon I have." He lowered his shotgun and tossed it to the ground.

"First Sergeant," a man at the far right called. "I got one up on the hill. He ain't lowerin' his rifle."

Crawford glanced up the hill. "Explain to him the error of his ways."

A single shot split the air and tree bark exploded in the face of the would-be sniper. He clawed for a handhold, then tumbled down the slope.

"Secure these men!"

Soldiers jumped from their horses and herded the miners against the south cliff wall. The sniper from the hillside got to his feet and joined them, prodded forward by the business end of a Springfield rifle.

"Private Nance!"

"I'm a corporal this week, Sarge." Nance tapped his upper arm near the shoulder when Crawford looked down at him.

"I guess I'm gonna have to look at your arm every week, so I'll know what to call you." Crawford smiled briefly, then turned serious again. "Burn this place down."

CHAPTER 40

"**W**AIT! THEY SAID THEY WAS headin' down to the Gila River to see if they could catch those Apaches."

The man with the holey undershirt added, "One of the boys here knew where that Indian chief made his home. Said he was tryin' to reach some mountain stronghold down in Mexico."

"The US Army thanks you for your cooperation," Crawford said calmly. He nudged his horse a few steps closer to the corralled miners. "Corporal Nance," he called, his gaze burning into the leader of the miners. "Burn it down anyway."

To the miner, he said, "I'm guessin' right about now you're regretting those things you said about Black soldiers." The miner didn't answer.

Within minutes, the soldiers had pushed fallen tree trunks into the caverns and sprinkled them with the miners' own kerosene. Then they set them ablaze. Soon smoke billowed from the entrances of each of the four mine shafts. As the wood used to shore up two of the openings in the hillside burned, the shafts collapsed under the weight of the dirt previously held in place.

The soldiers pulled the log shacks down and dragged the wood and all the mining equipment and supplies to the center of the valley. Last, they broke down the miners' weapons until they were useless. The pile of debris burned quick and fierce.

"Keep that blaze under control, Corporal. We don't want to set fire to the whole mountain."

When Crawford was satisfied nothing left was usable, he ordered the men to smother the flames with dirt. An hour later, Crawford led his men out of the mining camp. He called Private Hendricks forward.

"Sir!" the man said smartly when he rode up.

"How long you been in my army, Private?"

"Two months, sir."

"Well, I told you before I'm not an officer, so don't call me *sir*."

"Yes, First Sergeant."

"That's better." Crawford nodded. "Take a message to Sergeant Wilcox. Tell him we're headin' straight south from here and aim to cross the river about ten miles west of his position. He's to round up any Sixth Cavalry men he finds and have a detachment escort 'em back to the fort hog-tied or dead, as he sees fit. That done, he's to scout down to the southern edge of the Animas Mountains and await my arrival. If he encounters either Chief Juh or Captain Taylor, he is to engage them and attempt to force their surrender. Clear?"

"Round 'em up, ride down south, and engage. Very clear, First Sergeant."

"Dismissed."

Crawford wondered if Captain Taylor and his men would be reasonable when confronted. The enlisted men were prisoners—most of them convicts. They wouldn't be eager to visit the stockade again. On the other hand, the captain had at most twelve soldiers remaining with him, judging by the number of graves Crawford had seen along the trail. Wilcox had twenty men in his Company E detachment and Crawford had twenty-four Company B and E men. By any measuring stick, that was more than enough to handle the prisoners of the Sixth and a dozen or so unruly miners intent on killing Indians.

CHAPTER 41

C APTAIN TAYLOR REINED HIS HORSE alongside the private riding point.

"What are you stopping for, Scout?" Taylor saw the answer as soon as the private shifted in the saddle. The young soldier nodded ahead.

Two older Indians, a man and a woman, lay in a tangled heap on the parched ground. Taylor figured them to be a husband and wife. One had collapsed and the other probably was unwilling to walk away from his or her life partner.

"Seventh and eighth bodies we've passed today, Cap'n."

"The weak ones are falling, and the rest of the tribe can't carry them along."

"Sir, I thought the Apaches didn't leave their dead behind like this."

"Probably have no choice. It's a hundred and twenty degrees out here. And we've got 'em running without supplies and water."

The private nodded. "That miner said they keep rations buried in secret places."

"Up in the mountains, perhaps," he said. "Except this time, we cut 'em off. Their only escape was across these flats."

Taylor looked ahead. Through the shimmering heat waves he saw low mountains above the southeastern horizon. He guessed their distance at about five miles. He'd taken far too long picking up the fugitives' tracks. He never figured they'd try to escape across such desolate terrain, especially in this deadly heat. By the time he realized the warriors that kept attacking with pestering hit-and-run raids were only leading his men astray, he'd lost two whole days on his prey.

The captain glanced behind him where Corporal Smith waited patiently with the rest of the Sixth and the miners. A sorrier bunch of men he'd never seen. Even the tough corporal looked done in by the sun. His head bobbed slightly with heat-induced drowsiness.

"Corporal!"

Smith snapped to attention in his saddle, his eyes focusing a couple of seconds later on Taylor.

"Rest the men and water the horses as best you can." Taylor glanced down at the tracks left by the escaping Indians. "Looks like we're only a few hours behind them now. We've got to catch 'em before they reach those hills out yonder. Likely they'll have supplies and weapons hidden up there."

Half an hour later, the column of soldiers started up their march again with their horses at a quicker pace, though not a trot. The men seemed energized, but Taylor knew the rush of excitement of catching up with their prey would soon fade as the heat sapped their energy again.

As he rode past the entangled Indians, Taylor saw the old woman move. She raised her head and looked at him through long, gray hair that draped down over her face. When she blinked, her eyes stayed closed for a few seconds and her head bobbed as she struggled to remain conscious. Her lips were cracked and whitened.

Taylor squinted against the bright glare of sunlight reflecting off the ground and pulled his Remington pistol. As he aimed at the old woman, he saw her open her eyes again and nod. Realizing her nod was gratitude, he tucked his gun away and spat at her.

"You can suffer a bit longer."

The old woman laid her head on the body of her dead partner. After Taylor turned in his saddle and continued to ride for a few seconds, he heard three quick shots. He spun around and headed his horse back to a miner who was putting his rifle back in his scabbard.

"What the hell are you doing?" Taylor shouted as he reined up beside the rangy, stick-thin man.

"Just making sure is all." The miner shrugged. "I saw her move—"

Before he realized what he was doing, Captain Taylor pulled his pistol and shot the man in the forehead. The miner's head snapped back and as the man fell from his horse, Taylor looked around at the rest of his men.

"Last year I came across three soldiers who'd been stripped naked and tied to a cactus bush, left for dead by these soulless devils. Any of you see any Indians dyin' out hereabouts, you're under orders to let 'em suffer. You understand me?"

The soldiers nodded or answered the command, but the miners sat in their saddles stunned. Taylor reined his horse around, sure he'd gotten his point across. Just as he faced forward, he saw a flash of light in the distance. He jumped from his saddle, screaming the ambush as he crashed to the hard, sunbaked earth. All around him, his men jumped from their saddles and scrambled for their rifles, but many seconds passed before he heard the sound of thunder rumble in from two or three miles distant.

Slowly, Taylor and his men remounted, still wary of an attack from Jason Peares's long rifle. A single black thundercloud hung ominously in the distance and lightning flashed repeatedly. Taylor straightened his cap on his head and cursed the half-breed outlaw savagely as he kicked his horse into motion. With every passing mile, he hated Jason Peares even more.

Four hours later, a loud thunderclap rudely awakened Taylor from his heat-induced nap. His reaction to the sound snapped his head back so fast he heard something pop in his neck. Instinctively, he reached up to massage the kink in the back of his neck as he looked around for his men. Somehow, he'd gotten ahead of them, even passing the point man.

Captain Taylor felt mist against his face, then realized with despair that the passing clouds had deposited rain practically everywhere else except on him. Panic gripped him and suddenly he wanted that fresh cool water more than life itself. He entertained the half-witted thought of chasing the storm cloud. Instead, he just turned forward again in his saddle and grabbed up the reins. Then he froze at the impossible sight before him.

Jason knew he was dying. He remembered his legs giving out, remembered falling to his knees. He had no idea how long he'd sat on his haunches or what brought him rudely out of his delirious sleep.

When he finally opened his eyes to almost total darkness, Jason realized he was sitting in a torrential downpour. He raised his head but couldn't see a foot in front of him. A brilliant flash of lightning illuminated the landscape, accompanied instantly by the loudest thunderclap he'd ever heard. Just as quickly, his world plunged into darkness again. In that brief instant of light, he'd seen what he needed to survive.

Rain fell in solid sheets of water. The ground beneath Jason's knees inclined in front of him and torrents of rainwater cascaded past him. He hadn't drank water as long as he'd been carrying the woman. He remembered the cycles of daylight and darkness, but he couldn't believe he'd survived days in the scorching heat without water. He recalled hearing the elder woman's musical voice almost the entire time, keeping him going. Perhaps she knew he needed a reason to keep moving. Otherwise, it would've been so easy to quit and just rest forever.

When he did collapse, Jason still held the woman in his arms. Now he rolled her off him and he leaned forward and lowered his face to the ground. He stuck his mouth in a tiny flow of running water and drank deeply. The water tasted muddy and powdery, but like a wilted flower suddenly watered, Jason felt his body coming alive again. He pulled off his hat and turned it upward to collect rainwater. He crawled over to *Ancient One* and poured handfuls of water across her lips. Her mouth worked a bit and her eyelids moved, and he felt a wave of relief that she still lived.

Another flash of lightning lit the area. In the darkness that followed, Jason reviewed the brief image his brain had cataloged. The Apache survivors were scattered up the slope of the near hill, cupping runoff water into their hands to refill their water skins. Grady stood nearby, head hanging low but not drinking. The travois still held the boy Jason had shot.

With his belt knife, Jason punched a hole in his hat and let the water pour into both his canteens. By the time the canteens were full, the trailing edge of the storm cell had passed over him and once again, the late afternoon sun beat down fiercely. The water stopped running downhill and seemed to simply melt into the desert. Within seconds the topsoil was almost dry.

Jason started to lean down to help *Ancient One* with more water, but hesitated. A feeling of warning tingled down his spine and he felt a presence behind him. He spun, reaching for his holster guns at the same time, and stared up into the dark, malevolent eyes of Captain Ambrose Taylor.

CHAPTER 42

F IRST SERGEANT LAFAYETTE CRAWFORD GAVE the hand
signal to halt, nudged his mount up beside the private
riding point, and paused. He glanced around out of habit
and noticed with satisfaction that the two skirmishers who rode
a couple hundred yards off each flank of the column had their
Springfield rifles drawn. Those four men, plus the point man
ahead and the two rearguard scouts riding alert the same distance behind the column, would be the first soldiers to engage
any attacking force that threatened the column. Unfortunately,
they would be the first men to fall from a surprise attack or a
hidden sniper. Either way, those men on the outskirts protected
Company B from ambush.

Long ago, Crawford learned to detach himself emotionally
whenever he encountered death. He'd seen a lot of it in his fifteen years in the frontier army, and he knew he'd see a lot more
before the Indian Wars ended. He dismounted to inspect the
body of an old Indian man, but when he turned the body over to
look for gunshot wounds, he found nothing.

"Looks like he dropped dead from the heat," he murmured to
Corporal Nance as the man walked up beside him.

"These Indians must be hurtin'. I've never known 'em to leave
their dead behind." Nance checked the body carefully. "He's got
no weapons, and his water skin and ration bag are empty. I'm
guessin' Captain Taylor cut 'em off from their normal supply

stashes up in the mountains. That's the only reason I can see for them to be down here in the valley bravin' this heat."

Crawford took off his hat and wiped his brow with his sleeve. He squinted into the distance where the tracks led. Shadowy mountains shimmered in the heat waves. The sky was fairly free of clouds, but he saw two distinct storm cells floating in the sky maybe ten miles away. He absently reached for his canteen as he fantasized about riding in the feathery downpour of the dark clouds.

Crawford drank a sip and said, "Hottest summer I've ever seen."

"No doubt."

As Nance drank from his own canteen, Crawford gestured with his canteen to his men waiting patiently several yards away. They drank sparingly as Nance pointed to the tracks in the crusty earth.

"Looks like Captain Taylor's followin' 'em southeast."

"Toward the Animas Mountains?"

"That'd be my guess. They probably got a stash hidden up there somewhere. If they get there first, they'll be able to hold off the captain until he runs out of supplies. If he gets to them first...."

Crawford finished the thought, more to himself than for Nance's benefit. "There's gonna be some more murdered Indians."

He squinted around the landscape again. The ground was almost completely bare. A tuft of grass lay here and there, burned black by the intense sun. What few bushes he saw were dry stick skeletons. Around him lay great patches of white and dark brown, sandy dirt, devoid of life.

"Shall we bury this old man?"

Crawford considered the question for a moment, then asked his own. "How far behind them you figure we are, Corporal?"

"Hard to say. Maybe six or seven hours."

Nodding, Crawford said, "I don't want to waste time. Won't hurt this fella none if we leave him as he is." Crawford mounted up. "I figure we'd head straight south. Skirt the west side of the mountains and wait at the southern foothills." He said it like a statement, not a question, but not quite a decisive command.

"You askin' my advice, First Sergeant?"

"I am."

Corporal Nance nodded. "The captain seems to have a burr stuck in his craw about these particular Indians." He paused. "They got this far without him catchin' 'em. If they get into the mountains, they can split up and hide out. Wait until the captain quits. The only chance he'll have is to stay hard on their trail, follow 'em up into the mountains. And if I recall, those are some particularly rough hills, mostly bare rock with some brush cover. There aren't many trees until higher up in pine country to the south. Ought to be reasonably easy for him to stay on 'em. If I were the captain, I'd just follow 'em from a safe distance and then catch 'em when they make a run over the flats across the last few miles to the border."

"Good," Crawford said, turning his attention to the private riding point. "Straight south then, Private. We'll meet up with Sergeant Wilcox if he's there, then round up the Indians and the captain at the same time."

Juh and his seven warriors almost rode right into Sergeant Wilcox's Company E. To make faster time, Juh stayed in the lowlands along the eastern flank of the Animas Mountains. Juh found a well-cut dry gulch that kept his war party hidden from the surrounding flats. Unfortunately, the depth of the dry channel also hid the soldiers from view until the channel shallowed out suddenly, less than a quarter-mile from the column of troops.

Just before Juh saw the soldiers, his mount whinnied. Juh knew horses well, and he recognized the sound of one animal sensing another. In one smooth movement, Juh reined his horse up and swung his legs over the animal's neck. He used his momentum to tackle the animal smoothly to the ground as he'd practiced many times over the years. He lay his weight across the horse's flank. Within seconds the other warriors lay their horses near Juh's.

The blistering heat from the ground scorched Juh's bare skin while the army formation rode into view and crossed the gully only a couple hundred yards away. There was little danger, Juh knew. From the soldiers' perspective, the war party would just seem like an ordinary part of the landscape obscured by the shimmering heat waves, unless the warriors or their animals moved suddenly or attracted attention.

The soldiers continued past, and Juh waited another hour before leading his warriors straight up into the middle section of the mountains. An hour later, he stood before the hiding place known as Two Pointed Rocks Rising Above A Flat Boulder. His men stood behind him, and he wondered briefly if they felt the same hope he felt. He hesitated for a second, allowing himself to wish the survivors of his people had passed this way. Unfortunately, the realistic part of his brain told him that was impossible. There was no way his people could have traveled that far afoot so quickly.

Despite knowing the obvious, Juh's heart sank quickly as he removed the rocks under the flat boulder. All the supplies remained untouched. He replaced the rocks carefully, without taking any of the supplies, since all his warriors carried plenty of ammunition and their ration bags were still nearly full, courtesy of the Jimenez Ranch.

Juh rose and faced his warriors, saw the disappointment in their faces as well. There was little to say that would comfort them. Without comment, he mounted his horse and kicked it into motion. All they could do now was ride north along their well-known trail until they found their people. Each step of his horse tore at Juh's heart. He couldn't explain the urgency he felt or the gut-wrenching anxiety. Without realizing it, he found himself pushing his tired horse into a run along the winding trail.

The animal lathered quickly in the thin air and wheezed noisily, spraying foam from its mouth as Juh urged it onward.

When Juh glanced behind him, he found his warriors in close pursuit. Minutes later he understood why he had felt the need to hurry. Distant gunshots fluttered on the wind.

Among the Apache people, Juh was well known for his accurate visions of the future. That was his gift in life, but he'd never *felt* a vision quite like he had moments earlier. He'd had a *feeling* that his people were in trouble, and they were dying. *Right now.* He pushed his horse faster.

Juh paused on a ridgeline and stared with horror into the distance. Helplessly, he watched another massacre unfold less than a mile away. The soldiers bore down on his people, shooting into them like target practice. He saw his last son, Daklugie, helping Grandmother up the hill.

Then Juh let out a cry of anguish as he watched a soldier ride up behind Daklugie and pull his sidearm. He aimed at the boy's back and fired.

CHAPTER 43

A S SOON AS JASON GRABBED his right gun, he mentally cursed his specially made holsters. When he was standing up, the extra-stiff leather pockets kept his weapons riding low on his thighs in perfect reach of his outstretched palms for the fast draw. That way, when he was in a gunfight, he didn't have to waste precious split seconds reaching up for a high-mounted gun in a belt holster like most other gunfighters.

When he was seated or was squatting, as he was now, his low-slung holsters were prone to dumping his guns on the ground. So he usually kept a leather loop hooked on the hammer of each gun unless he was in a situation where he knew he would need his weapons.

Sitting on his haunches, he faced Captain Taylor, totally unprepared for a gun battle and he couldn't pull his guns free. Rather than waste time unhitching the loop, he instinctively reached to his belt for his backup guns. Then he remembered he'd given both the Colts to the Apache boys.

Fortunately, Taylor and the men behind him all seemed as surprised as Jason. None had their rifles ready. Clearly, they had ridden through the brief storm not knowing they were so close to their prey. Taylor shouted the ambush and reined his horse around. Then he and his men fled in a disorganized gaggle into the distance. Jason unhitched his right gun, but in those few seconds of delay, Taylor was out of range and Jason didn't want to waste his ammunition chasing the man with errant shots. Besides, he knew he had precious few seconds to act.

Captain Taylor was no fool, Jason knew. The officer had many more men than Jason expected. He'd regroup quickly, no doubt respecting the range of Jason's Spencer rifle. He'd spread his men out wide across the desert and charge, racing their horses erratically here and there as they closed the distance. No way Jason could hit more than a few of the soldiers, even with the Spencer. In a few minutes, Taylor and his men would be all over him and the Apaches.

Jason had to get to high ground to try and delay the soldiers until the few Indians with rifles could help cover the others. If the Apaches got up into the foothills, at least a few of the survivors had a chance to live. Otherwise, they would all die. Desperation hit Jason with the distant memory of all his .50-caliber shells reflecting sunlight as they tumbled down the steep slope days ago. He remembered staring at the dozens of tiny reflections at the bottom of the gorge, pinpoints of light that had taunted him, reminding him of his carelessness.

As the Indians scrambled up the near hill, Jason ran to Grady. He pushed aside the young boy who was trying to lead the weakened horse to safety. With no time to waste, Jason tore loose the travois and pulled the girl and two older women from the animal's back. Then he jumped onto Grady's bare back. He didn't need to glance behind him. He heard the thunder of the approaching soldiers' horses. In a panic, he kicked his heels savagely into Grady's flanks and the horse raced forward. He had to get to high ground, or his Spencer was useless.

Daklugie ran back toward *Ancient One*. As Jason raced past, he called out, and the boy removed the Spencer rifle that had been tied over his shoulder and tossed the rifle at Jason's outstretched hand. He caught the weapon smoothly where the stock met the barrel, right behind the scope.

For half a minute, Grady kept up a strong pace, but halfway up the hill, Jason found himself leaning forward, pleading with Grady to keep running. No amount of begging or kicking could dredge up another ounce of energy from the spent animal. Grady slowed to a crippled walk, and Jason jumped down and ran the last hundred yards to the top of the first hill.

Scrambling into the prone position, Jason brought his Spencer to bear on the approaching soldiers. Still racing on adrenaline, Jason removed his hat and took several deep breaths to steady his aim. Already, the soldiers charged toward the hill, weaving all over the land and shooting into the running Indians. Jason got lucky with his first two shots as he downed men who were careless and predictable with their zigzag, then he realized how hopeless the Apache's plight was.

Though less than five hundred yards away, he couldn't hope to hit the fast-moving dodging targets. Every time he thought he had a good bead on a killer, the soldier reined his horse around and messed up his aim. So Jason waited and watched painfully as the Apaches died. He had to wait until he was sure every shot would count.

He had only four shells left, but there were more than two dozen targets. He tried not to give in to the hopelessness, but he saw absolutely no chance for these people to survive.

CHAPTER 44

J ASON FOUND A TARGET FINALLY. A soldier who stopped his horse in front of a trio of elder Apache. He swung his rifle like a club and caught the old man across the skull. When the man flipped his rifle for the killing shot, Jason fired. By the time his scope lined up in front of his eye after the recoil, the soldier had already been slammed from his saddle. The two Apache women helped the stricken elder onto the soldier's horse and the three rode up over the hill to safety.

One shot. Three lives saved. Three shells left.

A scream drew his aim to the left where he saw Ishton and the young pregnant girl running. Ishton held the girl up by one arm, and the girl supported her huge belly with her other arm as they ran.

A soldier dismounted on the run and kicked the girl to the ground. He grabbed Ishton by her hair and tossed her down too. He stuck a boot against her back, pinning her down as he yanked upward on her hair. She screamed again and clawed at his hand, a futile attempt to escape as he holstered his gun and drew a knife. At just over a hundred yards, Jason aimed a snap shot without using the scope, and the soldier's head disappeared in a splatter of bone fragments and pink flesh.

Ishton glanced at Jason briefly, then helped the pregnant girl up the hill. Two more lives saved. Two shells left.

Jason just turned his attention back downhill when his side vision registered his hat move on the ground beside him. He heard the zip of the sniper's bullet at the same instant and knew his time had run out. The army sniper had found him and could put two bullets in the air in the time it took Jason to lock home a single shell.

He went through the motions anyway, refusing to give up. The sniper had missed by a mere twelve inches. He wouldn't miss a second time. Jason rammed home a cartridge and put his eye to the scope. He found the sniper even as he heard men race over the hill just yards to his right. Unseen warriors yelled their war cries to distract the soldiers.

Through the scope, Jason saw the army shooter laying way out in the flats. The man fired, but incredibly he did not shoot at Jason. A warrior screamed in pain close by, but Jason kept his attention on the sniper even as the man quickly worked his lever and switched his aim back to Jason.

The army sniper didn't use a scope. He simply made a quick thumb-screw adjustment on a vertical, flip-up lever calibrated with the front sight on the rifle's short barrel. Jason knew the sharpshooter's mechanism was just as accurate as a scope at any distance under five hundred yards, which was precisely where the army shooter lay.

Letting out half his breath, Jason gently squeezed the trigger. At the same instant, he saw the sniper's muzzle flash. Then the Spencer recoiled, and he felt the wind of the sniper's bullet streak by his left cheek. The sniper had missed, though just barely, but when his scope dropped back down in front of his eye, he found that his own shot hadn't missed.

One shell left.

He searched the hillside for his last target and tried to decide which of the Apache would die and which would live. He saw the two boys dragging the travois up the hill. An old woman ran up the hill carrying an infant child in her arms as two soldiers bore down on her. Daklugie and *Ancient One* struggled uphill ever so slowly.

Jason sighted on the mounted soldier looming up behind Daklugie even as the man pulled his holster gun and took aim at the boy's back. The boy's attacker was the closest of all the soldiers and, therefore, the most certain kill. Besides, he hadn't carried the elder woman halfway across the state for days just to let her get shot.

Jason aimed quickly and squeezed the trigger but flinched at the last moment at a sudden movement behind him, *right on top of him*. He knew without looking through the scope he had missed, and he heard the soldier's gunshot eclipse the gut-wrenching war cry in his ear. Then a flock of long, brown hair descended over him.

He'd used his last cartridge. The soldiers were far outside the range of his handguns, so there was nothing more he could do for the Apache except try to save his own life. He rolled and pivoted on his butt. He reached for his right gun at the same time, but a strong hand clamped his own so tight he couldn't pull the gun free. A hot metal blade pressed against his neck and Jason found himself looking up through a curtain of brown hair into the most fearsome and sinister eyes he'd ever seen on a man.

CHAPTER 45

W HEN JASON LOOKED INTO THE dark brown eyes above him, he saw nothing but pure hatred. He saw in the warrior's eyes the decision to cut Jason's throat even before Brown Hair moved the knife. The warrior's arm tensed, but he froze at a flurry of words shouted from a hundred yards away. Jason heard Ishton's voice, decisive and commanding.

Brown Hair glanced over at her briefly, almost without moving his head and then narrowed his eyes. He looked back down at Jason and grunted a raspy sound that seemed to originate from deep in the man's soul.

The warrior stood, ripped a skin sack from his woven leather belt, and dropped it to the ground beside Jason's Spencer. Then he was gone. Confused, Jason opened the sack and found his .50-caliber cartridges. He wasted no time thinking. He just reloaded and set his sights again on the soldier near Daklugie and *Ancient One*.

He expected to find them murdered, but they still lived. The soldier had missed a point-blank shot at the boy. Jason's previous shot grazed him in the side, almost knocked him out of his saddle. In the few seconds while Brown Hair attacked Jason, the soldier regained his seat and took aim at the boy again.

Brown Hair bounded down the slope, his muscular legs covering the distance toward the soldier in great, ten-foot strides. He yelled and waved his arms, brandishing a knife in his right hand with his Winchester in his left. His brown mane waved in the hot breeze. Though he was too far away to attack the soldier, his presence and his fearsome war cry distracted the man. The soldier tucked away the gun he was ready to use on Daklugie and brought up the rifle he carried in his other hand, preparing to snap off a quick shot at Brown Hair.

With a scope on the Spencer's forty-four-inch barrel, Jason could hit a man over fifteen hundred yards away. For a stationary target at two hundred yards, Jason didn't even need to use the scope or check his breathing. He just snapped off a quick shot easier than child's play. He hit the soldier squarely in the center of his chest with a definite kill shot. The soldier was slammed out of the saddle, and he thumped onto the ground face up, his dead eyes staring into the sky.

The sudden appearance of the warriors caught the bloodthirsty soldiers and miners by surprise, caused them to retreat again into the distance. Jason found three more targets with the Spencer, before finally recognizing Captain Taylor's straight-backed figure riding away. He took careful aim and fired. When the barrel bounced back down in front of his eye, he mentally counted the seconds. Watched his bullet take the rider next to Taylor off his horse when both men jogged their mounts suddenly to the left. He fired two more shots, but missed, and within seconds, the soldiers and miners were far out of range.

Jason counted six shells left in the sack. He stood and tied the sack to the front of his gun belt, then collected his Spencer. As he brushed dust from the weapon, he watched Brown Hair walk down the hill and pause by the dead soldier who almost killed Daklugie. The warrior worked on the dead man with his blade for a moment, then cut loose his scalp. The warrior tossed aside the flock of hair with a cry that seemed more anguish than anger, then he started back uphill.

Brown Hair exchanged a few words with Daklugie and the elder woman. The boy said something and nodded toward Jason, and Brown Hair followed the boy's nod. He held Jason's gaze for a few seconds, then leaned over, lifted *Ancient One* effortlessly in his arms, and carried her the rest of the way up the hill. Jason saw the old woman speaking, no doubt about him, and Brown Hair tossed him another glare while she spoke.

As Jason scanned the hillside, he saw fifteen dead bodies. Five were Apache and ten were from Taylor's detachment. The warriors collected their wounded and dead and congregated in a gathering on the hilltop a dozen yards away from Jason. When the group began their trek farther up along the trail, Jason walked toward Grady. The horse still stood where Jason had left him, just over halfway up the hill. The horse wavered back and forth but made no attempt to move toward Jason's call. Grady was all done in.

Jason felt useless and alone. He realized he was unneeded. The survivors had their warriors to protect them now. All Jason had was a sick horse, two canteens full of water, and maybe a couple hundred mile walk to any kind of town.

Captain Taylor would certainly keep pursuing him, especially if the renegade officer realized Jason was afoot and alone. His stomach growled and he realized how hungry he was. Unlike the Apache, Jason wore no ration bags and had no food. He'd let Daklugie carry what he foraged when they began their trek, what seemed like a week ago. That seemed to be the job of a warrior's assistant. The desperateness of his predicament struck him at that moment.

He comforted Grady as best he could as he watched another group of Apache men ride down from the high trail. All fierce-looking warriors, they dismounted and first embraced Brown Hair and his warriors, then the survivors. Next, he watched a man leave the group of warriors and walk over to Ishton.

Jason instinctively knew this man was the leader of the tribe, the man the army called Chief Juh. It was clear from the way he carried himself, the way he offered a tender word for each survivor. He hugged Ishton for a long time, then reached out a hand to Daklugie. The boy joined the hug.

Jason watched the tearful reunion and knew he was seeing a private side of these people outsiders never saw. He'd never considered that these men, so feared as vicious warriors, could share the gentle emotions of love and happiness. He realized they were not only warriors. They were also husbands and fathers and brothers fighting and dying to protect their wives and children.

Feeling like an intruder to the reunion, Jason turned his attention back to Grady. The horse fidgeted his left front leg, pawing softly at the ground. Its flank muscle trembled continuously. Jason poured precious canteen water into his hat, and with his finger he plugged the hole he'd cut in it. He knelt and stuck the hat under Grady's snout, but the horse wouldn't drink.

"Dammit, Grady." Jason drank some of the water and let the rest trickle back into the canteen. Then he stuck his hat back on his head. "You've carried me through hell and high water, and you've taken real good care of me."

Jason knelt and leaned his head against Grady's. He heard the familiar musical voice of *Ancient One* close by and smiled without opening his eyes. Only her voice had kept him moving across the desert all those hours or days. He'd been ready to give in to the heat many times and just lie down and die. He would have too, if she hadn't kept talking to him. It was like she knew his need and felt his desperation.

He opened his eyes and looked over at her and Daklugie. They stood behind him, slightly uphill. She gestured at her people farther up the trail and made a motion for him to join them. They all seemed to be waiting. Jason nodded and stood. He tugged on Grady's reins. The horse took a step and stumbled, then fell onto its side. It didn't try to get up.

Jason sighed and knelt beside the horse. He'd buried his entire family more than ten years ago—victims of frontier racism. When he hunted down and killed the murderers, he found himself an outlaw for killing those men. Since that time, Grady had become the closest thing to a friend he'd had, at least for the last two years. Now, he had no one left to lose. Jason stood quickly and pulled his gun. He took a deep breath, then cocked the gun and shot Grady in the head.

Ancient One spoke again as he packed his gun away. He

stood and caught sight of a woman cradling the limp body of the boy Jason had shot. A sudden wave of grief brought him to his knees. Tears welled up his eyes.

"Where is your God now, Crawford?" Jason muttered. "How could He let a boy suffer like that and die by my hand and then let me live?"

Jason closed his eyes and grabbed his head between his hands. His hat fell off and he felt the scorching sun on the back of his neck. The old woman's voice soothed him again as she knelt beside him and pulled him into her lap. He wept like a child. For the dead Apache boy and for Grady. For his own dead family that he'd never made time to cry for all those years ago. For the innocent people who died because they happened to be close to an outlaw named Jason Peares at the wrong time.

Through it all, he heard the woman's singsong voice talking to him, comforting and soothing him. For a long time after he felt all cried out, he remained curled up next to *Ancient One*, his head cradled in her lap. Finally, he collected himself and stood. Then he helped the woman to her feet. Maybe Crawford's God had sent this old Apache woman to take care of him.

Juh approached and Jason judged him to be about forty. The man held a look of deep compassion in his eyes as he regarded Jason. Juh exchanged words with *Ancient One*. Jason looked around and saw the rest of the Apache people were moving up the trail over the near ridge. The sun sat low in the sky and would set within an hour.

As much as he wanted to see this battle to the end and somehow punish Captain Taylor and his men, Jason realized the wisdom of leaving that task to the army, if they cared enough to arrest Taylor. If he stayed involved, he'd just get in the way, maybe get himself killed. He'd done what he was supposed to do. He'd saved innocent people from being massacred.

The thought occurred to Jason to ask for one of the captured army horses and some supplies, but he had no idea how to communicate the question. He was just trying to figure out how to deliver his question in sign language when Juh startled him with a question in Spanish.

Jason answered. "Yes, I speak Spanish."

"I am Juh." He pronounced his name *Hoe*. "We are of the Nednhi Apache tribe."

"You're the chief?"

"I'm no chief." Juh shook his head. "Only the *White-Eyes* call our leaders *chief*. I was elected by my people to lead."

Jason absorbed this knowledge and nodded as he watched after Daklugie and *Ancient One*. Then he watched the woman carrying the dead boy and closed his eyes for a moment.

"That boy saved my life, and I killed him for it."

Juh nodded. "I've been told of that unfortunate event. As a result of his sacrifice, you lived to save my last surviving son and my first wife and many others. Without your help, there would be no more Nednhi Apache."

Somehow, that revelation didn't make him feel any better. He asked for a horse so he could be on his way, but Juh declined. He nodded to where Daklugie stood with Ishton.

"*Jay-sone Peer* is known throughout the Apache land as an honorable warrior. Join us for a feast tonight to celebrate those of my people who have survived."

Somehow, he wasn't surprised the child-warrior who'd stuck by his side throughout the ordeal was the son of the leader of the tribe. He grabbed the Spencer and followed Juh and his family higher into the mountains.

"Captain Taylor and his men won't quit," Jason said after a while.

"They never do," Juh returned.

CHAPTER 46

PEACE REIGNED FOR TWO DAYS as Juh led his people higher into the Animas Mountains. They camped the first night at Two Pointed Rocks Rising Above A Flat Boulder and had a quiet feast of horsemeat, vegetables from the Jimenez homestead, and a kind of coarse bread Jason didn't recognize.

Earlier, when Jason followed Juh and his family, he'd seen a few of the women and children falling back. He knew they were going back for Grady, but he pretended not to notice. The Apache left no usable resource behind, and Jason knew the horsemeat could sustain the survivors for several days.

Jason found the size of the cavern that held the hidden supplies impressive. He saw dried vegetables and fruit, grains and plants for cooking and other needs, as well as enough ammunition to hold off a small army. In fact, the boxes of ammunition were stenciled US ARMY.

The Apache had also positioned a huge wooden bowl to collect rainwater from storms. The bowl was full, and Jason watched as women filtered the water through fabric before filling everyone's water skins. Afterward, warriors hid the cavern so skillfully with rocks and brush it looked completely natural. Jason figured he couldn't have found it even if he'd been told exactly where to look.

At the feast, Ishton directed a few of the women and children to carry bowls of food to Juh and the warriors. *Ancient One* sat directly to Juh's right, so Jason figured she must be someone of importance, maybe even Juh's mother or grandmother. Brown Hair, the only warrior with his long hair unbraided, sat to Juh's immediate left, and Jason mentally gave him the title of second-in-command. The young warrior kept looking at him, peering at him with his head cocked forward and a bit to the side, allowing his dark eyes to almost hide below his prominent brows. The look suggested contempt.

Ishton had organized the seating in a clearing away from the cooking fires. The elders and warriors sat on both sides of Juh and spread out in a circle. The rest of the people, about two dozen in all, sat scattered behind the members facing Juh. Jason sat several paces farther away. He was the last one served with food.

Juh rolled a leaf with some kind of tobacco, lit it, and blew smoke to the four directions. Everyone watched silently and Jason got the feeling it was an important ritual. Then the group ate in silence. When everyone had finished, Ishton again took charge, leading some of the women and children away. Juh began speaking quietly to the elders and warriors.

Jason retired deep into the brush to find a comfortable place to bed down. He'd become a part of the survivors' lives temporarily, but he still recognized the familiar loneliness that was typical of his life. By the habit of many years, he kept himself always on the outskirts of whatever group he happened to be near. He only felt truly safe when isolated from other people. That way, he didn't have to trust anyone, and he never had to wonder who might be a friend or an enemy. He never had to fear turning his back on anyone.

For a while, Jason listened to the muffled sound of somber Apache singing that filtered through the trees. The sound of the many voices held sadness and despair. Brown Hair visited him near midnight.

From his years of outlaw life, Jason learned to sleep light and on his back. He had a gun resting on his chest. He heard the warrior's careful approach long before he opened his eyes to scan the darkness. Unsure of the man's intentions, he cocked his gun and sat up. Brown Hair squatted next to him.

Jason gazed into the warrior's dark eyes. He couldn't quite figure out this man. He had seen gratitude in Juh's eyes, warmth in Daklugie's and Ishton's eyes, but Brown Hair's eyes showed a mixture of hatred and what he now guessed might be grudging respect. The warrior said nothing, but after a long moment he held out his Winchester in both hands. Jason took the weapon and Brown Hair stood and walked into the darkness.

Jason let himself slip into a light sleep. The next morning, he awoke as the sky lightened and imagined the feast from the previous night returning the strength to his body. He still felt tired from the long, hot days walking in the sun, but he was no longer weak from lack of food and water. When he approached the camp, Juh's gaze immediately caught the Winchester. He seemed to recognize the weapon and cast a glance over at Brown Hair who rested with some of the other warriors leaning leisurely against tree trunks or on the ground. Juh nodded at Jason with the barest hint of a smile.

"Brown Hair climbed down the canyon to gather up your bullets," Juh said. "He intended to kill you and take the long rifle." He paused. "Brown Hair hates all *White-Eyes*."

At that moment, it occurred to Jason that, with his light brown eyes, he fit into that category of people despised by the Apache.

"He almost did. I think your wife told him to spare me."

Juh nodded. "As you saved her and our son, she returned the deed. She declared you off-limits to all Apache warriors. No one is to harm you."

He smiled and Jason got the feeling Ishton's declaration was a powerful statement and was not to be ignored. Juh stood and motioned for Jason to follow him. He led the way along a path through the brush that ended on an outcrop overlooking the entire valley west of the mountains. He sat and patted the boulder next to him. When Jason sat, Juh continued.

"When I was younger than Daklugie, my father brought me

to this very spot. He told me of a day long past when everything you can see from here was land the Apache claimed as home. Grandmother tells of times when no one had ever seen a White man." He paused and shrugged. "Or a Black man."

The elder woman's leathery face filled Jason's mind. "The woman I carried...she is your grandmother?"

"Not *my* grandmother, but the grandmother of our people. She is the oldest living Apache known to all the tribes, everywhere in the land. She represents all we are and all we have ever been. Ishton told us you carried Grandmother across the desert for three days. By doing so, you have done our people a great honor."

Juh turned his head to face Jason. "And now Brown Hair hates all *White-Eyes* except one." Juh looked at the Winchester. "A warrior never surrenders his favorite weapon. Ever. He honors you with this gift." Juh indicated the clean but well-used Winchester. Jason liked the weapon. It fit comfortably in his grasp.

Jason nodded to the Apache leader. He understood the importance of the honor of receiving the gift. He and Juh sat in silence and gazed over the vista far below them. The scorched brown desert certainly wasn't quite to his liking. He preferred the lush green mountains of northern New Mexico and Colorado, but as he closed his eyes for a moment, he enjoyed the peaceful tranquility. He heard a few birds fluttering around but mostly heard only peaceful silence. When he took a deep breath, he savored the hot, dry fragrance of the land. He tasted both the sweet and pungent smells of high mountain scrub brush.

When he opened his eyes, Jason caught movement to his left. The long procession of the Apache families had come into view just below the ridge.

Juh nodded at the line of horses and people. "That is why I can't spare a horse for you. I have to get my people into Mexico where they'll be safe for a while. Killing the soldiers that murdered my people no longer matters. I know now there will always be more to take their place."

Jason sat silently. He studied the dark countenance of the warrior seated next to him.

"Tell me, *Jay-sone Peer*. Why does the White man hate us and drive us from our home?" Juh swept his hand over the distant valley that seemed to Jason utterly uninhabitable. "Why does he claim to own this land when he will never build a camp here?"

"I've heard that in the lands beyond the oceans, the governments that own the most land are viewed as the most powerful." Jason shook his head and looked away. "It doesn't matter if they will never use the land. If they could win a war against Mexico and Canada, they would probably claim those lands as well, and they'll kill anyone who threatens that claim."

During their journey the evening before, Juh had told him of the massacre and how these two dozen survivors were all that was left of his tribe of over a hundred. Jason tried to explain that the plan was to capture the village and force the warriors' surrender and that Crawford and his Buffalo Soldiers would never have murdered women and children. Juh responded that all soldiers were the same. They were trained to kill, and they'd continue to do so until there were no more native people to kill. He said that even if Jason had managed to kill Captain Taylor, another would take his place and the wars would continue.

"We are the *Indeh*," Juh muttered. "The Dead."

The two men stood and faced each other. Jason was about to speak, but instead nodded over Juh's shoulder. In the distance to the north, he saw Captain Taylor's men cresting a ridge about three miles away.

"We may still need your long rifle," Juh said as he led the way back to the main path.

They rejoined the procession and Juh sent a warrior ahead to tell everyone to hurry. In a few hours, they'd descend off the ridge. Then they'd have five miles of foothills to cross to get to the safety of the Mexican border.

Juh sent Jason to the front with two warriors to cover the women and children with the long rifle during their dash to the border. The rest of the warriors would ambush and delay the pursuing soldiers. Jason wasn't all that comfortable with the plan and preferred to be in the rear to face the main threat of danger, but he didn't argue. He supposed after a generation of eluding the army Juh knew what he was doing.

Jason and the two lead warriors jogged down the switchback trail into the scrub of the lower foothills. Late in the afternoon, sporadic gunshots echoed down from the high trail as Juh and his warriors skirmished with Captain Taylor's men. At the bottom of the switchback, the trail crossed a wide-open, bowl-shaped valley rimmed by six-hundred-foot ridges. The footpath meandered to the east a bit, then turned south toward a canyon opening that Jason made his objective.

The path crossed a sandy draw, and Jason paused to check for tracks. He'd lost sight of the two warriors, for they had easily outpaced him during the jog downhill. The prints of the two warriors ahead shuffled close together as if the men stopped to consider their options. Then one warrior veered up the draw to the left, while the other warrior went straight ahead across the draw, continuing along the path toward the canyon opening.

For no particular reason, Jason decided to move to the right, down the draw, since it also seemed to head indirectly toward the canyon opening. The soft sand of the dry creek yielded silently under his hard-sole moccasins as he jogged across the valley. The gunfire from the high trail picked up intensity, so he increased his pace as much as he could without becoming winded.

Jason ran with the Spencer in his left grip and the Winchester in his right. Being in unfamiliar territory, he had unhooked the loops securing his holster guns out of habit to prevent getting caught unprepared. The thought of his previous botched opportunity to kill the captain made him wonder if Taylor's men would find another way down into the valley before the Apache people escaped.

Glancing around during his jog, Jason knew immediately where he'd find a perch for his Spencer. A couple of boulders stood out atop the west wall. Concealed there, he could cover the entire valley. No way Taylor's men could get past him.

Turning his attention back to the path, he leaped over a dead tree trunk that had fallen across the creek bed. As his feet hit the sand again, a flurry of movement from a narrow draw off to the right distracted him. He dropped both rifles and grabbed a holster gun at the same time as the soldier grabbed his carbine. The man turned from his perch on the trunk of a dried-up bush growing out of the side of the embankment where he'd been resting his elbows. He dropped the spyglass he was using to study the distant battle. His Springfield was cradled over his left elbow, and he swung it around in one smooth movement at nearly point-blank range. Too late, Jason realized the soldier trying to kill him was Corporal Silas Nance. Both men fired at the same time.

CHAPTER 47

NANCE'S SHOT THUDDED INTO THE embankment behind Jason, but Jason's shot slammed Nance into the bush he'd been standing on. The corporal screamed in pain and started cussing. He dropped his weapon and fell to the sand. A yell came from several yards up the draw, around the bend.

"Corporal? You all right?"

Jason thought he recognized the voice. The other soldier called out again.

"Corporal?"

Jason decided quickly to take responsibility for the accidental shooting. "Over here," he called. "Nance just got shot."

By the time Private Hendricks came running, Jason had put away his gun and was cutting away the wool blouse of Nance's uniform with his belt knife.

Nance grunted in pain. "Thirteen years I been fightin' Injuns and never even got so much as a cactus needle stuck in me. Now, I go and get shot by one of my own kind."

Jason probed the area under Nance's right armpit. "I missed. Didn't even break the skin." The corporal grunted again as Jason moved his arm. "Creased a rib, I think. That's why it hurts so much."

"You sure? Feels like that lead is stuck in my chest somewheres."

"Trust me, I missed."

"What're we gonna do?" Hendricks said. "Them Injuns likely know we're here now."

"Help me get the corporal on his feet," Jason said. "Let's get him back to your camp."

"Git offa' me!" Nance waved off the helping hands and grunted his way to his feet. "You scared the hell outa me, comin' up on me like that. What're you doin' out here anyways?"

"Running from Captain Taylor. What're you fellas doing here?"

Private Hendricks answered as he retrieved Nance's Springfield and brushed dirt and sand from it. "We're huntin' the captain. And those Apache fugitives."

Jason thought to challenge the private's opinion but held his comments. He walked with the men but decided to leave his rifles behind. Nance held his right arm against his side as he led the way down the draw. Hendricks walked beside Jason. His lips were dried and cracked, and his dark face was ashen from lack of water and too much exposure to dirt, wind, and heat. Jason wondered how long the men had been out in the sun.

"Who's in command?" Jason said.

"That'll be First Sergeant Crawford," Nance said. "He's got scouts from Companies B and E lookin' all over these canyons for signs of those Injuns or the captain's men. I'm guessin' we just found 'em."

"That you did." Jason said nothing more until they met Crawford by the wagons half a mile outside the canyon exit.

One of the covered wagons held two huge water barrels while the other carried supplies and doubled as an ambulance for transporting wounded, if necessary. Crawford and another sergeant stood as Jason, Nance, and Hendricks approached. Jason shook hands with the big man.

"Glad to see you're still in one piece, Jason."

"Good to see you too, Lafayette." He almost called him L.C. like Shelton. That thought reminded Jason of the blue-eyed mulatto and he glanced around. "Where's Levi?"

"In the cemetery at Fort Bayard."

"Sorry to hear that," Jason said. "Seemed like a good man."

"He was." Crawford motioned at the shorter soldier at his side. "Sergeant Wilcox, Jason Peares." The men shook without speaking.

Crawford seemed to sense the same tension Jason felt. To Corporal Nance, he said, "Are those Apache up in that valley?"

"I suppose that's them up there trading shots with Cap'n Taylor's men," Nance said, nodding at Jason. "Didn't get a good look, though, before he came along and shot me."

"Shot you?" Crawford looked first at Jason, then at Nance's cut blouse.

"Accident." Jason shrugged. "Came upon each other by surprise and we both took shots."

"Except he didn't miss," Nance mumbled. He turned and headed toward the supply and ambulance wagon. "Thirteen years fightin' Injuns...." His voice trailed off.

"He just got a bruise, fortunately," Jason offered.

Crawford nodded. "Could be worse, I suppose."

He dismissed Hendricks, then he and Wilcox stood facing Jason. Crawford glanced down at the Apache ration bags hanging from Jason's belt. Daklugie had made them for him the day before and stuffed them full of extra food supplies. A similar pouch held his few remaining Spencer cartridges. Crawford's gaze drifted down to Jason's moccasins. He lifted an eyebrow in question.

"Looks like you got converted and done gone native on us."

"Lost my boots and most of my rig scrambling all over the mountains out yonder." Jason gestured to his belt and moccasins. "Just did what I had to do to stay alive, that's all. These moccasins are a heck of a lot tougher than boot leather, that's for sure." He paused for a moment and considered the distrustful look on Crawford's face.

"I'm not taking sides here, Lafayette. I'm just trying to help some innocent people avoid getting murdered. I think you know that's the captain's intention."

Sergeant Wilcox interrupted. "Innocent? Tell that to the Jimenez family."

Jason looked at the man. "Who?"

Crawford answered. "Seven ranch hands at the Jimenez Ranch murdered. Six children too. Apache war party raided the place, stole horses and food, and then burned the place down. Looks like it was Chief Juh's raiding party."

"I don't know anything about that," Jason said. "But what do you expect? You lure all the men away from camp, then ride in there and murder their unarmed women and children. I believed you when you said the army doesn't make war on women and children."

Crawford stared at Jason for a moment. "That was Captain Taylor's doing. He ambushed my men when we tried to stop him."

Jason broke the eye contact, suddenly feeling awkward. He knew in his heart Crawford could not have participated in mass murder.

The first sergeant continued. "I lost my lieutenant and seven good men. Four more seriously wounded."

"Sorry," Jason muttered. "Is that how Levi died?"

Crawford shook his head and walked a few steps away from Jason. "Levi took a poison arrow in the back. Warriors hounded us almost all the way back to the fort."

Jason stepped over to Crawford and laid his hand on the man's massive shoulder. He felt the same camaraderie he felt a week before, like the beginnings of a deep and lasting friendship. He sensed they both wanted to do the right thing.

"There aren't but a couple dozen of 'em left, Lafayette. They're just old men and women mostly, and a pregnant girl who looks like she wants to drop a baby any day. There's only half that many men left to protect them. Captain Taylor's huntin' 'em down like animals." He paused. "All they can do is run. They can't even really put up any kind of defense." Jason shrugged. "They're all fought out."

Jason pointed to the hills in the distance. "They just want to get home without getting killed. They're no longer a threat to anyone."

"I have my orders." Crawford shrugged Jason's hand from

his shoulder and turned to face him. "I'll have Captain Taylor, his men, Chief Juh, and all his Indians in chains before I ride back to the fort."

"Everything else has been taken from them." For a moment Jason spread his arms out, palms up, pleading. "Can't you just let them go in peace?"

"My orders are to end these Indian Wars. That won't happen until they're all stuck away on a reservation so they can't run around doing any more killing."

Crawford pointed a finger at Jason. "If you've got any influence with them, tell 'em to surrender." He looked up at the late afternoon sun. "Come first light tomorrow, I'm going in after 'em. Anyone holdin' a weapon is gonna get shot. Make sure they understand that clearly."

Jason stared at Crawford for a few seconds. Finally, he nodded, knowing he had little choice in the matter.

"I'll convey your instructions, but I reckon I don't have much influence with them. The only thing I have in common with the Apache is that Captain Taylor is hunting me too. I'd just as soon ride away from here, and if the captain wants to pursue me, I welcome the opportunity to have a one-on-one conversation with him."

He turned away and started walking back toward the canyon entrance. Jason glanced to his right and left. About thirty of the Buffalo Soldiers stared at him. Some had pitched their A-shaped tents against shrubs for shade. Others stood in the hot sun watching him. He could see they didn't trust him. Being soldiers, they would distrust anyone who looked to have taken up Apache ways, even if it was just to survive.

Even his new friend, Lafayette Crawford, didn't have an open mind about frontier survival. When all else was stripped away, Jason wasn't a soldier, and he wasn't an Apache. Same as with every other part of his life, he was involved with both and part of neither. He felt very much alone as he walked back into the canyon.

CHAPTER 48

JUH, BROWN HAIR, AND JASON sat silently in the same draw where Jason wounded Corporal Nance. He'd retrieved his rifles two hours earlier and continued up the draw, quickly finding the main group of Apache survivors. Jason guessed the other two warriors he'd come down the mountain with heard the gunshots and gathered everyone together, while other warriors scouted around to find the army waiting for them.

Jason relayed to Juh the conditions dictated by Crawford, then waited while the Apache leader consulted with his warriors and elders for a few hours. Sporadic gunfire occasionally ripped through the night as warriors played cat and mouse with Captain Taylor's men half a mile up the switchback.

The survivors gathered in a tight group, and Daklugie and the younger children slept curled up on the sand. A few paces away a single warrior, only visible as a shadow that rarely moved, kept watch on the approach from the canyon entrance. Jason figured another guard kept watch beyond the silent group.

The survivors were relatively safe down on the floor of the valley. Jason had discovered during the day that the valley was covered with dozens of dry gullies caused by storm water runoff from the surrounding canyon walls and hills. Some of the draws were too narrow for a person to navigate without walking sideways, while others were several feet wide. Some were barely shallow enough to allow crawling, yet others were almost ten feet deep. They joined and crossed each other, creating a maze of paths and hiding places. Crawford would discover the same maze at daybreak. He'd need twice as many men as he had available to find an enemy determined to remain hidden. That revelation gave Jason an idea which he conveyed to Juh in Spanish.

"If your men allow Captain Taylor to come down into the valley at sunrise, your people can sneak back up the switchback to the ridge while Taylor's men fight with the Buffalo Soldiers."

Juh remained silent for a while, then nodded. "The soldiers you met with will see us moving up the hillside. They'll have long rifles, won't they?"

Jason nodded. "Probably."

Judging by Crawford's seriousness earlier, he couldn't guarantee the Buffalo Soldiers wouldn't shoot at the escaping Apache. Captain Taylor certainly wouldn't give it a second thought. Now that he considered his own strategy in detail, he acknowledged it wasn't much of a plan. If the Apache were spotted heading up the switchback, whoever started shooting would have easy target practice.

Juh continued. "Are you willing to use your long rifle against the Buffalo Soldiers?"

Jason remained silent for a while, then shook his head. Juh and Brown Hair sat cross-legged, facing Jason. They began to converse in their own language. Jason picked up his Spencer and began cleaning it with a well-worn kerchief retrieved from his back pocket. While the two men talked, he pretended he was too distracted to notice he'd been dismissed.

"This is the end I've seen in my vision," Juh said to Brown Hair. His voice was almost a whisper. "If we fight, they'll kill all of us."

"If we surrender, they'll kill all of us," Brown Hair countered.

Juh nodded his head toward Jason, who was busy cleaning his rifle. "He thinks the Buffalo Soldiers won't kill us. He says Sergeant Crawford is a man of honor."

Brown Hair growled his contempt. "You cannot trust the

Black soldiers. They make war on us just like the White soldiers do. They treat us the same as the White soldiers treat them."

Juh sighed and shook his head. "You would think the Blacks would fight *with* us instead of against us. The elders say the same things that have been done to us have also been done to them."

"The Blacks are smarter than the Apache," Brown Hair muttered. Juh heard despair replace anger in the young man's voice. "They know the White soldiers can't be defeated. There are too many of them. So they joined them and learned their ways."

Juh nodded. "Years ago a traveler from an eastern tribe told my father he'd seen towns where Black settlers live with no White people among them."

"None?"

Juh shrugged. "They owned their lands and their houses, and they kept the crops they farmed and the animals they raised."

"They weren't herded onto miserable reservations like the Apache?" Brown Hair said. Juh shook his head, and the young warrior continued. "I don't understand how people claim to own land that's not theirs to own. Only *Ussen* possesses the lands."

Juh shrugged. "I don't understand it either. I just know it's one of the many ways our cultures differ. Maybe that is why they live, and we die. We concentrate on winning battles, but they always win the wars. They want to own everything. They buy everything with paper money, coins, and gold. If the Apache are to survive, we must learn to live in the White man's world like the Blacks have." He fell silent for a few moments before he continued. "You think if we surrender, they'll let us own some towns and some houses and farms that aren't on a reservation?"

"The Great White Father let Cochise own his reservation but didn't let him keep it. You've said this many times, Juh. And he promised Victorio his Warm Springs reservation forever if he would end his wars. And when he stopped fighting, they took back the lands they promised. Why would they let the Apache keep a reservation, or have even a small town? Even if they did, they'd probably only let us own the most worthless land they can find."

"But it would be *our* land," Juh said. "Maybe we could have a town with only Apache and no *White-Eyes* like the Blacks have."

"Then we'd have to farm crops like they do. And raise filthy animals."

Juh shuddered at the distasteful thought. "I know it's not the Apache way, but it's the sacrifice we must make to survive. It's what we must do to get the rest of our people to safety in Mexico."

At first, he wasn't sure if Brown Hair heard him, because the young man didn't react at first. Finally, Brown Hair looked over at him, confused. Juh continued.

"I will surrender to the Buffalo Soldiers—"

"I will never surrender!"

Juh saw Jason look up at the young warrior's outburst. The other warriors and most of the women and elders looked over also.

"I know. But *I* must surrender to save our people. The soldiers will not be satisfied without capturing me, but if they have me maybe they will leave this land. You and one other warrior will take everyone who can travel fast. Go up over the hills," Juh said, pointing with his nose to the high canyon rim where the moon was just rising. "I know it's a very hard trail, but those who are able can make it at night. Go east a ways until you're sure the Buffalo Soldiers won't see you and hurry south into Mexico. The soldiers can't follow you across the border. It's their law."

Brown Hair said nothing, just stared at Juh for a moment before looking at the sand again. Juh knew what the young man felt. Brown Hair no doubt believed those who stayed behind would never be seen alive again.

"Promise me one thing," Juh added quietly. Brown Hair looked up. "Don't let them kill my wife and son. If you're caught, don't give them a reason to murder the others."

Brown Hair looked from Juh to Jason, who had gone back to cleaning his Spencer.

Juh continued. "I know your heart is hard with hatred for the *White-Eyes*, but if they find you, don't force them to attack." The young man looked away. "Brown Hair, you are a great warrior, the most skilled fighter I've ever known. I know you may not feel ready yet, but I need you to be a great leader also. Please, do this for our people. Don't let them die."

Brown Hair closed his eyes tight and finally nodded. Juh sensed that was the hardest decision the young warrior ever had to make.

"I promise."

Brown Hair looked up briefly, and Juh saw the young man's watery eyes glisten in the moonlight as he fought with his emotions. Juh understood completely. While Juh had been elected into leadership, this young warrior now had that responsibility thrust upon him. The task of saving his people now fell solely on his shoulders. Still young and full of fight, Brown Hair wanted only to kill the enemy, not to think strategy or make sacrifices for the survival of the others.

Juh and Brown Hair rose and explained their plan to the warriors and survivors. Farewells were brief, though intense. Juh stood before Ishton silently. He held her cheeks in the palms of his hands for a moment. They stood toe-to-toe, foreheads resting against each other, noses touching. He gazed into her dark brown eyes as his mind swam into the past, remembering all the happy times and the hard times. He knew he shouldn't show his affection openly in front of the people, but he couldn't turn himself away. He knew he would never see Ishton again.

He released his gentle hold and turned wordlessly to his son. He gave Daklugie the same long gaze he'd given Ishton. Minutes later, the Apache survivors hurried into the darkness, led by a single warrior and followed by Brown Hair.

Juh watched them for a moment, then he turned and faced the few Apache who stayed behind. He walked over to Jason. Putting his Spencer aside, Jason stood and faced the leader.

"I will surrender," Juh said.

CHAPTER 49

C APTAIN TAYLOR LOOKED DOWN INTO the darkened valley. Every now and again, he saw a spark of light. Seconds later, he'd hear the distant report of a Winchester. The moonlight made the shadows seem even darker. Only the tops of trees and bushes were lit. The Indians moved with impunity in the blackness under the trees. He felt frustration boiling inside his chest. He'd barely been able to see the warriors with a spyglass during broad daylight. His men had no chance to find them at night.

The Black soldiers were down there somewhere also. He'd seen a patrol move through the canyon entrance earlier in the afternoon. There was probably a whole company camped out yonder, waiting for a report of the whereabouts of the Indians or himself.

Taylor considered this unfortunate development again. He figured he had at least as many men as the force camped beyond the canyon entrance. On the other hand, while that commander wouldn't know Taylor had picked up almost two dozen armed miners, Taylor knew he really had no tactical advantage. The miners were nothing more than gold-hungry Indian haters. Trained cavalry soldiers would tear them apart in a confrontation.

Now, Corporal Smith had more bad news for him. He felt the uneasiness of the man standing at attention behind him. Captain Taylor lectured to him without turning.

"These savages are geniuses. They were made for this land.

They know how to survive out here without food or water and they can slither around bushes to keep from being seen. Even their skin and clothing blend in with the terrain."

"Yes, sir," the soldier said quietly.

Taylor sighed and turned to face the man. "What's your report, Corporal?"

"We've lost four more men, sir. One private and three miners. Some of the other miners are talkin' about pullin' out and headin' back north."

"No great loss there," Taylor muttered.

"One more thing, sir. As you ordered, I sent a man out looking for another trail down into the valley."

"He found one?"

"No, sir. But he saw some Indians sneaking over the ridge out yonder." Smith pointed to the southeastern edge of the bowl of steep-sided hills. "Mostly women and children, a couple of old men, and two warriors."

Taylor looked to the south as if he could see in the dark. "Only the ones that can travel fast. They'll be in Mexico by noon." He thought for a moment. "That Chief *Hoe* is a smart man. The rest of the old folks and the wounded are goin' to surrender to the army."

"Sir, if they surrender, we won't be able to get at them or Jason Peares."

Taylor nodded to the darkness and faced Smith again. "Gather all the men together. Put that skinny private—Hodges, isn't it?" Smith nodded, and Taylor continued. "Put him in command of the retreating miners and send them north. Tell him the rest of the soldiers will cover the trail behind them if the Indians or the Ninth try to follow."

Smith hesitated. "But we're not followin'?"

Taylor shook his head at the obvious. "You and the other men are going to have to make an adjustment in your thinking." Smith raised an eyebrow. "We're not soldiers any longer, Corporal. We're fugitives now. We're outlaws. Those Black soldiers are gonna hunt us down because we killed their officer and some of their men." He paused to let his words sink in.

"The Indians down there are safe, and so is Jason Peares as soon as they surrender, and there's nothing we can do about that now. We've lost that battle. We've got to get down off this rock and hide out in Mexico. When it's safe in a month or two, we'll ride up to Silver City and get the gold from the bank. Clear?" He knew he was presenting a dangerous lie. If his men discovered the only gold available was what he carried on him, he was a dead man.

Smith focused his sharp blue eyes on Taylor. "That wasn't part of the bargain, sir."

"I know." Taylor sighed. "I certainly didn't anticipate this turn of events, but because of the situation, Corporal, the bargain must be modified. We have no choice. On the good side of things, your share of the gold gets larger as soon as the miners head north."

Corporal Smith flicked an eyebrow at that revelation and turned to his duties. He had the miners organized and headed north within fifteen minutes. An hour later, Captain Taylor led his men to the east, searching for a trail out of the mountains.

"What about those Indians that escaped, sir?" Smith said as he rode beside Taylor.

"They're headin' for the border also." Taylor guided his horse carefully around boulders and brush, trying to scout a path. "When we get down outa here, we'll try to pick up their trail. Maybe we'll get lucky."

Taylor accepted the frustration of the turn of events. At least Senator Bennington's plan had succeeded, though not quite in the way he'd wanted. With Juh's surrender there would be no unified Apache nation to wage war or dictate peace terms with the US Army. Unfortunately, without any written orders, Captain Taylor had no evidence that he was operating under the command of the senator, a fact he was sure was part of Bennington's plan.

Ambrose Taylor was about to be fed to the wolves. Of that, he was certain. He had to figure out a way to turn the tables on the shrewd senator.

CHAPTER 50

J ASON LAY ON HIS BACK and watched the sky brighten. Sleep eluded him all night. For the second time, he found himself considering how different his life might be now if he'd rode the other way when he first encountered the Apache survivors on the West Fork of the Gila River. That was never his way, though. Time after time he always stuck his nose in other people's troubles. He always helped those who couldn't help themselves.

Trouble. It was his old friend and shadow, his constant riding companion. He used to think trouble always came looking for him. In reality, he usually found trouble on his own without searching too hard.

When he was a kid, his father inspired him with stories of Black men who became educated politicians or social leaders, pillars of good character in the community and in government. He'd dream of someday becoming someone important, someone special, a leader crusading for the rights of others.

The chuckle he felt growing inside became quickly stifled by sadness. Jason's dream came true, though not in the way he imagined it would. On the trail of the men who murdered his family, he discovered—quite by accident—that he possessed deadly skills with a gun. He never dreamed he would kill four men at the young age of sixteen. He never dreamed he'd eventually become one of the highest bounty outlaw gunfighters in history.

Famous, he finally was.

Now, years later, he again found himself right in the thick of things, riding with his partner *trouble* yet again. He'd simply been trying to do the right thing without taking sides in a war that had no clearly defined friends or enemies.

He'd watched most of Juh's people walk into the darkness the night before, and the leader hadn't seen fit to explain to Jason where they were going. Later, the remaining warriors sat together and conversed for a while. Again, Juh didn't relate to him what was going on and Jason considered what that meant. The leader didn't trust him and neither did Crawford. Perhaps the secrecy was wise. Jason couldn't tell Crawford where the rest of the survivors were if he didn't know.

As the sky brightened, Jason heard the warriors whispering. They gathered their weapons and jogged away in all directions. Juh remained alone with Jason and the Apache survivors who couldn't travel fast.

"I will surrender now," Juh said.

"They'll keep hunting for the other warriors." Jason realized the warriors intended to keep the soldiers looking for them so they wouldn't ride after the Apache who had fled into the night. Those people were likely heading toward Mexico.

Juh nodded with a single movement of his head. "The soldiers won't find them."

Over the years, Jason had seen a lot of gun action, but he'd never seen or fought in a war. He imagined the conclusions of all wars must look a lot like the present moment. The victorious commander strutted around issuing directives and dictating terms, while the conquered commander, a proud leader in his own right, groveled for leniency and mercy for his people.

Jason wanted to say something comforting, to show his distaste for the whole business of war, but he remained silent. Carrying his Spencer in his right hand and Brown Hair's Winchester in his left, he turned and led the way toward the canyon entrance.

Ancient One hobbled alongside him, and he kept his pace slow for her. She muttered in her musical voice and almost instantly, Jason felt comforted, like he was not so much a part of the war or like he was immune from the miserable treatment these native people seemed destined to suffer. He thought he finally understood why this old woman was so special to the Apache.

With a backward glance, Jason saw that Juh followed a distance behind the rest of the survivors, leading the four army horses liberated from Captain Taylor's men. The warriors must have tied them a short distance up the draw, away from where the people slept.

Jason had always considered himself keen on noticing the tiniest details, but the Apache seemed almost mystical. He'd forgotten all about the horses. Now he wondered about other things. They must have taken the time to eat and drink, but except for the celebration feast the previous night he couldn't remember noticing when the group ate during the day. He never saw them make water or attend to other private business during their weeklong trip. As Jason glanced back again at the survivors, they didn't seem quite so mystical any longer. They looked defeated.

Jason saw the mounted Buffalo Soldiers blocking the canyon entrance long before he walked up. He led the survivors and Juh through a gap created when two of the soldiers nudged their horses aside. First Sergeant Crawford and Sergeant Wilcox had been summoned and stood waiting a hundred paces outside the canyon. A dozen soldiers encircled the small band of Apache, rifles pointed threateningly at the group. The eight survivors, including the pregnant girl, who looked like she was laboring, huddled close together in fear behind Jason and *Ancient One*.

Juh pulled the reins of the horses and walked up to Crawford carrying his Winchester in his right hand. He extended his arm and offered the weapon and the reins of the army mounts to Crawford. Jason translated the words Juh spoke.

"He surrenders to the United States Army and asks for merciful treatment of his people."

Crawford looked over the group. "I thought you said there was a couple dozen of 'em left."

"Counting the warriors who ran off into the darkness last night, there was about twenty-four or so, including these ten."

Ancient One kept singing in a voice Jason could just barely hear. The pregnant girl held her enormous belly. A young, wounded warrior with a heavily wrapped leg leaned on an elder man with long white hair. The warrior's leg had been shattered at the knee during the skirmish with Taylor the previous night. Five other elder women stood waiting for the army to make them prisoners. Juh spoke again.

Jason said, "As a gesture of honor, he presents these horses he took from the officer that murdered his people."

"Honor," Wilcox spat out. He stepped forward and slammed the stock of his Springfield rifle against the side of Juh's head. The Apache leader fell to the ground unconscious. Immediately, all the Apache huddled closer together and began singing what sounded to Jason like a mournful dirge.

Jason didn't speak or move, aware any action might get him arrested for sympathizing with the enemy. He sensed Crawford watching him.

The first sergeant spoke. "Sergeant, hogtie the chief, and get these people ready to move out." Wilcox pointed out four of the nearby soldiers as Crawford issued orders. "Then I want you to take Company E and half of B and clean out that canyon. Shoot any Indians you see. It's clear they aren't prepared to surrender."

"Yes, First Sergeant."

"And pursue Captain Taylor. If he saw us, he's likely running to the north. Send a scout back as soon as you pick up his trail. I'm sending these Indians back to the fort with a wagon, a water barrel, and a detail of four. I'll take the other ten men and a wagon with the other water barrel. We'll get ahead of the captain's men as soon as you discover which way they're headed."

"Yes, First Sergeant." Wilcox began barking out orders. Within minutes, all but ten of the Buffalo Soldiers rode into the canyon.

Jason heard a stream of obscenities from one of the soldiers herding the Apache survivors over to the wagons ten paces beyond Crawford. A private shouted repeatedly at *Ancient One*. She kept nodding and singing. For a moment Jason felt sorry for the old woman, but then realized she didn't understand the foul words the private showered upon her. When the private drew back his hand to strike the old woman, Jason stepped forward and shouted at the man.

"Hey!" he said. The private froze, stopped by the authority and the danger in Jason's voice. "Don't you dare hit that old woman." The young soldier glanced uncertainly at Crawford.

"Best you don't take sides here, Jason," Crawford said quietly. "Just let us do our job." Behind him, Jason heard the metallic sounds of rifle actions being worked.

"I told you I wasn't taking sides, Lafayette," Jason returned, exasperated. "C'mon, that woman's a hundred years old!"

"Woman?" the private said. "Come on, Sarge. She's an Indian. With all the people they done killed, they deserve to be hit."

From the corner of his eye, Jason saw Crawford shake his head at the private. "As you were, Private. Leave her be."

Jason took a deep breath. "Thank you."

"Look, Jason. These people are prisoners, and I intend to treat 'em as such." Crawford took a step forward and placed his giant hand on Jason's shoulder.

"Yeah, I know." Jason nodded and accepted the inevitable.

"You did your part, my friend. You kept 'em alive and safe from Captain Taylor and his men. I have my orders though, and I aim to follow 'em. Maybe it's time for you to leave. Take one of the captain's horses. The army won't miss one animal. Pick up some water and grub for your trip." Crawford nodded at the supply wagon where the Apache were being tied by the wrists.

Jason watched two of the soldiers drag Juh by the feet. They flopped the Apache leader down behind the water wagon and tied his ankles to his wrists behind his back. It occurred to him that if the army had captured a White officer of an opposing army, they'd treat him decently rather than like an animal.

Jason shook his head sadly. Crawford was right. He didn't want to stick around and witness how the prisoners would be treated, especially since he'd become emotionally close to them. The army was the victor, and the Apache were the conquered. If the situation were reversed, Jason was sure the Apache would treat the soldiers the same or worse.

Jason cradled the Winchester and the Spencer together under his left arm. "I'm obliged for the water and food, and for the horse."

"See the quartermaster." Crawford nodded at a corporal messing around the supply wagon. Then he peeled off his glove and offered his hand. Jason returned the handshake.

Five minutes later, Jason mounted up and departed without farewell and without looking back. Four hours later, he rounded a foothill and struck north.

Before he stopped in Silver City with Crawford and his detachment, he'd been heading up to Colorado in search of a place called Rosebud—one of the few Colored folks' towns west of Oklahoma and Texas. He figured he might as well ride that way again.

Jason soon found himself in that region of consciousness between heat-induced sleep and distant hypnotic awareness. His body motion blended with the rhythm of the horse's gait, the clip-clop of the animal's hooves the only sound his brain registered. He jerked upright in the saddle and reined up his horse. He'd seen something out of the ordinary, something that didn't belong on the desert floor.

Reining his horse around, Jason scanned the ground until he saw what he was looking for. The large, deep tracks of nearly a dozen big army horses followed alongside moccasin tracks. Noticeably absent were the tracks of the smaller, locally bred horses that the miners rode.

Somehow Captain Taylor had escaped out of the mountains and picked up the survivors' trail. For a moment, Jason considered following the tracks, but he knew he would have limited effectiveness alone against a dozen armed men. He needed help.

The tracks indicated that the soldiers were riding their animals at a walk, a smart tactic in the extreme heat. Without doubt, they'd overtake the Apache survivors that were afoot, so they really had no need to hurry. Jason spurred his horse into a run and headed back toward Company B. He could only pray that Crawford and his men hadn't already ridden off to intercept the miners who were obviously a decoy retreat force.

He hoped the first sergeant would find the compassion in his heart to prevent another massacre.

CHAPTER 51

CAPTAIN TAYLOR STUDIED THE TRACKS from his saddle. Corporal Smith cursed.

"We done been suckered, sir."

Taylor nodded. It looked like a dozen Indians had passed that way, but the tracks were too orderly, and they were headed in the wrong direction. The false trail gradually curved straight east when it should have led south if the Indians intended to escape to Chief Juh's mountain stronghold.

Taylor led the column of eight soldiers to the top of the low hill and signaled a halt. A couple hundred yards downhill, a lone warrior hopped and skipped down the hill, planting his prints side by side. Occasionally, he dragged his feet as if trying to give the impression of old or tired travelers.

"Ingenious," Taylor muttered. He looked down at the tracks again. He'd been so excited to find, and finally kill, the last of the Apaches, he hadn't looked close enough to notice that all the tracks were made from the same size foot. "This means the rest of the Indians are probably already in Mexico, somewhere southwest of here."

"We still headed that way, sir?" Smith said.

"That's right. At least we know the Ninth Cavalry can't follow us across the border."

The corporal pointed ahead at the warrior. "Don't look like he's got any weapons."

Taylor nodded. "They knew we were following. I figure he

knew we'd catch up to him, so he left his rifle with the others. Sacrificed himself so the rest could escape." He felt a tinge of respect for his enemy and shuddered, hoping his men didn't hear it in his voice. The Indians were animals. They deserved no respect.

Beside him, Corporal Smith started to pull Hansen's sniper rifle from the scabbard near his left knee. He froze when Taylor cast him a bone-chilling look.

"I thought we had an agreement about *not* killing the savages."

Corporal Smith stared at him. "You want him alive, sir? We can't even talk to 'em."

"I don't want him alive," Taylor said. He paused for effect, then continued loud enough for all the men to hear him. "I want him to suffer. Wait here."

Without waiting for a response, Captain Taylor pulled his Remington sidearm and put his horse into a slow trot down the hill.

Jason slowed his horse as he neared the camp of Company B. The animal protested and tossed its head from side to side, foaming at the mouth and throwing lather. Jason reined up in front of the supply wagon and swung his leg over the horse's head even before the animal stopped completely. He tossed the reins blindly to the soldier serving as quartermaster for the expedition and ignored the man's cursing admonishment of his treatment of army property.

With controlled desperation, Jason headed straight for the only tent that looked large enough to hold Crawford. At the entrance, he gazed inside to find the first sergeant and his three senior enlisted men. He vaguely caught enough of the conversation to understand that Company B was about to ride around the west side of the Animas range to trap Captain Taylor and his men on the north end.

"First Sergeant," Jason interrupted forcefully. "A word, please." He turned away from the tent and moved off several paces so no one would overhear their conversation. On his race back to camp, Jason had decided not to count on the army man's compassion. He knew he'd need a more forceful argument.

As he waited, Jason glanced over to the group of Apache survivors tied up by the wrists behind the water wagon. *Ancient One* and the others sat beside Juh, casting shade over their conquered leader.

Juh lay hog-tied on his side, his hands and feet tied together behind his back. A thick branch from a bush had been forced between his jaws, keeping his mouth wide open. Rope attached to both ends of the stick was tied behind his head so Juh couldn't wiggle the obstacle from his mouth.

Jason shuddered at the sight. He'd been similarly hog-tied five years ago after being captured by a posse. That day wasn't nearly as hot as what Juh had to endure. He turned away as Crawford stepped up beside him.

"What is it, Scout?" the soldier said harshly.

Jason stared at the man for a moment, realizing finally that the budding friendship he had imagined growing between them was nothing more than a faded dream, a casualty of war. Still, he could not let go of his sense of goodness in the big man standing before him.

"Lafayette," he said gently. "I'm not your enemy."

Crawford said nothing for a while, just stared at Jason through dark eyes. Jason matched the sergeant's stare. Crawford's gaze softened, and he looked away.

"I know that, Jason, and I apologize." His eyes searched the ragged canyon entrance absently. "Fact is, I was hopin' we'd become friends after all this business with the Indians is done with."

Jason nodded. "I had similar thoughts."

Crawford said, "I ain't gonna be in the army forever. And now that Levi is gone, I'm a bit short of friends."

Jason appreciated Crawford's confession, knowing his words

were as close to an emotional appeal as he'd ever get from the man.

"You want Captain Taylor, right?"

"That's a fact."

"You won't find him up north," Jason said. Crawford's eyes narrowed. "I figure he sent the miners and some soldiers up north to get you to follow them." He paused as the first sergeant considered the logic of the deception.

Jason continued. "I ran across his tracks east of here. I reckon he knows he's a hunted man. He's heading down into Mexico."

CHAPTER 52

FIRST SERGEANT CRAWFORD TURNED AWAY immediately and then hesitated. Without turning back to face Jason, he said, "You darn near killed an army horse just to get back here to tell me where Captain Taylor is?"

It wasn't really a question, but Jason answered anyway. "Well, not exactly." He pushed his hat up a bit, then kicked at a tuft of desert grass.

Crawford turned to face Jason. "They're chasing the Indians, aren't they?"

"Yeah."

Twice, Crawford acted like he was going to say something, sucking in a breath and opening his mouth as if to speak. Finally, he threw up his hands and stomped back to his tent. Before going inside, he turned.

"I don't give a hoot about those damn Indians. You best get outa here before I have you roped up like those Apache." He stooped and entered the tent.

Jason waited a few seconds, then said, "But you want Captain Taylor, don't you? You want him because he killed your men." He paused. "And he killed your friend."

Almost half a minute passed while he played the waiting game. He almost turned away by the time Crawford stepped back out of the tent.

"Where is he?"

"It'll cost you." Jason held his ground, knowing Crawford already knew the price.

Crawford angled his head so the soldiers inside the tent would hear him. He ordered a corporal to form up a detachment of ten men.

"We'll find the captain's tracks on our own."

Jason agreed. "Sure, but I can save you two or three hours." He paused. "It's mighty hot out here, Lafayette, and you'll be wantin' to catch up before they cross the border. I know which direction they're headed." He wasn't sure at all about the last, but if he had to lie to keep Taylor from murdering the survivors, so be it.

"If I come across those Indians, I'm bringin' 'em back as prisoners."

Jason nodded. "At least they'll be alive. And when you find the Apache, you'll find Captain Taylor." He turned toward the quartermaster's wagon. "I'll be needin' another horse. That one," he nodded at the horse he raced in on, "is all tuckered out."

Crawford grunted but didn't argue and Jason switched his saddle to a fresh horse tied up with the picketed animals. Jason checked the Spencer rifle and tied it on the right side of the pack behind the saddle. Then he tucked Brown Hair's Winchester in a loop of rope on the left side of the saddle. It wouldn't be convenient if he had to get to it in a hurry, but at least he had it with him. Confident those weapons were loaded and ready, Jason checked his Schofield holster guns.

Jason mounted up and paused beside the water wagon. Juh looked up at him. He looked in considerable pain because the stick in his mouth was too long to allow him to lie on his side without crooking his neck, with his face toward the sky. Even worse, he couldn't lay on his back on account of the way he was hog-tied, a fact that was obviously intended by his captors.

He reined his horse around and took his position beside Crawford as the detachment rode to the east. After a few moments, Jason experimented with conversation. It felt oddly uncomfortable after more than a decade of being alone with few friends to make conversation with.

"I suppose an active army life doesn't blend well with making a lot of friends," Jason said. He didn't know how to convey that he understood how war sometimes snatched those friends away, but he figured Crawford knew what he meant.

The first sergeant glanced at him. "I wouldn't say that. Usually, we have plenty of time to sit around and get to know each other." He gestured with a hand toward the men following them. "This month, the patrols have been out of the ordinary."

"Really?"

"Usually, we spend nigh on two weeks a month on patrol and never see hide nor hair of these Indians. Time we get a report of them killin' somebody or stealin' somebody's animals, they're long gone. When we cut their trail, they done already crossed over the border. Either that, or they lay false tracks. This month, we've been on the go constantly for almost five weeks now."

"The way people talk over in Texas, I thought the conflict with the natives out here was pretty severe."

Crawford nodded. "That's why they sent the Ninth Cavalry out here a few years back. The Tenth stayed over in Texas—"

"That's the other Black cavalry?"

"Yeah. We got the Comanches pretty much under control out there, and the Apache were starting to cause trouble out in Arizona and here in New Mexico." Crawford paused, as if reminiscing.

"First it was Cochise and his Apaches that had to be subdued. I heard he was a tough old chief. Smart too. The old wise ones always wanted to talk peace rather than risk a war they knew they couldn't win. I think it was the Sixth Cavalry that finally got his people tucked away on the San Carlos reservation.

"Then we—the Ninth—got involved when Victorio moved into the Black Mountains north of Fort Bayard. We've covered a lot of miles trying to find him." Crawford paused again. "It's the young chiefs who cause all the trouble nowadays. They aren't afraid to run around the frontier killing. Still think they're invincible. Then there's this new warrior chief named Geronimo."

Jason nodded to himself. "I've heard of him."

"Keeps running away from San Carlos, causin' trouble here and there. We keep a patrol after him, but he always seems to find his way back to the reservation. Army's not too worried about him. I doubt anyone will even remember his name ten years from now. He ain't half the leader Victorio is. Or that wily old Nana."

Crawford grunted a sound that Jason interpreted as grudging respect. "Now there's a crafty old warrior, Nana is. I heard from the Mexicans he's got some woman-warrior with him who can sniff out soldiers and ammunition. He keeps hittin' supply wagons and gets away clean every time. Never falls for the decoys, thanks to that woman."

When Crawford fell silent, Jason asked, "So what keeps you out here?"

"What's a Black man gonna do out here if he ain't in the army?"

"Well," Jason shrugged. "You could always be an outlaw." He chuckled.

"You got a point," Crawford said with mock seriousness. "Lots of opportunities for extended travel and mountain camping." They laughed.

"That's right. I've actually been to both borders, top and bottom, as well as the Pacific Ocean, and pretty much everywhere in between. Of course, I never got to enjoy a place for very long, and I don't collect much in the way of friends. Except for the lawmen and posses and bounty hunters, of course."

Crawford chuckled. "I suppose every occupation has its bad side."

Jason was about to say more when they cut the tracks of Taylor's horses. They had followed the trail south for an hour when the trail curved eastward.

"Hold on a minute," Jason said. Crawford halted the column and Jason dismounted to study the tracks closer.

"Does seem like they're headed the wrong way," Crawford agreed.

Jason stood and nodded. "I've seen this trick before." The Arapaho warrior he rode with a couple years back used the same method of deception over in Arizona. "One warrior lays these tracks, makes it seem like a whole crowd went this way. Meanwhile, the others wiped their tracks up and went that-away." He stood and gazed to the southwest.

"You sure?"

"Positive," Jason said as he mounted up. "We'll have to ride back to where the trail turns, then spread out and ride across the terrain. I'm guessing we'll pick up their trail about a quarter-mile after that."

Jason led the detachment as he had suggested and within half an hour, he found the trail of the survivors.

"Looks like they're moving fast." He urged his horse into a trot and the column did the same. "Fifteen people plus one warrior, assuming the second warrior's the one who led Taylor astray."

Private Hendricks spoke up from the column, his voice filled with doubt. "You can tell how many there are from all these messed up tracks?"

Jason didn't slow his horse. "No, I saw them leave last night."

An hour later, Crawford called the detachment to a halt. "This is as far as we go."

"Excuse me?" Jason must have worn his feelings of ridicule all over his face.

"See those hills yonder?" Crawford said. Jason scanned the hilly landscape and picked out a set of three tall hills half a mile away. "That's the Mexican border."

"The Apache won't stop at the border," Jason countered. "And I can guarantee you Captain Taylor won't stop."

"The US Army cannot conduct operations on foreign soil," Crawford said as he pulled his reins about.

"Lafayette, Captain Taylor won't be too far behind those survivors. If he catches them before they get to high ground...."

Jason pointed to the distant peaks that shimmered in the heat about five miles away. "There *will* be another massacre."

"I'm sorry, Jason. We'll be headin' back."

Jason watched the column turn away. "I'm not in your army, Lafayette. I'll be goin' forward." He spurred his horse ahead and heard Crawford call after him.

"Not on an army horse, you won't."

CHAPTER 53

JASON STOPPED HIS MOUNT AND turned to face Crawford as the man rode over to him. The first sergeant was a no-nonsense man in command of a military operation, and he wouldn't back down. He couldn't back down.

"You figurin' on stoppin' me?" Jason said.

"Hell no." Crawford shook his head. "I've seen that look in your eyes a couple of times now. I reckon you're about as stubborn as I am." He stuck out his hand. "I'll wish you good luck."

"I'm grateful." Jason reached out and accepted the handshake. "And I hope to be seein' you again, my friend."

Crawford paused for a moment. "Look, I know you don't believe in my God, but I hope He blesses you anyway."

Jason thought about *Ancient One* and nodded. Then he reined his horse to the south. A half hour later, the tracks veered around the east side of a set of craggy hills that exploded from the desert floor. Jason decided to save time by taking the direct route over the hills. At the top, he gazed into the distance and saw the strung out line of tiny figures disappearing behind a low hill. Waves of heat shimmered off the desert floor making the Apache look like undulating shadows.

About a mile east of the Apaches, a single line of horsemen raced across the desert. They'd catch the Indians out in the open behind the hill, but there was nothing Jason could do about it. At two miles distance, they were far outside the range of his Spencer.

He yanked his canteen from a hook on the saddle pack and drank deeply of the hot liquid. Then he spurred his horse into a run down the hill and up the second hill. When he reached the top, he saw nothing but empty land. The Apache and the soldiers had completely disappeared.

Or had they? Jason saw a discoloration in the landscape about half a mile away, like a faint shadow painted across the desert floor. A rift or a crevasse, probably wide and deep from the looks of the shadow.

Taylor was either extremely confident or very foolish for following the Indians into the rift. Did he know only Brown Hair protected the survivors? Some of the elders carried rifles, but Jason knew they'd only survive a short time against Taylor's heavily armed men.

Jason ran his horse toward the west edge of the depression. He found a way down that his horse could manage, then proceeded cautiously toward the east. He pulled the Winchester free and checked to make sure a round sat in the chamber.

Scanning the thirty-foot-high walls of the canyon, he almost felt trapped. The valley floor was a jumble of rocks and boulders, extremely hard to navigate while looking above for an ambush. The whole valley snaked back and forth, and huge boulders jutted out from the walls so Jason could never see more than a dozen feet ahead. Jason decided to dismount. He ground-tied his horse and moved forward cautiously.

An explosion of rapid gunfire sounded like it came from just around the next boulder. Jason scrambled up the north wall a bit, trying to find a perch on a boulder. He just got a foothold, preparing to climb onto the rounded top of a huge rock, when a face suddenly appeared beside him. He reacted quickly and for the second time in as many weeks, he found himself pointing the business end of a Winchester at Ishton's chest.

Jason immediately angled the rifle away and helped Ishton through the space between the rocks. Behind her, several elders and children followed. The Apache obviously knew this rift well. Ishton led her people through the pass beside Jason's boulder to the next leg of the winding canyon, shielded from the closely pursuing soldiers by the curve in the rock walls.

Climbing atop the rounded boulder, Jason looked for targets. About twenty feet below him, he saw Brown Hair retreating, covering the escape of an elder, gray-haired man. The old man moved well for an aged warrior, navigating quickly and deftly up the steep side of the canyon toward Jason. Every now and again, they'd both turn and shoot in the direction of advancing soldiers Jason still couldn't see from his position.

When the old warrior had made it to safety, Brown Hair backed his way up the incline, still shooting until his rifle was empty. He turned, tossing the Winchester aside, and scrambled through the pass as Jason sighted on a Sixth Cavalry private taking aim at the warrior's back.

Jason fired, hit the private in the center of his forehead, and the shooter vanished behind the rock he had used as protection. Almost immediately, Jason heard the pounding of many hooves and knew Captain Taylor was going to brute-force his way to victory.

Taylor and four mounted soldiers charged into view while the remaining three skirmishers opened up on Jason's position. Bullets pinged off the rocks near him. He tried to roll off the boulder but slid off the side instead. He flailed at air until he hit the ground. The rocks on the steep canyon wall gave way under his boots and he tumbled several more feet to the valley floor.

What should have been a mild tumble turned disastrous when he banged his head and left elbow against rocks. The Winchester bounced out of his grasp. His arm went numb immediately, and his head felt like he'd been struck by a hammer.

Jason almost blacked out. He heard a deafening ringing in his ears. Then a shadow moved toward him and descended over him. Lying on his back, he finally focused upside down on the face that sneered down at him. He recognized the sharp-featured face but couldn't remember the soldier's name. The man grinned and pointed his Springfield at Jason's head as horses thundered by. In a panic, Jason grabbed for his right gun, but without the leather loops in place, his right gun had fallen out of its holster during his tumble. His left arm was numb and completely useless.

The soldier aimed his rifle and pulled the trigger.

CHAPTER 54

T HE FLASH OF FLAME BLINDED Jason. The explosion of
sound echoed in his ears. There was no time to react or
move, and he had no chance to reach across his body
with his right hand to grab for his left gun. Somehow, the soldier
missed from point-blank range!

He rolled slowly to his knees and saw the soldier's dead body
lying faceup on the rocks a few feet from him, his chest a bloody
mess. Then he heard a familiar voice boom into the rift from
above. It was First Sergeant Lafayette Crawford.

"That'll be about enough, Captain Taylor. By order of Colonel
Hatch, commander of the Ninth Cavalry, I call upon you to surrender your arms." The man paused, and Jason got the feeling he enjoyed his announcement immensely. "You are under
arrest."

The captain and his mounted men had already passed Jason
on their way to overrun the Indians. The two remaining foot soldiers had yet to catch up and stood near Jason and the dead
soldier, surprised by the sudden appearance of the Ninth.

Crawford had the high ground. The renegade soldiers knew
this and looked around for cover or escape. Taylor seemed to
examine his diminished tactical options. He and his men were
caught like fish in a barrel. From the ridge thirty feet above
them, there was no way Crawford and his men would miss.

Only problem was, he was right in the line of fire. He counted
only four men with Crawford. The other six were probably moving

up both ends of the rift. No doubt Taylor saw the same trap, so he pulled his Remington sidearm and fired the first shot.

Jason balled himself on his side into as small a target as possible. He didn't want to catch any stray lead. He heard a brief exchange of gunfire, two volleys from above, then silence. When he looked up, only Captain Taylor remained on horseback. His other soldiers and their horses lay dead.

Jason collected his Winchester, then moved his left arm around as the numbness slowly subsided. He saw Captain Taylor still holding his pistol pointed up at the soldiers on the ridge, waving it back and forth as if trying to decide on a target. As he finally lowered his gun, he looked around at his dead men.

Clearly, Crawford had ordered his men to capture the captain alive. Taylor caught Jason's gaze and hatred radiated from his dark eyes. Jason saw the captain's decision to act in the flicker of his left eye, long before the man shifted his pistol over to take a shot.

Jason had just located his Schofield and tucked it away in its holster. He still had his hand hovering near the low-slung gun butt. Taylor only had to move his own pistol a few inches for the shot. The captain had already thumbed the hammer back. He simply shifted his aim.

Jason didn't think or contemplate consequences or possibilities. He simply reacted as he had in hundreds of quick draws. He pulled his Schofield and fired as Taylor's eyes widened in surprise at the speed of his draw. His bullet slammed the captain from his saddle.

The mounted Buffalo Soldiers converged from both ends of the rift about the same time. Crawford scrambled down the steep slope, under cover of his four soldiers above, and barked out orders. The cavalry quickly rounded up Brown Hair and the other survivors, then they buried the dead prisoner-soldiers of the Sixth Cavalry under a pile of rocks.

Crawford stepped over to face Jason. Jason shook his hand.

"I sure am glad you had a change of heart, Lafayette."

Crawford shrugged. "Would've had to listen to Corporal

Nance's whining all the way back if I left you out here without help."

Jason glanced over Crawford's shoulder where Nance stood supervising the other soldiers. Hearing Crawford's comment, Nance flashed Jason a smile and winked.

Crawford added, "I've seen some fast gun work before, but I've never seen a man pull a piece like you just did."

Jason shrugged. "Got good at it over the years."

"Except I wanted him alive."

"I'm sure you'll find he's still alive, unless he broke his neck fallin' from his horse."

They walked over to Taylor who was beginning to stir. He had blood soaking into his right shoulder, near his officer's insignia.

"Private Hendricks," Crawford called to the nearest soldier. "Secure the captain to his horse."

"Yes, sir."

Crawford shot the private a look of disapproval that the man didn't see. Taylor opened his eyes just as Hendricks bent down as if to help the man to his feet. Instead, he deliberately laid his boot hard across the captain's head. Then he stood over the unconscious officer and looked sheepishly at Crawford.

"Sorry, sir. I must've slipped."

"Quit callin' me sir."

"Yes, First Sergeant."

"And see that you watch your step from now on." Crawford added a smile as he turned away.

"Yes, First Sergeant." Hendricks wrestled Taylor's unconscious body across the saddle and tied his hands behind his back.

Farther up the rift, Jason saw Brown Hair and the other Apaches being led away, all tied to each other by the wrists. Four hours later, the Buffalo Soldiers led their prisoners into the camp at the south end of the Animas Mountains. As they approached from the southeast, the new arrivals didn't see Juh tied up until they came upon the first group of prisoners behind the water wagon.

Brown Hair let out a wail of anger, what Jason guessed was his war cry. In a flash of movement, he produced a small knife hidden in his hair, cut himself free, and ran the last few steps to his leader. Instantly, the four soldiers standing guard covered him with their rifles. The rest of the prisoners shuffled quickly over and protectively surrounded Brown Hair and Juh. The mounted cavalry raised their weapons to cover the group.

Crawford dismounted and pulled his sidearm. Pointing it through the group at Brown Hair, he motioned for him to step aside. Brown Hair froze with his knife poised to cut Juh's bonds. He glanced down and moved to continue but stopped again when the click of Crawford's hammer split the silent air. Though still tied to some of the other Indians, Ishton stepped in front of Crawford's gun and Daklugie stepped in front of her.

The first sergeant grabbed the boy and shoved him aside so hard he tumbled to the ground with several other survivors tied to him. Then Crawford pointed his pistol between Ishton's eyes. She raised her chin in defiance and closed her eyes.

Jason sat on his horse, knowing there was nothing he could do to stop what was happening. The scenario before him could only end one way. The war and hatred between the army and the Apache had lasted for many years and would likely last many more. Jason couldn't interfere. Even if he did, he wouldn't make a difference. He'd just get Apache and soldiers killed, probably including himself.

The conqueror and the conquered. It was the way of war.

Jason nudged his horse away from the rest of Company B and looked off into the distance. He waited for the gunfire.

CHAPTER 55

BROWN HAIR STILL PEEKED BETWEEN the people who stood over him, but now he rose up and spoke a single word. He tossed the knife at Crawford's boots and shoved his way toward the first sergeant, arms wide in surrender.

Jason saw the Buffalo Soldiers exchanging nervous glances. Two shifted their aims to cover Brown Hair as he stepped forward. The warrior repeated the same word, edging between Ishton and Crawford. He knelt down on one knee and bowed his head, arms still spread wide. The first sergeant nodded and holstered his gun.

"Corporal Nance," Crawford said, finally lowering his Remington. Nance stepped up with his Springfield pointed skyward. "Cut the chief and the others loose."

Nance elbowed his way toward Juh. With his belt knife, he cut the rope binding Juh's wrists and ankles, then none-too-gently sliced the rope holding the branch in his mouth. While he worked, Nance looked up nervously at the Indians around him as if wary of a sudden attack. When freed, Ishton knelt beside her husband and pulled the stick from his mouth, then began massaging his arms and legs.

"Corporal Nance—"

Crawford seemed about ready to say more when Captain Taylor shuffled over from the supply wagon. Shackles bound his hands behind his back, and he dragged his leg-iron chains noisily as he stutter-stepped forward. He spat in Crawford's face and cursed him.

"You should've killed all those goddamn savages!" When Crawford didn't respond, the captain continued. "That's why you Black bastards will never be worth anything in this great nation of ours. You can't ever make the tough decisions."

Taylor took a deep breath and looked around at the Buffalo Soldiers. "This country would be better off if all of you went back—"

Jason had dismounted and stepped over close to Crawford and launched a vicious sidekick that struck Taylor in the gut. He yelled with the effort, put all his weight behind the kick, all his anger and frustration. Taylor's breath exploded from his chest with a loud grunt, and he doubled over.

Jason said, "Maybe the first sergeant has to listen to that crap from you, but I don't." He grabbed Taylor by the back of his uniform and shoved him to the ground.

Hands shackled behind his back, Taylor fell face first. When he thrashed about, trying to get back to his feet, his face ground into the dirt. His boot kicked Brown Hair's knife near the feet of the defiant warrior. With a very slow and controlled motion, Brown Hair picked up the weapon and slowly dragged Captain Taylor to his feet by his hair. He put the blade against the man's neck.

Brown Hair and Crawford locked gazes. Neither man spoke a word.

CHAPTER 56

A COUPLE OF THE BUFFALO SOLDIERS started forward, but Crawford stopped them with a single motion of his hand, his gaze still on Brown Hair.

"Corporal, have the men stand down."

"First Sergeant?" Nance took a halting step forward. "Did I understand you correctly?"

"You did."

Nance paused, then repeated the military orders. Around him, the Buffalo Soldiers raised the barrels of their rifles toward the sky. Crawford took two steps forward and pulled his pistol. He placed the barrel of his Remington firmly against Brown Hair's face, just left of his nose.

"Scout, tell him to let the captain go."

As Jason translated the command into Spanish, the rest of the prisoners shuffled out from behind Brown Hair. They seemed to know that Crawford's bullet would pass straight through the warrior's skull.

Juh got to his feet with Ishton's help and in a scratchy voice, translated Jason's words into the Apache language. Brown Hair stared at Crawford and spoke a few words.

"He says your Black soldiers fight with honor. He asks permission to kill the man who murdered his people."

Crawford glanced at Jason. "He asks?"

Jason spoke to Juh who nodded with a single movement of

his head. With a nod, Jason said, "That's what Juh says. Brown Hair is asking your permission."

"This man is a war criminal," Crawford said, shaking his head. "He has to stand trial for his crimes. If people know what he did, he'll be punished. That might stop others from murdering Indians."

Jason translated, and the warriors exchanged words. "Brown Hair doesn't trust the White man's law. He wants to use the Apache law."

"Tell him this isn't Apache land anymore. It's my country. And everyone—White, Black, and Red—follows my laws. Tell him if he kills this man, I will shoot him."

Jason translated, and the two men continued to stare at each other. Brown Hair nodded and spoke.

After Juh translated, Jason said, "Brown Hair says he respects your command. He will not kill Captain Taylor."

The warrior moved the knife upward, away from Captain Taylor's neck. He kept raising it and stopped the blade at Taylor's forehead. Then he pressed the sharp tip into the man's skin.

Taylor's eyes bulged and he screamed in pain. He squirmed and jerked, but the muscular warrior had a firm grip on his hair. Brown Hair looked deep into the captain's eyes and very slowly he raked the blade around the right side of Taylor's head to the back, then reached around the left side and repeated the motion. Even above Taylor's high-pitched squeals of agony, Jason could hear the blade grate against the captain's skull.

Nance stepped forward, aiming his Springfield. "First Sergeant! You gotta do something. He's an officer!"

"As you were, Corporal," Crawford answered. He stepped back and holstered his gun. "This man is no officer in my army. He's a murdering criminal. If this is Apache justice, I'd say no one deserves it more."

"Senator Bennington!" Taylor shouted. "He gave me orders. I can prove it. I'll tell you everything. Make him stop. Please!"

Crawford said nothing, but Jason stepped forward and put a hand on Brown Hair's arm to stay his knife.

"Where can I find the senator?"

"El Paso. He said he was going back there."

Jason thanked him and nodded at Brown Hair. The young warrior spoke in the Apache language. Juh translated.

"He says that for the rest of this man's life and wherever his spirit goes in the afterlife, the murderer will be forever dishonored and disfigured."

Brown Hair turned Taylor away and held him by his hair at arm's length. Even as the captain begged for mercy, Brown Hair placed his foot against the man's back and shoved. Hairless, Taylor hit the ground with a whimper at Corporal Nance's feet.

Brown Hair raised his face to the sky and yelled a long wail of agony. In the end, the warrior looked at Crawford again and tossed the knife and the scalp at Taylor's twitching body.

"Corporal Nance, wrap a bandage around that mess. I don't want him dyin' before we get him back to the fort for trial." He paused for a moment and then added, "And round these people up and get 'em ready to move out."

Nance relayed orders as Private Hendricks stepped forward.

"Uh, sir, move 'em out where?"

"I'm not gonna tell you again, Private."

"Sorry, First Sergeant."

"Sarge will do just fine."

"Well, Sarge," Hendricks said hesitantly. "What'll we do with 'em?"

Crawford looked at Jason then at the Apache. Jason studied them too. There was no fight left in any of these people, not even in the fierce warrior, Brown Hair. They'd seen almost their entire tribe wiped out. On a last run for freedom, they'd been captured and forced to see their leader humiliated and gagged like an animal. Now they huddled together, looking pitiful and defeated.

Jason finally understood what Juh had tried to tell him over the last couple of days. The Apache had accepted their fate. They'd live or die at the whim of First Sergeant Lafayette Crawford of the US Army.

Crawford looked back at Jason. To Hendricks, he said, "Get 'em the hell outa my country."

"Sarge? You mean, let 'em go?"

Crawford looked at Hendricks for a few seconds. "Form a detail of two and escort the Indians to the border. Shoot anyone who strays from that path. Otherwise, take no action against them. Is that clear, Private?"

"Perfectly, Sarge."

The Apache survivors were quickly gathered together and led across the desert. With mixed emotions, Jason watched them leave. He'd lived with the Apache for only a short time, but still he had built a kinship with them. He saved some of their lives and they saved his.

Now they were nothing more than vanishing shadows in the heat waves. They didn't look back. Not Daklugie, or his father, or his mother. Not Brown Hair or Ancient One. He didn't know whether to be sad or relieved. A part of him wanted to acknowledge their kinship and have them acknowledge it. Another part of him never wanted to see them again.

Jason turned to First Sergeant Crawford. "Doesn't seem like the army way, Lafayette."

"Field commander's prerogative," Crawford said. "My standing orders are to stop the Indian Wars. Those people aren't going to be doing any more warring." He paused. "Besides, I'll need my resources to hunt down those warriors that ran off and also to round up those miners."

Jason looked away to the east, and Crawford seemed to read his mind.

"You figure on lookin' after the senator?"

Jason looked him in the eye and nodded. "I aim to have a talk with him."

The first sergeant looked at him for a long while, then said, "During that conversation, be sure to give him my regards." Crawford paused. "And Levi's."

"I'll do that."

"Be careful, Jason. The senator likely has powerful friends

and that could mean some measure of trouble for you." Crawford managed a grin.

"Me and trouble, we go way back." Jason paused. "You goin' back on the trail?"

"I don't know." Crawford shrugged. "We'll get the captain back to the stockade, and he'll get transferred somewhere he can get a fair military trial. Me, I got a couple days leave coming, then I suppose we'll ride out again on patrol." He was silent for a long time, and Jason returned his gaze.

The first sergeant said, "I have to admit, Jason. I do believe I've had my fill of this damned war."

Corporal Nance reported that the troop was ready to ride to the northwest to meet Company E. Crawford and Jason both mounted up and shook hands.

"You're a good man, Jason."

"If you decide it's time to do something other than soldiering, look me up in Colorado. Place called Rosebud."

Crawford spurred his horse to take the lead position of his company, and Jason spurred his mount into a walk, heading east. For a moment, he thought about just turning around and riding north with the Buffalo Soldiers. Maybe he could take a stab at keeping some friends for a while. Then he realized that his appointment with Senator Bennington couldn't wait.

As he'd become accustomed over the years, Jason Peares became a part of the landscape, blending with the heat waves of the desert. His friend and shadow, trouble, was never far away.

TO BE CONTINUED

If you enjoyed this adventure, check out the next book in the Jason Peares saga at JeffreyPostonBooks.com or wherever you buy books. Please let other readers know what you thought of the book by leaving a brief review at your favorite retailer. It only takes a moment and reviews are very valuable to authors.

THE MAKING OF WARRIORS

Warriors is chronologically the third in the four-book Jason Peares historical western series. This is a work of fiction, but the conflict between the (Black) Buffalo Soldiers of the Ninth Cavalry and the Apache warriors in the early 1880s was very real and well documented in history books. This was not just a two-sided conflict, though, because there were political and economic factors regarding the business of war that heavily influenced the continuation and outcome of the conflict.

What I've tried to capture in this story are the thoughts and feelings of the characters on all sides of the conflict as they live through this adventure, in essence to give you, the reader, a glimpse of what life and war were really like for the Apache warriors and the soldiers during their struggles to fight and survive. The characters are fictional, but they're based on the journals of military officers and enlisted men who served during the frontier wars, and of politicians who influenced government strategy during that time period, as well as interviews with Apache survivors who lived and fought during the 1880s.

ABOUT THE AUTHOR

Jeffrey Poston is the acclaimed author of the Jason Peares historical western series, as well as the fast-paced adventure thriller series *American Terrorist* and *Call Sign: Raven*. Blending traditional and revisionist historical research, his historical westerns have been praised as "fast-moving" (Kelton) and "exciting, page-turning" (Zollinger) and "among the best writers of westerns" (Biblio.com). His thriller books are lauded as "so realistic," "powerfully intense," and "action-packed page turners." He is a self-described *Rambling Man* and writes his novels wherever he happens to be in his travels.

Find Jeffrey at http://www.jeffreypostonbooks.com/

Amazon.com: http://amazon.com/author/jeffreyposton

Facebook: http://www.facebook.com/JeffreyPostonBooks

Twitter: http://www.twitter.com/BooksByJPoston

Goodreads: http://www.goodreads.com/JeffreyPoston

ACKNOWLEDGMENTS

As writers, we often go into our creative caves to compose a book, but when we come out, there are often dozens of people who help refine a story and turn it into a really good book. No writer can succeed without this special group of people—critical readers, cover artists, professional editors, marketing and PR specialists, and publishers.

I especially want to thank my critical reader and sounding board, Dr. Stephanie McIver. She's helped me through many of my books, offering insight and analysis that added depth and breadth to my characters and my plot.

Special thanks to Debra L. Hartmann, The Pro Book Editor, and her team for copyediting and proofreading. I also want to give a shout-out to the cover art designers of my books: Deanna Dionne.

I'm also thankful for the active imaginations (and the suspension of disbelief) of all the readers who enjoyed my Western and Thriller adventures. I'm especially grateful to the dozens of beta-readers who previewed the book and sent back invaluable advice. Your help means the world to this author!

www.ingramcontent.com/pod-product-compliance
Lightning Source LLC
Chambersburg PA
CBHW020348120726
47904CB00002B/506